Found myself totally immersed culture of a place close to my own narrative design of two parallel distinctive location and ethos — colonial India of the British Raj, and Oxford (England) in the late 1990's — pulled me deep into the lives of the protagonists. Sylvia Vetta has written a book which fundamentally traces the philosophical and moral dimensions of a journey which crosses racial and religious boundaries.

Rebecca Haque, *Professor of English at the University of Dhaka and Daily Star columnist*

This is an impressive book with excellent characters and an engaging story. In this well researched novel I especially like the warm picture of Ashoka, one of my heroes.

Simon Altmann, *Emeritus Professor at Brasenose College, Oxford*

A page turning love story – I was hooked. Harry and Ramma are hugely endearing and I hoped their relationship would be strong enough to overcome the prejudice they both faced. It reflected my life of gifts and travails of a mixed-race relationship.

Polly Biswas Gladwin, *TV and documentary editor*

Sculpting
the Elephant

by
Sylvia Vetta

CLARET PRESS

www.claretpress.com

Claret ▶ Press

I dedicate this book to anyone anywhere whose partner was born in a different country, a different culture, a different religion or who has a different skin tone. Sculpting the Elephant was written to acknowledge what had happened in your lives in order for you to meet in a particular place at a particular time.

Simla

Delhi

NEPAL

Lumbini

Sravasti

Kushinagar

Sarnath

Patna

Khajuraho

Varanasi
(formerly Benares)

Nalanda

Bodhgaya

Sanchi

Ujain

Kolkata
(formerly Calcutta)

INDIA

Mumbai
(formerly Bombay)

Part 1: Oxford

Part 2: India

Part 1: *Oxford*

CHAPTER 1: Deco-rators

Oxford, 1997

Harry stared at the brush. The colours at its end were drying. The blank canvas yawned at him. 'Today, I'll make a start,' he told himself, but then was interrupted by the telephone. He grabbed at it.

'Deco-rators. This is Harry King. Can I help you?'

A deep voice on the other end said, 'My name's Charles Carew. I have some things I need to sell and you come highly recommended. Would it be possible for you to come over and take a look?'

While Kathy, his business partner, looked after the shop, Harry set off for North Oxford in his battered old Volvo estate. As he drove past The Jericho Tavern, he smiled at the memory of himself as a teenager at Radiohead's first local gig there in 1986. Not that he knew how special it was at the time, but he did remember the buzz of excitement. Only last month, Radiohead had burst onto the world stage and now that venue was a mecca for musicians. Harry's stylish art and twentieth century design shop was situated just one hundred yards away, and the pub was now his local. Jericho, once a working-class enclave in Oxford, was being gentrified and attracting creative artists. Every builder's sign he passed on the way reminded him of how lucky he was to get the shop lease two years ago.

Leaving behind the rows of terraced housing, Harry signalled right and was soon driving down the broad streets of substantial Victorian Gothic Revival houses. They'd been built for married dons moving out of the colleges at a time when servants were plentiful.

He knocked on the red front door. It was opened by the

1

owner himself who, Harry assumed, was well into his seventies. Charles Carew looked untidy but had the bone structure of a handsome man. Harry was shown into the library. At one end was an equally distinguished-looking chest of drawers, obviously custom made considering it was eight feet wide.

'That is what we need to sell,' Charles said. 'We have to move. The bungalow we're buying is spacious but this house is overflowing with a lifetime of possessions. We need to part with some of them. That twelve-drawer chest is where we want to begin – that and its contents.'

Harry hesitated before replying. 'I'm sorry but Deco-rators doesn't go in for Victorian furniture, no matter how charmingly quirky. But those vases on the top are another matter.' His eyes caressed the nineteen-thirties wonders that he recognised immediately, even without lifting them to see the name underneath. 'I can offer you a good price.'

*****

Harry set the alarm for 4:30am and tried getting an early night. Sleep came at last when delightful images of his newly acquired black basalt vases faded.

At 4:35 sharp, Harry downed a strong cup of coffee, pulled on his faded jeans, trainers and Radiohead T-shirt, shrugged himself into his soft leather jacket and headed off to Portobello Market. As the M40 cut through the Chilterns, the sun rose ahead of him. He drove towards the light bathed in optimism – a feeling he'd thought was lost to him. 'It's crazy how the antiques trade likes ridiculously early starts,' mused Harry. Then a smile spread across his face. 'There's method in the madness. Driving through London at five in the morning is a delight and a madness.' That word echoed a sign in the Oxford Antiques Centre where he'd first met Kathy. *Beware those of sound mind who enter here.* And they'd bonded over the shared laughter.

He needed to stop his mind wandering and concentrate on the road ahead. His hand went out to the CD play button and the distinctive sound of Radiohead and *Paranoid Android* smothered his thoughts.

An hour later, he'd set up his market stall. While his shop displays had witty originality and panache – which was why people asked for his advice on interior design – there was no artifice involved in today's haphazard arrangement. He might as well have emptied the boxes straight onto the trestle. He smiled as he remembered his first encounter with the dealer, Ingrid Lindberg. She'd been doing the same thing and blushed when she'd realised he'd witnessed her lack of reverence. Despite the vast difference in their age and background, he counted Ingrid a dear friend. What Harry loved most about her was her enthusiasm: she looked to the future with schoolgirl delight and tried to enjoy every moment. She had a passion for antiques that came with a story. Antiques filled with stories prompted a vision of Charles Carew's stonking eight-foot-wide hunk of furniture.

He muttered to himself, 'It sure came loaded with history, but why on earth did I let myself be persuaded into buying that chest of drawers?' Its presence could not be ignored. All twelve drawers were carved with acanthus growing like whiskers from the lion-faced handles. Hand-made from solid oak, it had tactile solidity. Not surprisingly, it was also the heaviest piece of furniture he'd ever bought. Harry had called on his mates to help him deliver it to the shop. Although unique, Kathy would think it uniquely awful. Ha! The old professor had called it well-travelled and said, 'It was custom-made around 1880 – went to India and back twice. The second time was in 1921, when it travelled with my parents to Mussoorie, where my father taught. It finally came back to England in 1934, when I was seven and it was fiftyish–'

His thoughts were interrupted by a hearty, 'Hi Harry, what's brought you down from the dreaming spires?'

In front of him was a giant of a man. Mike Wells could have

walked off the film set of *Indiana Jones and the Temple of Doom*.

'Yeah, I don't think I've been here since we opened Decorators. It's like this, Mike. I was called out by a couple who are downsizing from a North Oxford house. They had two Keith Murray pieces that I really had to have. In fact, one of them is every Murray fan's dream piece: black basalt vases. I offered well over the odds but they wouldn't sell them to me unless I bought a huge chest of drawers and its contents! It was all or nothing, so now I have to dispose of these.' Harry waved his arm over the trestle table. 'I hope I can interest you in some scientific instruments.'

Mike picked up a strange looking piece. It had a brass watch-like case with a thermometer attached to it. 'What's this?'

Harry shook his head. 'Haven't a clue. Don't you know? I thought scientific instruments were your speciality.'

'Yes, but I haven't had one like this before. It's probably an altimeter.'

Harry was none the wiser. 'What's that when it's at home?'

'Home's a mountain.'

'Come on then, demonstrate some of your Roadshow expertise. How does it work?'

'Okay, let the camera roll.' Mike looked earnestly at the altimeter and then struck a pose at an imaginary lens. 'In the pioneering days of mountaineering, the only way you could measure height was by the time and temperature needed to get water to boil. My guess is that this was intended to do just that.'

'You're kidding.'

'No, seriously. But I can't be certain. Who were the people who sold it to you?

'Two retired academics, Professors Charles and Judith Carew. She said the scientific instruments and photographs belonged to Charles' grandfather, who did some exploring in the Himalayas.

'I'll buy this,' said Mike, holding the grubby height-measuring device. 'What do you want for it?'

'£30 any good to you?'

'Done,' said Mike, automatically pushing his hand forward to shake on the deal. Then he dropped the device into a zip-up bag and scrabbled for some notes in his pocket.

'I'd be interested in knowing a bit more about the grandfather... provenance and all that. Then I might buy some of the other stuff too.'

'I'll give Professor Carew a ring when I'm back in the shop,' said Harry.

'You look pretty damn cheerful. Got yourself a woman at last, Harry?'

'Got my eye on you, Mike.'

Mike grinned and made a suggestive gesture as he hurried away.

CHAPTER 2: A Mysterious Disappearance

Oxford, 1868

My attentions have long been diverted by the attractions of the Natural History Museum, so my 1st in Classics was astounding. Father's pride & delight provided me with an opportunity to broach my suggestion. When he sent me to Harrow & Oxford, it was with the intention that I should go into politics; reading Classics was to prepare me for the Commons. I did not utter the truth that such a career is not my vocation. Father was amenable, however, to my suggestion that to be effective I needed greater experience of the world. He agreed that I could go to India. James, the little blighter, is showing an interest in the mill so I hope not to be the chosen son. No regrets, however, about the experience I gained working on the maintenance of the looms in the holidays. Good training & all that for the adventurous life for which I yearn. I hope to live up to family motto: Discere Faciendo. I was taken aback when father handed me this leather-bound diary. He made me promise to write in it religiously & he, in turn, promised me he would never ask to read it. It should be a private communiqué between God & myself, & help me with the thorny problems I shall apparently encounter. Father says that making observations & mulling them over will increase my knowledge of myself. I cannot quite believe that this has been so easy. Writing a diary seems a small price to pay for this opportunity to work for the Empire.

Opening the door of Deco-rators a few hours later, Harry was overwhelmed by the presence of the chest of drawers that screamed 19th century. It clashed with the image they were trying to create for the shop. The general rule was that stock had to date from 1920 to 1970, apart from Harry's own paintings and other contemporary artwork.

Harry's business partner looked furious.

'There you are. Damn it. I opened the door this morning to find this monstrosity. I thought we had an agreement? I hope this is some bad dream and you have a customer lined up to get rid of it pretty damn quick. How about now? Why didn't you warn me?' Kathy sported a 1930s hairstyle and vintage fashion. Her usually breezy manner matched her 20s plastic jewellery.

'I'm sorry. I should have told you. Look over there,' Harry pointed to the tapering matt black vases in the glass cabinet. 'You know the call out to that professor's house on Leckford Road? I've been trying for years to find a Murray black basalt piece that I could afford and suddenly there were two!' Harry's eyes didn't stray from the achingly elegant examples of Murray's creations. 'I just couldn't risk losing them.'

Kathy huffed but a little more softly.

'The Carews insisted I take everything they wanted to sell or else they would all go into Whittaker's next auction. I know it isn't our style but the chest is saleable. And it can store all the other things from the Carews inside the drawers.'

Kathy looked askance. 'What other things?'

Harry opened one of the drawers and pointed at a camera from the 1870s. 'Scientific instruments, ephemera... Don't look like that! What else could I do? I sold some of them in Portobello this morning. I'll give Dr Groth a ring. He does collect that sort of thing, doesn't he? Please, forgive me.' Harry blew her a kiss. 'And do brew up a welcome for me – I had an early start.'

'Don't talk to me like I'm your maid, Harry.' But still she swept into the little kitchen and filled the kettle. Despite the hard tone, Kathy was grateful to him for giving her shares in Deco-rators, so she couldn't remain angry with him for long.

Meanwhile, Harry unloaded the unsold stock from the boot of his car. He unpacked the collapsible boxes and had begun putting the contents back into the chest when he noticed some of the drawers were lined with old newspapers. He took them out to read later, bits falling like petals. He smoothed them gently on the table, idly scanning the faded columns. When Kathy returned with the tea, the shop was tidy.

Remembering his promise to Mike, he phoned Professor Carew. 'Sorry to bother you, sir,' Harry began, 'but would you mind if I asked a few questions about the things you sold me? I mentioned that scientific instruments are not my forte. You said they belonged to your grandfather? Can you tell me his name and why he had them?'

There was a long pause before the professor answered. 'My grandfather's name was Bartholomew Carew. He was an explorer with a fine scientific mind – always collecting, measuring and excavating.'

'Where did he explore? Mountain ranges?' asked Harry.

Another pause. 'India mostly and the Himalayas in particular.'

Harry tried to elicit more information but the professor seemed surprisingly reticent about his grandfather. 'That's helpful. Thank you, Professor,' Harry said reluctantly, and then put down the phone. Bartholomew Carew. The name rang a bell. One of the Indian newspapers? Harry picked it up and, sure enough, the story at the bottom of the page was about him.

Bartholomew Carew is reported missing. The intrepid archaeologist and advisor to the Viceroy of India on matters of scientific interest was last seen to the west of Mount Kanchenjunga. Major Lewington of the Bengal Lancers expressed his astonishment at finding the Professor alone. Carew had been strongly advised to return with the patrol to their camp. The Major was of the opinion that it would be difficult for the Professor to survive without supplies in such hostile terrain. The Professor declined the offer but agreed to join the Major in three days. He explained that he had sent his men back to Darjeeling and had sufficient tinned food and water for four days. The explorer did not rendezvous and Major Lewington sent out a search party. We regret to inform our readers that they failed in their efforts to locate him.

CHAPTER 3: Encounters

March 21, 1869

We land in Bombay tomorrow. I am impatient for my first encounter with India. Lord C drummed into me my duty to spread the blessed rule of the Queen Empress. 'Never forget the privilege you bestow, Carew. Whatever you do, do not let her down.' Over & over was this repeated. It instilled some anxiety in me that I might not live up to expectations. My appointment with Henry Thuillier is in Dehra Dune. If I pass muster, who knows what adventure awaits in the Himalayas working on the Great Trigonometrical Survey! The chart produced as observations & measurements are taken is unique. This huge undertaking started at the beginning of the century & I am to be part of one of the greatest achievements in physical geography. No map in the world can rival it for accuracy and scale, & deo iuvante, I will help create it. The excitement leads to vigour & a sudden sense of freedom arouses in me the desire to pit myself against the might & majesty of the Himalayas. I must confess to no small degree of regard for my own abilities in this matter.

Professor Allen ushered in his DPhil student, Ramma Gupta. Since arriving from Mumbai eighteen months ago she had worked at a prodigious pace. He offered her a cup of tea while he read through the notes and references she had produced during the past week in the Bodleian Library. She was following his advice to search out diaries written at the time, as well as academic and official papers. He looked over his glasses at her eager face.

'Miss Gupta, while I fully support your choice of subject, I still remain unclear about how you intend to pursue your scholarship given the lack of primary sources.'

Ramma inhaled deeply.

'Thank you, Professor, for your support. Ashoka in effect created Buddhism, the world's third biggest religion, but few people know about him. A glance at reports from Transparency International is enough to realise the need for the kind of good governance of which he was an outstanding example. So my topic is hugely important. I envisage my dissertation having a positive impact on India's present day governance.'

'Miss Gupta, you are engaged with historical scholarship, not political activism.'

'Yes, sir. I want to emphasise how knowledge of him was lost for a thousand years and focus my DPhil on how he was rediscovered during the Victorian era.'

Her tutor nodded.

'So what new have you got to tell me about how Ashoka was brought to light?'

'I found an 1837 paper by James Prinsep,' said Ramma, handing a copy to the professor.

'Mmm, that is definitely quotable but it has been in the public domain for 161 years. What can you tell us that we don't already know? To get a doctorate, you need to make an original contribution to the field.'

Ramma's smile faded. She blinked back tears of frustration. Dr Allen squeezed his lips. He would be doing her no favours by not being honest.

'Miss Gupta, you have the enthusiasm and the ability to write an outstanding thesis. But I suggest that you read over the papers you've gathered and see if one aspect inspires you. Walk and think. Concentrate on what is missing, what you need to seek out. Come back in two weeks' time and we can discuss it more.'

He showed her out. She ran down the stairs and out of Trinity College. She headed across the road and ran straight into a cyclist. He didn't fall off his bike but had a few choice words to say.

*****

Wanting to appease Kathy, Harry began his rearrangement of the shop by angling the chest of drawers in an attempt to make it appear less prominent. Then he set about refreshing the window display. The previous month's array had been inspired by artists and illustrators from the thirties, including Vanessa Bell and Eric Ravilious, and Harry wanted to create a glamorous and intriguing arrangement to surprise Kathy and distract her from the great lump of oak.

He glanced at his world music collection. 'That's it,' he thought, 'I'll transform the window with an international theme.' Harry's sharp eye surveyed their stock of Egyptian-influenced pieces. Open on his desk was a book about Picasso and glancing at it, he was reminded that the links he was making were not a coincidence. The 20s were a time when artists and designers were looking with admiration, rather than disdain, at African sculpture. He chose a CD at random but the strains were not of Mali, as he thought, but of India; the rhythmic sound of a morning raga. He must have mixed up the sleeves. Liking it, he left it playing and continued his work. Fifteen minutes later, he added the finishing touch to his display by placing a large 70s Troika lamp base at the back.

He opened the door and stepped outside to admire the effect, almost knocking over a young woman, who was staring intently at a Deco bronze figure in the window. As she regained her balance and looked up at him, her gaze revealed the longest eyelashes he'd ever seen. Trying hard to compose himself, Harry brushed back his unruly hair with the back of his hand and said, 'Oh sorry! Are you okay? I got rather carried away and had my eyes on the objects not on you...'

Looking at her, Harry wondered why on earth his attention had not been on her but said, 'Do you like the bronze?' She nodded.

'Do you want a closer look? My name is Harry King, by the way.'

'And I'm Ramma Gupta. I like your shop.' She addressed him in the charming singing tones of the sub-continent's English, which modern Indians referred to as 'Hinglish', the Hindi version of the language that had taken on a life of its own.

Harry ushered her in. As she leaned forward, the almond shape of her face was emphasised by dangling gold earrings, and a delicate little necklace was suspended just above her cleavage.

'That's Ravi Shankar.' A surprised Ramma glanced at Harry and became aware of the sensuous blue of his eyes.

'World music inspires me to be creative in new ways. That's one of mine,' said Harry pointing to a vibrant abstract. Then he stopped mid-stream, wondering why he was telling her all this, and then opened his mouth and said some more. 'I'm an artist as well as a dealer.' He stopped again. What was he going on about? And with horror, found his mouth opening to speak again. So he coughed. Then he covered his mouth with his hand. Both actions took supreme concentration.

'The rhythm's hypnotic, do you not think? I wonder, please tell me about the golden goddess in your window?'

Harry carefully took the figure from the display. 'She's an Amazon; I guess she is like a goddess. She was inspired by Diana, the huntress. I love her windswept hair.'

'I thought it was the same one we had at home but on closer inspection, I see it is similar but not the same.'

His fingers stroked the smooth bronze curves. Then noticing what he was doing, he snatched his hand back and stuffed it into his pocket. Inside, he groaned with embarrassment. But he expressed his enthusiasm in words.

'It was designed by a French sculptor called Marcel Bouraine. Etling, the company he worked for, took quite a risk. These Deco bronzes were expensive to produce. All of Marcel's women were powerful.' It sounded so suggestive. All that was missing was a nudge-nudge wink-wink. 'I meant to say, Bouraine's sculptures of women were powerful.'

Ramma failed to notice. Her response to the sculpture was personal. 'Daddy-ji bought ours. He said it reminded him of my mother and... yes, she was strong but slight. Her power was of the heart.'

Harry thought she was going to cry. Instinctively, he put out an arm to comfort her, but concerned that she might misconstrue his motives he strode off to make her a cup of tea. After she admired the rest of the shop, they settled into a pair of comfy 30s tub chairs, to drink their tea. Harry apologised for the Bob the Builder mugs.

'Kathy, who shares the shop, has two young children. They're into Spiderman now so we've inherited these. So, you've a Bouraine statue at home?'

'You are kind. Thank you...' said Ramma, a shadow passing over her face. 'The sculpture means much to us as Mata-ji died five years ago.'

Harry rubbed the ring on his little finger as he listened.

'Daddy-ji is alone now. Not alone. Daddy-ji does not live alone, not in India. I am shocked by how many people live alone in this country. People are always coming and going in an Indian house. You are not allowed to be lonely except... ah, I do miss her.'

She seemed to be somewhere else for a minute and Harry guessed that she experienced the same ache as he did. Then her attention returned to the bronze. 'How much is it?'

Harry didn't want to lose this customer. 'Your father has good taste. This one is in fact only one thousand because the tip of one of her fingers is missing a tiny paint chip and the spear has lost some of its golden patina. His pieces can fetch up to eight thousand in auction, and there's a buyer's premium on top of that.'

Ramma brightened up. 'Yah. I must tell Daddy-ji. He gave it to an aunt to remember my mother. She should insure it. You are not just trying to impress me? It really is that much?'

Harry was a trifle hurt by the doubt in her question.

'I know some of those television programmes give the impression that we are all a bunch of grasping idiots,' he said. 'There are bad apples in every walk of life. When I joined the trade, I was taken by surprise by how genuine most dealers are. Their passion for art, antiques and history is like a magnet, and the hunt for the right stock becomes a way of life. They don't want to jeopardise it by being dishonest.'

Harry glanced at his stock book; he had paid £750 for the bronze. To see this softly-spoken vision again, he'd willingly give it away. 'I can see you really like it. How about 800? It is more of a discount than I normally give but somehow it looks right for you.'

Ramma laughed a light musical trill. 'In spite of your sales pitch, will you keep her for me? I am a DPhil student only. Daddy-ji gives me a generous allowance and if need be, I could sell these earrings. They are large rubies and should fetch a good price. Will you keep the Amazon for me?'

'Can you find a deposit of say, £200? I'll deliver it to you personally and you can pay the rest in instalments. I may be able to find a buyer for the rubies.' This was something he only did for regulars whom he knew he could trust, but he wanted to see where Ramma lived in the hope that he might get to know her better.

It was only when she left the shop that he became aware of the swing of her hips in her tight blue jeans. Feeling surprisingly up-beat, Harry felt he could even tackle his accounts so he sat at the desk and ran the finger wearing his mother's ring down the list of outgoings.

CHAPTER 4: Waiting for Ramma

Calcutta: November 1869

What good fortune! I have the support of Henry Thuillier. Yesterday, I collected the altimeter I ordered. It arrived in excellent condition. Well packed, thank heavens. Not long now before I shall have my first glimpse of the Himalayas. I had the immense good fortune to meet Nairn Singh Rawat when he came to visit Henry Thuillier. We discussed his legendary journey to Tibet. His mission is to survey that secretive country & he has made enormous strides. The Tibetans would not permit him to measure or map, & as such he employed simple but inspired decoys. He used a Buddhist rosary as a measure & hid his compass in a prayer wheel. Ingenious! He succeeded in meeting the Buddhist leader, who is called the Dalai Lama. Singh Rawat's exploits began with his recruitment by the Schlagintweit brothers, German geographers. Would the Raj post-1857 have given a village boy such an opportunity?

Henry Yule says Nairn Singh Rawat has added more knowledge to the map of Asia than any other living man. How then is this intrepid explorer described as 'wily'? If his skin were white they would parade him down the Mall!

Post scriptum: Now that I think about it, after a leisurely brandy and cigar, I've decided that the Raj did hire Nairn Singh Rawat. The East India Company hired Hermann Schlagintweit & his brother, Adolph, to make the measurements necessary to increase the speed and efficacy of its trade routes, & the Schlagintweit brothers did so — by hiring Singh Rawat. I wish he were here with me now and I would heartily clasp him by the hand as a fellow employee on our great project.

Harry shook his head as the waiter approached. Feeling on edge, he eyed his watch. Ramma was late, very late. And that made him anxious. Since that day, five weeks ago, when he'd nearly tripped over her outside Deco-rators, they'd met often and never parted without arranging another meeting – like this one at the Moonlight restaurant on Cowley Road.

He checked his watch again. Nausea engulfed him as he realised that this evening – June 4, 1997 – would echo that other June 4 when Harry had screwed Helen's letter into a tiny ball and thrown it against the wall. Like an animal in pain he had stumbled in front of that picture of the two of them embracing at Kathy's wedding. He'd taken it off the wall and turned it face down and stalked off. Then he'd hesitated, turned on his heel, picked it up again and smashed it on the floor, shattering it so his smile in the photograph was as broken as his optimism. Helen had gone from girlfriend status to a private hurt that he gnawed on, overthinking and re-analysing until it became a quiet obsession.

Since meeting Ramma, he'd finally managed to form an explanation for Helen dumping him: she loved New York more than him. Did he love Oxford more than her? Possibly. At last, he could admit to himself that he could have moved to the USA to be with her. In theory, but he'd just signed the lease on the shop and was locked in for ten years. To top that, his mother had been diagnosed with breast cancer so even if he had been free to move he wouldn't have left her to face it alone. If that wasn't the universe telling him something, then he didn't know what else it could be.

He steadied himself with a vision of his black basalt vases, the Keith Murray pair he'd bought from the Carews. Their family's story was all bound up with India. Surely that was no coincidence? Last night he had dreamt of the vases, and emerging from a tapered neck, like a genie from a bottle, was a belladonna-eyed Ramma.

'Why should she feel the same about me? Maybe this is her way of dumping me,' he thought to himself. But that wasn't fair. Ramma was no coward. She would tell him face-to-face; he was certain she wouldn't tell him in a letter. Were they even in a dating relationship? He wasn't wholly sure. Apart from shameless flirting, erotic enough for Harry to break into a sweat, they'd been platonic. They'd done little more than hold hands at the movies. This wasn't how he normally went about these things. No beery nights at the pub, no raucous clubbing, no raucous anything. He wasn't complaining – just confused.

But then, all of a sudden, there she was, walking gracefully towards him, and the tension drained away. Ramma was dressed in an Indian cream silk suit embroidered with tiny pearl beads and a matching pair of pearl and gold pendant earrings. As an artist and antiques dealer, Harry had over time acquired an eye. His female friends were surprised when he noticed and remembered what they wore.

'Hi gorgeous.' Then he whispered to her, 'I've opened an oyster and discovered a pearl ... my girl with the pearl earring.'

'Maybe I need to take one out?'

Harry gently ran his index finger down her right ear. She shivered. 'Shall I do it for you?' Holding his breath, he gazed into Ramma's eyes and allowed himself to take a risk. He bent forward for a kiss – but just before their lips could touch the waiter interrupted.

'Ready to order?' The previous week he had persuaded Ramma to try her first sip of wine. She had screwed up her face a little before saying, 'Wine drinking is natural for you, Harry, but for me it is not accha. It is not an Indian thing.'

Harry was becoming familiar with the odd Hinglish word and knew *accha* meant 'okay' or 'good'. He scrolled down the drinks menu and decided to order a cold white wine. It was a trifle sweet for him – he preferred red – but he thought it would be an accha choice for Ramma. Like many Hindus she was vegetarian.

It wasn't a problem for him; it had been a long time since he'd eaten red meat. Still, he worried about ordering fish or chicken for himself but Ramma reassured him. 'We Hindus do not go in for proselytising.' she said.

'What do you mean?' said Harry not wanting to reveal his ignorance.

'The Indian religions have no creeds. Hindus and Buddhists, to a great extent we determine our own beliefs. Some Hindus even think like atheists but are still regarded as Hindu.'

'How can you be a Hindu and an atheist?'

'Well, Daddy-ji is, actually.'

'Is he that rare thing, the only one?'

'I happen to think he is unique but not as a Hindu atheist. The Vedas, India's holy books, are among the earliest ever written. Can you imagine, 1700 or 1600 BCE is when it is thought they were started in Sanskrit. The four books are a philosophical debate, each having different ideas and the fourth even proposes that there is no god.'

Harry gave a quiet chuckle of surprise. 'I like that. So what's the difference between a believer and a non-believer?'

'Whatever our preferences, we have a respect for all living creatures but some Hindus do eat meat, apart from beef. Daddy-ji may be an atheist but he is also a vegetarian. If you come to India, and go to a restaurant, they will ask you if you want 'veg or non-veg'. It is your choice if you want to eat meat or become a vegetarian. I shall not try to persuade you, but these idlis are good.'

Ramma held out a forkful of the South Indian rice and lentil dumpling soaked in spicy samba for him to try. As he took it off the fork, he winked lasciviously at her. She blushed.

Suddenly nervous, he told her about Bartholomew Carew.

'The contents of that twelve-drawer chest, they mostly concern him,' Harry began. 'It's full of his papers, letters, photographs as well as some nineteenth century scientific instruments. Quite an archive. He must have been an interesting man but then he just disappeared off the face of the earth.'

'I am working in the Indian Institute next week. Perhaps I can find out some more about him?' suggested Ramma.

CHAPTER 5: Ramma's Regrets

Simla, August 1872

Niraj desires to write a tribute to Radhanath Sikdar. His request for me to check some calculations affected my judgment and has led to his humiliation. I invited Niraj to discuss them at the club. He came but they refused him entry. Their reason? He is Indian! By heavens, this is India. Of course there's an Indian in India.

Sikdar, the great mathematician, measured and identified the world's highest mountain. In his wisdom, Andrew Scott Waugh named the peak 'Everest' in honour of General George Everest. The former Director of the Survey deserves honours galore for his epic achievement surveying the meridian arc from the southernmost point of India north to Nepal - a distance of about 2,400 kilometres. It took from 1806 to 1841 to complete so he should be given every honour the Raj can bestow. Honourable man that he was, Everest objected to Waugh's proposal as he had nothing to do with working out which was the world's highest mountain. That was the work of Radhanath Sikdar. Everest expressed his admiration of Radhanath. Apart from mastering the usual geodetic processes, he invented quite a few of his own.

I apologised as profusely as I was able to Niraj. He replied that it was nothing new. Radhanath had related similar stories of his treatment despite Everest's high regard. I have vowed never to set foot in the club again unless they allow men like Sikdar and Niraj to join.

Received a letter from Mother. She says I should marry. Apparently when the fishing fleet arrives in Simla, an army of matchmakers set themselves to work. The old hands here

have Indian families and they appear to be happy ones. Life,
however, for the children of miscegenate marriages has come
under a shadow. They are no longer accepted as equals by
the British and the Indians also ostracise them outside work.
It would be unfair of me to pursue Sumitra.
Her parents are about to arrange her marriage. Niraj has
noticed the attention that I paid to his sister and was quick
to tell me about his parents' choice of husband.

Ramma was feeling unsettled at the Bodleian the next day. She stood in the queue to pick up a book, head down, and didn't see her tutor coming towards her until he almost bumped into her. People bumping into her was becoming a habit.

'Hello Ramma,' he said, somewhat surprised that she was so unaware.

She looked up and hoped he hadn't noticed the embarrassing flush of heat rising in her cheeks. Her thoughts had not been on her work nor had they been on her surroundings. They were on Harry.

'Sorry, Dr Allen, I followed the advice you gave me about spending some time outside of the library – until today that is.'

'I look forward to hearing about your ideas at our tutorial tomorrow,' he replied.

The librarian was still explaining to a new reader the significance of a copyright library. 'The Bodleian is given a copy of every book published in the UK, so we need a mile and a half of new shelving every year!'

'But it doesn't look big enough to house that many.' The new reader's voice was sceptical. The librarian smiled.

'Appearances are deceptive. It doesn't appear big enough to hold five million volumes,' explained the librarian. Recognising Ramma she added, 'But this young lady knows us well and can tell you how, when you cross the road, you are walking over miles of books.'

Suddenly aware that the librarian was including her in the conversation, Ramma's fingers slipped from her ear, which she had been fondling as she remembered Harry's amorous gesture in the restaurant last night. She pulled herself together. 'That is right, but I was told that the space will run out sometime in the not-too-distant future.' Spying an opportunity, she handed her order to the librarian. 'I reserved this last week: James Prinsep on *The Laws of Piety* in Brahmi.'

While she waited, she pictured the strange but effective delivery system of conveyor belts made in the 1930s that would bring the book to her. Ramma's tutor had given her a tour beneath Broad Street into the New Bodleian, and she had seen for herself the labyrinth of rooms below. She'd felt overwhelmed knowing how few of those books, stored beneath the tarmac, she could read in her whole lifetime. Insignificance in the face of so much knowledge humbled her, but at the same time transplanted some backbone. She might not get through all of them, but given a chance, she intended to make quite a dent.

Her passion for history monopolised her. She knew she couldn't give it up; it was the driving force in her life. The past was her future and India's as well. She just had to figure out how to meld the successes of the past to what lay just beyond the millennium. The 21st century could belong to India. That India was changing was not open to debate. The question was, in which direction? To what end? Celebrating which identity? And how?

Ramma dug in her bag for her notes on Brahmi, the language that Prinsep had interpreted. She really should be reviewing them until they became muscle memory. Standing there, easing her weight from foot to foot, her eyes fixed on the sheet, her mind wandered again.

When she had come across some of her father's books written in a foreign language, she'd asked him about them. 'When we next visit Delhi, I shall show you a pillar within the courtyard of the Qutb Minar,' he had said. 'It has the appearance of steel, and yet it was made in the Gupta period when Pali and Brahmi were the spoken languages. The engravings are still as fresh as when they were written, but few people can read them.'

'Why is that?'

'From 500 AD the use of Brahmi became rare,' her father had explained. 'And just as well, because otherwise those pillars would have been destroyed. Aurangzeb demolished thousands of Hindu and Buddhist temples in the north, but these minaret-like pillars, which did not tarnish, fascinated the invaders. We are fortunate that at least they survived.'

Her interest was piqued. Then that interest grew with her studies. Much of India's ancient history had been lost or suppressed during the centuries of invasions and colonisation. Ramma believed the country's identity could be enhanced if this new generation connected to its pre-Mughal and colonial past. And the past that interested her most was the time 250 years BCE, when Indian culture had spread throughout Asia without violence or oppression, although Ramma took that with a grain of salt, as there were considerable battles fought and won before pacifism was announced as the only way forward. Myth had it that Ashoka converted to Buddhism while walking the battlegrounds littered with the dead and the dying, and swore that in the future he would convert solely by moral force. Instead of violence, he offered tolerance, rights and diversity. Ashoka's influence stretched from Afghanistan to China.

But what had been forgotten could be rediscovered. If she could find a way to highlight its successes, then she, Ramma Gupta, would be part of the answer, part of the new future that India was forging.

And then there was her father. She so wanted him to be proud of her. He hadn't been able to study as he'd wanted, but instead had to work. If her DPhil were a success, he would fly over from Mumbai and watch her with tears in his eyes as she received her doctorate in the Sheldonian. That image was so strong in her mind she could visualise each and every moment. To be wholly truthful with herself, the fear that it might not happen, the toe-curling shame of failure and the certainty of her father's forgiveness despite her failure, was no small part of what drove her on.

Her lips twisted in wry humour. Fear and ambition were the foundation of her career researching the strength that comes from peace and tolerance.

And she needed strength. Nothing was going as planned. In that vast subterranean maze of paper, she'd found nothing original, nothing insightful, nothing really at all. That seminal book that she wanted to write on the rediscovery of the Emperor Ashoka? So far she wasn't adding much. Maybe her tutor was right after all. Frustration was undermining her confidence.

And then there was Harry. He kept swirling around in her head, jostling for space and taking up too much of it. She tried to push his image down but it kept resurfacing. Until now, her drive had been firm. Why had she been so stupid and allowed herself to be swept up in these uncontrollable desires?

She forced herself to imagine the excitement James Prinsep must have felt in 1839 when he succeeded in translating the inscription on an ancient Ashokan stone pillar, except in those days no one realised the pillars were Ashokan. Then she pictured her twelve-year-old self on her first visit to the temple in Bodhgaya where she had seen mysterious inscriptions in Brahmi.

'Few people can read them,' her father had said to her. 'You would make me so proud, Ramma Beti, if you become one of those few.' That day her dhamma was written.

Twelve years of education later, and eighteen months after saying goodbye to her father and arriving in Oxford, she'd set herself a blistering pace. She worried she was becoming obsessive. The world of Ashoka and the Victorian explorers was becoming more real to her than Oxford's dreaming spires. She entered the library at sunrise, ate her meals hunkered over a digital reproduction in a semi-obscured room, then left to go back to her own room in the dark. If she was lucky, it wasn't raining.

Obsession got the work done. Thanks goodness for obsession.

In spite of that, uncertainty about her ability and loneliness chipped away at her and lowered her confidence. That was why she'd decided to take some time off to explore the delights of the city. And that was how she had come to peer in the window of Deco-rators, frozen by the sight of the bronze which reminded her of home and her mother. Harry said that he had placed it there only moments before. She'd been the first person to see his new window display.

In India, it was unusual for a twenty-four-year-old woman to be neither engaged nor married. Perhaps because Mummy–ji had died, it had not occurred to her father to arrange a marriage for her. She was comfortable about her status. She was adamant that she didn't want to be a housewife, she wanted to remain free in order to establish her career, and her father supported her ambition. Although she didn't admit it aloud, she knew that time was of the essence. Her father might not want another man in her life right now but Ramma felt sure that at some point he would want grandchildren. Certainly, if she did meet someone, her father would expect her to seek his approval. Until then, she had an opportunity to make a difference, and show that she could make a contribution as a thinker.

Meeting Harry had changed everything, and now she wasn't so sure about anything anymore. She was now obsessing about the wrong thing and that could prove disastrous.

Now, she wondered if it would have been better had she walked past the shop ten minutes earlier.

CHAPTER 6: Revelation

Calcutta, November 1873

I presented my report to the Survey. They showed no curiosity over my drawings of the strange pillars but immense interest in the rock samples. I feel gratified that the fossils are destined for the Natural History Museum in Oxford. Indeed only last week I enjoyed a discussion with some of my colleagues about Darwin's theory. They were suitably impressed that I had been in the audience at that debate in 1860, an occasion an enthusiastic student could hardly forget. What a year that was! The contentious election for the Boden Professorship of Sanskrit occurred only six months later, where the great Indologist, Max Muller, was passed over in favour of Monier-Williams. Williams had no difficulty convincing the board of his Christian credentials but it was hard for Muller to sound sincere on that account! After his appointment, Williams declared that the conversion of India to the Christian religion would be one of the aims of orientalist scholarship. I read a paper in which he predicted the demise of the Hindu religion & called for Christian evangelism to ward off the spread of Islam. Complete bunkum! Damnant quod non intellegunt! As if England, or indeed any foreign power, could overturn philosophical ideas established over 3000 years ago. These so-called men of learning have no sense of India. When I explored Bombay, I encountered a Gothic Church, a temple to Hanuman, a Mosque, a synagogue, a Jain temple, a Zoroastrian fire temple & a Sikh Gurdwara, all within a couple of miles of each other, all co-existing with no friction. The Zoroastrian Towers of Silence alone would lead to riots in England. Although the Queen–Empress has not travelled to India she has an admirable understanding of the sub-continent. She has wisely declared that all her subjects must have freedom of religion.

As Harry recorded his takings the following evening he realised that everyone who had come into the shop had bought something. He pursed his lips and whistled, 'Oh, for a good mood every day!'

Almost giddy, he phoned Ramma and made a suggestion. 'It's about time you introduced me to your father, Ramma. You mentioned he was a singer, have you got a video? How about bringing one around tonight? I'll cook supper.'

*****

When they couldn't meet Harry missed Ramma with an intensity that surprised him. Tonight, when she arrived he was singing along to Radiohead's 'I promise'. As he put the finishing touches to the meal using only fresh ingredients, his mood was as light and bright as the food. He waved her into the living room. A few minutes later, he placed a bowl of creamy tagliatelle on the table. He'd garnished it with parmesan and a sprinkling of the basil which he'd managed to cultivate on the window ledge outside his kitchen. He glanced towards Ramma who was looking at the photographs on top of a bookshelf. Ramma picked up a photo of Harry, aged eighteen, with his mother.

'I see you are your mother's son.'

Harry hoped that was true because he certainly didn't want to take after his father. Harry surprised himself by opening up to Ramma. Before he knew it, he had told her most of the story.

'So yeah,' he concluded, 'he walked out on us and never came back. To make things more desperate, he withdrew all the money from their joint bank account.'

'What did your mother do? I've heard the British courts can chase men like him.'

'She reported him missing but we never discovered whether he was alive or dead.'

Concerned that Ramma might think that he was like his father, Harry said, 'I don't know why I'm telling you this, Ramma. I'd rather forget it all but I can't. It's something I can't fathom.'

'This is no consolation, but as a historian I should caution you against trying to figure out motives. You can't know what was going through his mind when he made his decision.'

'It feels odd because most of my memories of him are of us having fun. I understand now that my mother was my rock even before he left. Afterwards, how she did it... she's amazing. She was amazing.'

What Harry hadn't told Ramma was that his mother's death coming so soon after Helen had announced that she was staying in New York had drained his river dry. Since then, throwing himself into growing his business and savouring the pleasures of art and design had been his method of taking his mind off his losses.

'My aunt Julie later told me how dire our financial circumstances were. So Mum had to cope with being penniless as well as the emotional hell. I guess that in India a large extended family would rally around, but she only had my aunt, who was in London most of the time. If Mum had even a slight indication of why my father left, then it might have been easier. But there was nothing that suggested he was planning to leave. Nothing, zilch! His disappearance was as mysterious as Bartholomew Carew's.'

After the meal, they sat on the sofa, Ramma stroked his hair and began to massage his neck as he said, 'I wish you could have met her. She spared me the knowledge of just how bad things were. Except that I guessed it when she took on a second job. It meant leaving me on my own a lot; so Mum encouraged my art and was the biggest fan of Hidden Secrets, the rock group I joined.'

'Hidden Secrets? You have kept very quiet about that, Harry. You have not sung to me even once.'

'That's because I wasn't a vocalist. Percussion: that's me. Most of my school friends were football crazy but music saved my reputation. A passion for visiting galleries was nerdy but drums were choice.'

Talk of Harry's mother led to Ramma expressing emotions she usually tried to hold back. She described her mother, Rani, and almost wistfully said, 'I still talk to her. It's like she is standing in front of me. Whenever I have a dilemma I have to tell her.'

Harry couldn't believe what he was hearing. He had never told anyone about his visits to his mother's grave. Every week he went there to talk to her. He knew most people would think it odd behaviour for a young man. He rubbed his mother's ring on his little finger and said, 'I thought I was mad because that is exactly what I do.'

Ramma tried to reply but no words came. Harry turned his head to kiss her and was stunned by the passion in her response. Then she withdrew suddenly, casting her eyes to the ground. She reached for the video she had brought with her. Closely curled up on the sofa, they watched the kitsch Bollywood film.

When the young and handsome hero sang his desire, Ramma surprised Harry. 'That voice belongs to Daddy-ji. At fifty-three-years old he is still the singing voice for twenty-year-old movie stars!'

Ramma tried to explain over the music until Harry, unable to focus on both, reached over to the VCR and pressed the pause button. 'Start from the top,' he genially ordered.

'You can look all you like to try and find him dancing around a tree with a female star, but to be aware of Daddy-ji's presence, you must use your ears. The stars are hired for their looks but most of them cannot sing well so the actors mime to my father's recording. Do not get the wrong impression; he is not ugly, but there is too much character in his face to be a Bollywood hero. But you, Harry, you would fit the bill if you had a hint of tan!'

He responded with a mock audition trying out some Bhangra dancing.

'You need a bit more practice, Raja Hari!' she laughed. 'Daddy-ji's situation as a playback singer has definite advantages. Unlike the actors, he need not hang around the set for hours on end but can record songs for all the studios in one place.'

'How do you become a playback singer in India?' And then Harry laughed at himself. 'I don't know how anyone becomes a movie singer in this country either.'

Ramma laughed too. 'I only know Daddy-ji's story. His own father had a bookstore that catered to foreigners and my father used to work in it and sing when it was empty, or what we would consider empty in India. Some of the customers and friends of the family persuaded my grandfather to bring him to prestigious hotels to perform. At first, he sang the ghazals of the great poet, Ghalib. Because of his proficiency in languages, bored wives in the consulates taught him the songs of their homelands. Homesick Russians wanted Caucasian folk songs and the French enjoyed Songs of the Auvergne and tunes you could hear in the nightclubs of Paris. Americans asked for Gershwin and Rogers and Hammerstein. Before long, his recitals were earning the family more rupees than the book trade. His ghazals were recorded and a Bollywood producer hired him. Once the singing contract was signed at the age of nineteen, his fate was sealed.'

'And how did someone like you, the daughter of a celebrated Bollywood star, come to Oxford?'

'After my parents married, between his income and her dowry, Daddy-ji hoped that he could indulge his ambition and study history. As a child in the bookshop he delved into the history section and tried reading it all. He's actually incredibly well read, and near as I can determine, has been since he was a child. But I was born a year after he was married in 1973. My birth was not without complications. My mother could have no more children. So I was hardly starved of love and attention. I was thoroughly spoiled, actually,' laughed Ramma. 'I asked for something, and it was given. Really anything. If the nanny or Mummy-ji didn't give it to me, then I needed to ask Daddy-ji only. He hoped I would not be burdened by the constant pressure to attend family functions; we have wedding invitations every weekend of the season! He suggested I come here to study at the British Library and the Bodleian.'

She almost added, '...and fulfil his ambition.' It lingered like a tune. But his ambition had long ago become her ambition too. 'I wanted to come here also. Oxford has an extraordinary collection of rare historical documents. Human nature has not really changed. The more I read, the more I perceive the same vices and virtues played out on different stages. My hope is that with more knowledge, we see with greater clarity, and then we can choose the better path to walk down.' It sounded foolishly naïve and Ramma blushed once the words left her mouth. With a self-deprecating laugh she said, 'I just emailed my father that if we could learn how to avoid conflict using knowledge of the past, how much more tolerant the world would be.'

Harry smiled broadly. 'I agree.'

'So I came here to figure that one out,' she concluded.

Between them, they got through a whole bottle of chablis. There was something romantically old-fashioned about the film. No violence, just unrequited love suddenly being returned. They had a few laughs at the stock villains and stern fathers but the music was surprisingly good, by a composer called A. R. Rahman.

Perhaps it was the wine or maybe the music but when the heroine died, they were both in tears. It was the first time Harry's suppressed hurt and anger over his losses dissolved. He put his arm around her. His pain had just begun to turn to pleasure when his newly-acquired Nokia rang.

'Oh, bugger!' said Harry as Ramma pulled herself away.

'I must be going, Harry. Shukriya. Thank you for a lovely evening.

CHAPTER 7: Beating the Dealer

Simla, March 1874

Father threatens to cut me off unless I stop my campaign for reform. My letter to The Times about John Company's destruction of the Indian textile industries has had repercussions. Orders are down & he blames me. Mother says he will calm down if I marry Dora. The arrival of Dora's letter at the same time felt like fate. My Indian friends have no problem with that idea.

Monier-Williams has named the native religion 'Hinduism'. It derives from Sindu, a name the Persians gave to the people of the Brahmaputra, sometimes called the Sind River. People brought up in the strict parameters of our Abrahamic religions are confused by native Indian religions, & confusing they are. Most Indians don't distinguish between Hindu, Jain, Sikh & Buddhist. That is alien to us but it's because there is no 'belief system'. The scene is mystifying, like the many arms of Shiva, because Indians flirt with different gods & philosophies. I tell newcomers to think of it as a way of life in which you can devote yourself to an avatar. For a Hindu that avatar could be Shiva or Krishna or even Jesus or Mohammed. Christian missionaries & Mohammedans are offended by this. The implied equivalence is blasphemous to them but it is actuated by tolerance. No one brought up in the Indian religions is disturbed if you don't believe there is a God. Those 'Hindus' have a scientific frame of mind in which they discuss the unity of life. Because of that they tend to make great mathematicians. It should come as no surprise that Indian mathematicians invented zero. Just as well I did not talk about the possibility of 'no God' while I was at

Oxford, they might have rusticated me like Percy Bysshe Shelley!

I shall try to overcome my prejudice & give the 'Hindu' idea of fate a chance. Dora has a scientific inclination, albeit for botany. My parents have a point. I must talk to William & ask for leave to return home.

Harry was in a buoyant mood when he opened the shop, despite that wretched phone call. Unlocking the shutters, he found himself singing silly words emanating from the Bollywood film and moved from side to side with the Bhangra beat.

'Hmm, pardon me.' He was interrupted by a commanding voice.

An embarrassed Harry turned around to see an over-dressed, over-made-up woman in her mid-forties. The woman marched past him into Deco−rators as if she owned the place. She was a bottle-blonde, too put together. As sleek and twitchy as a weasel, she stalked her way around the store, fingering the goods.

'You the owner?' she asked.

'Yes, I'm Harry King. How can I help you?'

She looked around with eyes that didn't really *see* anything. Then she introduced herself.

'I'm Davina Green from LYNX TV. The good news is that we are in Oxford today looking for a location for our exciting new antiques show. Your shop looks perfect.'

'Nice to meet you, Davina. If you're thinking of making a programme about Art Deco and twentieth century design, you can see that's exactly what Deco−rators is about.'

Davina's eyes glinted with steel but she smiled broadly. 'I'm delighted you're enthusiastic because our idea will be good for your business. We will pay you for the use of your shop.'

Harry felt a frisson of anxiety creep over him. 'Perhaps you'd better tell me about your programme.'

'We have selected two couples to spend a week with Joe Buy learning the antiques trade. Each team will trade from your shop for a month and the couple who make the most money for Joe will be given £10,000 to start up in business.'

Davina maintained her artificial smile but Harry's expression hardened. He knew of Joe Buy, the TV front man for antiques, and guessed this programme was going to be another smug addition of this celebrity. The trade disliked Joe's dumbing-down and lack of interest in design qualities and social history. Joe Buy's only interest was making money.

Despite his unease Harry managed a courteous reply. 'What are you calling this show?'

For the first time, Davina hesitated. 'We haven't finally decided. One suggestion is "Beat the Dealer".

People who didn't know Harry well admired his cool and humorous way of handling difficult situations. But he had an edge. His face reddened as Davina's remark brought on an unwelcome memory. He saw himself, aged eleven, caught sitting alone sketching at school and being beaten up by a gang of boys.

'B-beat the dealer, f-flog the d-d-eeler,' he stammered. 'Isn't g-grievous bodily harm a crime?' Taking a deep breath he recovered his composure and looked Davina straight in her eyes. 'Do you mean to say it's alright if the victim is an antiques dealer?'

'Come, come, Mr. King,' Davina replied, snorting slightly. 'You're taking this too literally. It's just a bit of fun, family entertainment. And it'll be worth your while.'

'I appreciate you thinking of me, but I must decline,' said Harry as he opened the door.

But Davina's feet stayed firmly planted in the heart of Decorators. 'Joe really wants to use a shop in Oxford and yours is the only one with easy parking. I have the contract. You can treat yourself to an exotic holiday – get away from it all while we're here. All you have to do is sign and you'll earn £2000 a week.' She tapped her fingers on her designer handbag. 'We'll pack up and store most of your stock.'

Harry could picture the elaborate furniture and the sharp-edged, heavy, cut glass beloved by Joe Buy. He made himself as tall as his slim five-foot-seven stature allowed and said quietly, 'The answer is still no. I'd like you to leave.'

Davina went towards the door then turned and pointed a finger with a blood red nail towards Harry. 'You will regret this. Joe Buy has a lot of clout in your business.'

Harry was incandescent. 'Clout? When Ingrid Lindberg introduced me to this trade, it was respected. Deals were made on word alone, and people were respected. Your company doesn't understand that. "Beat the Dealer". No way do I want Deco-rators to be associated with anything so degrading.'

'You used to be a teacher, I believe. You should think about returning to the classroom. Short-sighted: that's the word for people like you, Mr. King.' And with the precise movements of controlled irritation, she left the shop.

An hour later, a couple came into the shop. Thankfully, Harry's good nature had returned and he was able to give them a warm welcome. The lady turned out to be a younger version of Ingrid Lindberg. Five-foot-four in her shoes and not short of a few pounds, her energy filled the space. Within minutes of entering, she was enquiring about the twelve-drawer oak chest and Harry launched into full storytelling mode.

'Did you know that civil servants and settlers on their way to the colonies were given an empty cabin? There was a sensible reason behind it. That way, they could take some of their own furniture and create a home away from home once they arrived. You can imagine there wasn't much available to buy in some far-flung destinations. You know the sort of place: Wellington, Vancouver... Oops, I'm sorry. Are you Canadian?'

'No, we're from Illinois.' Then she turned to her husband saying, 'but the Mid–west was pretty undeveloped in the 19th century, wasn't it, Jerry?'

'Sorry, I haven't introduced myself. I'm Harry King and I share Deco–rators with another dealer.'

'I'm Marge and this is Jerry. Charmed.'

'The chest of drawers was my find. You seem interested?'

'Possibly,' said Jerry, 'but please tell us a bit more about it.'

'The previous owners, the Carew family, took it to India and back, not just once but twice! You can see how big and heavy it is; it's made from English oak. But the weight didn't matter to the shipping lines, only the volume, the space it occupied. The Carews would have filled the drawers to the brim with clothes and practical items. They probably also took pieces of campaign furniture – the kind that came apart and could be re-assembled in minutes.

'I bought the chest of drawers from Professor Charles Carew, who was born in India. He was seven when his parents returned home from running a school in Mussoorie in the foothills of the Himalayas and settled in Oxford. He was already a history don when he inherited it and it was still housing his grandfather Bartholomew's collection. Bartholomew was a bit of a pioneer, it seems.'

'In what?' asked Jerry.

'In India's history and archaeology. But he was also an engineer and interested in the sciences. He was a polymath.'

'If it can go to India in the 19th century, Jerry, it can easily travel to Illinois in the twentieth.' Then turning to Harry, she said, 'Our sabbatical in Oxford is coming to an end. We leave in a month's time, but we want to take something home to remind us of a memorable year.'

She anticipated Harry's question. 'We live in Champaign-Urbana.'

'Wow, what a great name. It sounds like my sort of place.'

'It's a campus town, south of Chicago. The chest is a lot more substantial than we originally had in mind but I love its story.

And I adore cats – so opening the drawers with those pussy head handles will be a pleasure.'

Jerry wasn't as enthusiastic until he looked at the price label of £400 and was pleasantly surprised. 'We're renting a 16th century cottage, built around the time the Mayflower sailed. I thought of buying a Jacobean chest we saw in Burford – that's more my period. I'm over here working in the Ashmolean. I was keen to see that American icon, "Powhatan's Mantle".'

'The famous one embroidered with shells?' Harry asked. 'It's a powerful work of art, truly from another world. That's what I love about antiques.'

'I agree,' said Marge, taking off her headscarf and sitting down on the chair proffered by Harry. She stretched out her legs clad in red slacks and made herself comfortable before continuing loudly. 'Most people don't know about King Powhatan, but do know something about his daughter.'

'Wasn't she Pocahontas?' asked Harry. 'And didn't she marry John Rolfe?'

'Exactly. That's why the mantle's so significant. She helped the James Town colonists survive,' said Jerry. 'You see why I wanted something from the seventeenth century but Marge has fallen for your Victorian piece.' Twinkling eyes peered over his glasses. 'I know when I have lost the argument so I will lose gracefully. See if you can get a competitive shipping quote and we'll come back and seal the deal.'

As they left the shop, Harry remembered the story of Pocahontas and John Rolfe. Ramma and I are not the first to be attracted despite our cultural differences, he thought to himself with quiet optimism.

Harry was soon on the phone to the shippers. Transporting the chest was not as expensive as he thought. It was still volume not weight that determined the price. Like the Carews, Marge and Jerry could fill the drawers at no extra cost.

They returned in the afternoon to get the quote and the

idea of filling the drawers appealed to them. They were soon drinking tea sitting on the tub chairs and agreeing a deal. Being a historian, Jerry asked more about the Carews.

'I recall reading something by Charles; a paper on the ideas of the French and American revolutions, but I'm rather taken by Bartholomew. Can you find out some more for me?'

'My girlfriend's a historian too. Ramma promised to look for references to Bartholomew at the Indian Institute. He seemed unusually open-minded for his time. The early East India Company men adapted to the Indian way of life, but that changed after the Mutiny in 1857, which the Indians call the First War of Independence. According to Ramma –' then Harry stopped. He was uncomfortable about calling her his girlfriend and then quoting her like she was one. He wasn't sure what Ramma would have said if she'd overheard.

So he turned to Marge. 'I read some of Bartholomew's papers. Before 1857, assimilation wasn't just a male thing. He wrote about a Welsh woman called Fanny Parkes who went on loads of adventures in India around 1834. I gather she was disapproved of not for her spirit of independence but for learning to play the sitar and for wearing a sari on her travels. White supremacy was regarded as essential in order to justify the Empire and deny influence to Indians in their own country. Enlightened people like Fanny and Bartholomew were described as "going native" and came to be viewed as traitors to their race and their country.'

Jerry examined some of the papers stored in the chest and said, 'I expect they tolerated him because of his brilliant mind. They probably excused his love of Indians and Indian philosophy as academic eccentricity. Find out what you can about Bartholomew. I'd love to know what became of him.'

Turning to his wife, with a mischievous smile, Jerry added, 'How about writing up his story, Marge, seeing as you will have such a huge reminder of him in the house?' He winked at Harry and said, 'Marge is a biographer.'

Harry laughed. 'The way you talk, it seems like this chest of drawers has a personality. It's as if you are giving it the chance to tell its stories.' Harry handed them his business card. 'Do keep in touch and I'll get Ramma to email you the results of her research.'

Marge and Jerry liked the idea and left discussing the lives of the previous owners. Harry felt that Davina's aura had been well and truly exorcised and Kathy would be pleased to find out that the chest of drawers was sold. All in all, it was turning into a better day that the morning had augured – even though he couldn't meet up with Ramma that evening. Instead, he phoned her.

'What shall we do on Saturday? Can I meet you after I close the shop? No, what a pity! Sunday morning is out for me, unless you can come with me? It's the Brookes Fair. It is only four times a year so I don't want to miss it as I buy well there. Afterwards, we can take a walk through South Parks. What do you think? How about lunch at the Bird and Baby?'

'Where is that?'

'The Eagle and Child. Sorry for the infantile sense of humour. I expect Tolkien and CS Lewis told their jokes in Anglo Saxon. They called themselves, "The Inklings". Shall we call ourselves the "Etlings" since it was an Etling figure that brought us together?'

Like most art and antiques dealers, Harry was independent-minded but sociable. He was a member of the regional association in the Thames Valley. That evening there was a committee meeting starting quite early at 6:30pm so they could follow it with a meal and a natter afterwards. Over dinner, Harry shared the experience he'd had with Davina. Quite a few members had known the TV celebrity, Joe Buy, when he was a dealer and they all felt he'd fouled his own nest.

Helen from Tetsworth said that they had been approached to be a location for one of his earlier shows. She sighed. 'I told the producer it was pointless coming to us. I said, "You can't buy something here today and expect to sell it at a profit in a general sale at a provincial auction house next week – especially after the auction house takes its commission. If you wait for the appropriate specialist sale you might make a profit but you wouldn't want to wait that long." Davina said to me, "Helen, that doesn't matter, it's just a game". I replied, "It may be a game to you, Davina, but we are in this for life. So, no thank you."'

Harry felt vindicated. 'I wish I had thought of that. Well done, Helen. Let's have a bit of fun in the quarterly newsletter. We could invite everyone to invent the most outrageous TV shows that would make us seem like absolute idiots. On second thoughts, perhaps not! Joe Buy might get hold of a copy and use them!'

CHAPTER 8: A Thing of Beauty is a Joy Forever

Halifax: August 1875

I am a married man. My sabbatical ends next week. Dora is eager to see India but the Himalayas are no place for a woman. Her passion to come with me threatens my resolution. But I have promised that, without doubt, I shall send for her once I am back in Calcutta next year. I shall miss our walks together. Dora has taught me the Latin classifications of plants. She is as animated by a desire to understand flora as I am by engineering & rock strata. However her anticipation of seeing the abundance of Indian flora & fauna must be put on hold for the time being.

The theodolite I shall be using has a telescope & measures the angle between fixed points. In addition, it can measure how metals behave at different temperatures. I am hopeful that it will be more accurate than my altimeter. My only concern is that the theodolite is of great weight, & many porters will be required for its transportation.

On Sunday, Harry was examining a charger on the stand of a dealer from Taunton when Ramma entered the hall. Eyes turned. She was so lovely; it was hard not to stare. Harry introduced her to the dealer and, in cheerful mood, he bought the tube-lined charger and said he would pick it up later. Ingrid Lindberg was in the well of the hall and Harry wasn't surprised to see her buying an inexpensive curio. Despite her diminutive size, she was easy to spot because of her weakness for colourful hats and bright beads. He waved to her and as she approached, all he could see was a circle of crimson floating down the aisle. Her felt hat was so firmly pulled down on her forehead she appeared like a headless woman. Ingrid greeted them enthusiastically.

'This must be Ramma, What a wonderful surprise. I've heard so many lovely things about you. Can I give you a hug?'

Harry suggested a coffee and the three of them were soon laughing together.

'Harry was only twenty-one when I first met him,' said Ingrid looking at Ramma. 'He answered my advertisement for accommodation to let. He was a poor student working at his post-graduate teaching qualification but he could afford to lodge with us because my sister and I didn't charge much rent.'

'Because you packed us in like sardines,' joked Harry.

'We hadn't much choice. Maud and I were tenants, too,' explained a slightly embarrassed Ingrid.

'I was only teasing, Ingrid. It was great fun living with you – an experience I'm unlikely to forget.'

Harry noticed a wistful look flash across Ingrid's face.

'It seems incredible that people like us could rent a vast Oxfordshire Manor House in acres of ground. In those days such leases were relatively inexpensive. Now only millionaires would stand a chance. Even so, we could only afford it because, as Harry has reminded me, we took in seven lodgers to cover costs.

'They were the good times. I'd invite you both to my house now but there is barely enough room for me and the cats: one up one down with a little extension for the kitchen and bathroom. It was hard moving there after living in the Manor House with its fifteen spacious rooms, but I'm alone now so it suits me really.'

Ramma hesitated before asking in a soft voice what had happened.

'Maud's health deteriorated and I couldn't manage looking after her and doing enough business to keep us afloat. I tried, but for a long time I didn't want to face reality. But you can never escape; Nemesis always knocks.'

As they parted, Ramma gave Ingrid an affectionate embrace.

After Harry put his purchases in the boot of his car, he took Ramma by the hand and led her towards South Parks to enjoy the panoramic views. On days like these, when a dappled sunlight set the golden stone of the dreaming spires glinting against a hazy blue sky, Oxford was at its most alluring. Harry couldn't think of anywhere on earth he'd rather live.

As they enjoyed the spring in their toes on the grassy hill, he made Ramma laugh with tales about life with Ingrid as a landlady.

'Ingrid's sister, Maud, had a domineering personality. You couldn't help liking her but you wouldn't want to contradict her. It was her idea to rent the manor house and trade informally from it. Almost all the contents had price tags and we ate from, sat on and read by the light of all their merchandise. And it worked. She did sell loads from the house. There were always people coming and going, looking at the furniture and turning over the pots. Thinking about it, I didn't have much choice but to be drawn into the trade, did I? She even put price tags on the curtains, but how Maud imagined anyone would want to buy them is beyond understanding. The aroma of cats was pretty powerful!'

Ramma turned up her nose. 'There is one thing I find difficult to understand about the English. People here adore animals but they eat them also. Accha! Anyway, now I know how you became involved in the antiques trade. It was all Ingrid's fault, was it not, Harry?'

'I guess so. Ingrid rented space at Hungerford Arcade, and she encouraged me to go with her on buying trips. She liked illustrated books and thought that, as I studied art, I may have an opinion worth having.'

'You bought books and pictures?'

'Actually no, but Ingrid did. I discovered inexpensive thirties ceramics. At that time regular antiques dealers didn't merit them. Antiques had to be over a hundred years old. To me, they were works of art on clay that even a poor student like me could afford to buy. I should've been warned that it could turn into an addiction. Once I had my own collection, I either had to stop buying or start trading.'

'That explains everything!'

'I began trading at the weekends while I was still an art teacher. Life is strange. If I hadn't lodged with Ingrid, I don't think I would have become a dealer and then, I'd never have met you.'

He was tempted to kiss Ramma but had to make way for two dog walkers.

'In India, it is called karma,' smiled Ramma.

They headed towards the river. Because the path was narrow, they couldn't be side by side so conversation faded until they sat by the river in University Parks. Even the gentle Cherwell failed to cast a spell over the suddenly restless Ramma.

'Harry, what are we going to do? I have to return home when term ends in June. I shall be back in October but once I have finished my DPhil, I must start my career in India.'

'Can't you start your career here?'

'My subject is ancient Indian history and I want to do the archaeology as well as write about it.

'What post will you apply for?'

'My mind is on my DPhil. Only when I have finished my thesis will I explore possibilities.'

'Are you sure that isn't a pipe dream, Ramma? How many openings for archaeologists are there in India?'

Ramma glared at him.

'Harry, you don't understand the sacrifices I have made to come here, leaving all my family and friends behind. Some college friends have already chosen marriage and motherhood. I too would prefer to have a close relationship and someday be a mother but not yet, my career must come first. You may think my passion not worth uprooting to come to Oxford on my own knowing no one. For me, the alternative ideas that Ashoka tried are important. Where my research will lead I have no idea, but I want to achieve something with my life, starting here in Oxford.

I intend to go on from here, achieving even more. If I don't, I couldn't go back to India; I couldn't face my father. And you don't seem to get that.'

'I get it. You want to chase your dream. You think I don't want to chase mine?'

'You told me that you are an artist but you are kidding yourself, Harry. You haven't really made much art. You don't make the time for it; you're too busy running a shop. Art is rarely – if ever – on your agenda.' Her voice trailed off. 'I can't make that kind of a compromise.'

The blood drained from Harry's face. 'You're rich. You don't have to make compromises. I do.'

He leaped to his feet and strode to the river's edge.

They'd begun as a flirtation and once they'd shared the trauma of their mothers' premature deaths he'd thought they had made a deep connection. 'Damn,' he thought, 'why did I let myself...?'

He swung around to confront her, his lips tight in anger. But then he noticed Ramma's watery eyes and knew that she too was hurting and angry.

He stared at the tranquil Cherwell. As the minutes passed, he realised he didn't want to think about her leaving or about her unkind comment. He wanted something else. Something that captured a little bit of her just for himself.

'Let me show you an artist at work. Let me sketch you. I'll start with your hands.'

Harry always carried a leather bound book with him. He took out a thick soft black pencil, opened his book and began sketching.

'When did you learn to draw like that, Harry?'

'I've sketched for as long as I can remember. In Mum's favourite photo of me, when I was only two, I was drawing. It became an obsession after dad left. I had this urge to kind of fight back but I didn't talk about it. You probably won't believe this but I didn't say much at all. You know, fourteen-year-old boys! I expressed myself with a brush or pen. It could've been a lot worse; some friends whose parents split up around the same time thought that drugs were the answer. Studying hands, I felt I was in charge, doing something, not being taken over. Do you understand?'

'Yes, I do. I loved reading epic tales as a child and throwing myself into studying helped me also.' But Harry wasn't really listening.

'Mum bought me a book about Leonardo and he also sketched obsessively. Knowing about him meant that it stopped feeling crazy. Eventually, I had hundreds of examples and became pretty good at it, even if I say so myself.'

As he sketched, Ramma asked him, 'Why sketch a hand, not a face?'

'I do both. In fact, I draw all parts of the body, but the face and hands more than anything else express powerful thoughts and feelings.'

'What do you mean about sketching all parts of the body?'

Harry answered while shading the underneath of her hand and without looking up. 'When I was a student, I became interested in Francis Bacon. Have you heard of him? The studio, in Soho, where he lived and worked had paint-splattered walls and the floor boards were buried beneath the remains of masses of art materials. I couldn't relate to his messy lifestyle but he intrigued me.'

'Are not his pictures disturbing?'

Harry rubbed his mother's ring before replying.

He showed her the sketch. There, in black and white, were her hands, the slender fingers twisted with anxiety. She blinked in surprise. It had taken so little time to make and yet there they were, the edge of the palm showing, the familiar length, and her quiet display of tension.

'You know this like the back of my hand,' she joked. And

he smiled as he put the sketchbook and pencil away. 'Bacon's portraits are not photographic images,' he continued as if the sketch has been nothing at all. They're inspired by poses, movement and emotion and yes, some are disturbing. When he was interested in a particular part of the body he ripped up photographs. He pasted them all over the room and called them "my models".'

'I do not understand. What did he mean?'

'Those scraps – his models – were a catalogue of examples. I've copied him. If there is a bit of "anatomy" in a magazine or newspaper that looks different, I cut it out. Last week I did that to a print of an Al Greco portrait in the Ashmolean that has a contorted looking hand. I'm not as spontaneous as Bacon.'

He turned and smiled at Ramma. 'Don't worry. I don't rip them out and glue them to the wall. I paste them in scrap books like a well-brought-up boy.'

What he didn't tell Ramma was that after Helen left, he sometimes found himself doing a Bacon and ripping out pictures of her from his sketchbooks and photograph albums. He had only stopped since he met Ramma.

'Can I see some of your scrap books?' asked Ramma.

'They're like working tools. I haven't shown them to anyone. But sure. Come back to Canal Street and I'll show you some.'

Instead of going to the pub as planned, they returned to the car, picked up some Lebanese food from a deli and headed for Harry's house. After enjoying a meal together, Harry said, 'I'll wash up and put things away and you can amuse yourself with these,' and handed a few of his scrap books to Ramma.

While he was in the kitchen, she began to flick through them... hands, noses, feet, faces, breasts, penises... Ramma was not a prude. She enjoyed the temples of Khajuraho but there, the sculptures were sinuous and beautiful. Had she misunderstood Harry? He seemed nice and normal but these... some seemed crude and besides, who were they? Ramma was confused because up until now she had found Harry unusually sensitive for a man, sensitive in noticing things and emotionally too. She appreciated the way he responded to her moods and feelings.

Harry returned carrying two glasses of sparkling wine and was about to make a funny remark when he was taken aback by the look of disgust on Ramma's face. He gave a wry smile of understanding.

'Ah – you think art should be beautiful. But what is beauty? And who says beauty has to be regular, symmetrical?'

Ramma relaxed a little.

'You know Keats, the poet? He said beauty was in the eye of the beholder and he was right. Take a look at this.' Harry pulled out a book on antiques. 'See these grotesques by the Martin Brothers? They were our first studio potters and eccentric geniuses. Sometimes I think that to be a great artist you have to be... obsessed. What do you think of these birds?'

'I see what you mean; they are ugly but also strangely attractive.

Harry realised that Ramma was still shocked by his sketchbooks. He put them back in the cupboard and changed the subject.

'How's your research going? Any news about Bartholomew Carew that I can pass on to those nice American customers?'

Ramma was apologetic. She had got caught up in another line of research and had forgotten.

'That's not so different from me sketching and getting carried away,' said Harry, and Ramma seemed to agree.

CHAPTER 9: Ramma in the Bodleian

Sarnath, March 1876

Translated the Ashokan inscription. What a notion! Governance without capital punishment. I have to admit that the horrors of 1857 & the punishments meted out are not forgotten. The Fealice Beato's images of the hanging of rebellious sepoys will not allow us to forget. Indeed in England, people queued to purchase his images of the sites of the Mutiny & of the cannons used in the retribution. While those who favour order are pleased about that retribution, I am unsure that it benefits the Raj in the long run. I need a heavy draft of Keats' hemlock to induce forgetfulness of such violence. That or distraction with artistry that can be celebrated.

My ardent desire to see Samuel Bourne's photographs of the mighty Himalayas has been rewarded. I purchased two of them. He told me that he needed 40 porters to get his equipment to 18,600 feet. Bourne has built his company's success on portraits including one of the last Mughal King Bahadur Shah Zafar but it is his scenes of nature's grandeur that attract me.

The Ashokan inscription gives me hope that Homo sapiens can be compassionate. That brings me back to the odd inscription I translated of a government so benevolent that it didn't discipline the populace with some form of execution. It does make me wonder if such a regime could survive for any period.

Ramma threw down her pen, squeezed her forehead and sighed. Embarrassed, she looked around but the readers nearby were all focused on their work. What was she thinking of? Not her work, that was for sure. Harry. Again. This wasn't the Indian way. You were expected to fall in love with your husband after marriage – not before it.

'How can an Englishman adapt to Indian family life, where family rather than the individual comes first?' she worried. From what little she'd seen in England, extended family life was not embraced in the way it was in India. 'What about any children we might have? Where would they belong?'

No one else in her circle of family and friends had faced this dilemma. She had no one to talk to, no one to help her decide. This really was her karma.

'How can I be so stupid even thinking about marriage? Harry isn't interested in marriage. Why should he be? He can have as much sex as he wants without any commitment. He made no mention of marriage. Or children. Or family. Or moving to India. He could be in it just for a good time. He knows I'll be gone by July and then he can pick up another girl next year. That's probably why he's still single at his age.'

The pages of his sketchbook turned over in her mind.

'Do I even know Harry?' She put her head in her hands. 'Oh Ramma, how have you created such confusion. You could have married any guy in college in Mumbai.'

After raging silently at herself for a while longer, she finished with, 'It is not love. I am just lonely and anxious. It is not love. It is hormones. I've been gone for almost two years. So I shall enjoy my time with him now and once I go back to India, I will forget him.'

The librarian returned with the Prinsep papers that she had been working on the previous week. Ramma did a little calming yogic breathing as inconspicuously as she was able. 'This is my future. This is what I will take back to India with me. Not a man but a DPhil.'

She started to read the article but her concentration barely lasted ten minutes. Yogic breathing wasn't helping much either. She pushed herself away from her desk irritably. She needed a distraction. Not work and certainly not Harry.

'What was his name? Bartholomew Carew?'

*****

Two hours later, Ramma stared incredulously at an article intended for a Victorian journal on archaeology written by one Bartholomew Carew. The article suggested that there may have been as many as 10,000 pillars and rock edicts in India erected between 272 and 231 BC by King Piyadasi. When Prinsep translated Pali he decided Piyadasi was another name for Ashoka. The pillars and rocks acted like billboards promoting non-violent government and the welfare of citizens. Huge numbers had been destroyed at the time of the Mughal invasions.

Among the many papers she had been handed by the librarian was a letter from Bartholomew Carew to a respected Indologist, John Muir.

> *If I do naught else with my life, I am determined to uncover more pillars and edicts. The Raj wants to spread Christianity. That's all very well. Jesus was like Ashoka in his pacifism. Could Jesus have heard of him? The big difference between them was that Jesus rejected political power and Ashoka decided to use it. Their ideas have been conveniently put aside by generations who came after. In the case of Ashoka, I would like to resurrect him — with your help.*

Why had not she heard of Bartholomew Carew before?

Ramma had begun to fear that her thesis would be perfectly mediocre. There would be no university position awaiting her; no funding grants; no post-doc at Harvard or indeed at anywhere at all. Mediocrity got her nothing.

So she couldn't believe what she was seeing and re-read it

twice to make sure she wasn't making it up.

But eureka! This was the breakthrough she'd been seeking. Was this karma? She would never have stumbled on it without Harry. Why had she made that cruel comment? She remembered reading about the explorer Nairn Singh Rawat, and how that village boy's destiny had been changed by meeting those German brothers.

She phoned her father to tell him the news. She wanted to hear his delight but he wasn't at home. What would Harry think about the amazing coincidence? She must ask him to introduce her to Bartholomew's grandson. Could her relationship with Harry resolve itself in just such a revelation?

Her melancholy evaporated. She ran to Deco-rators only to find Ingrid.

'Is Harry in his studio?' asked Ramma.

'No he's out on a buying trip. That's why I'm standing in for him as Kathy has to be at a school show. Don't look so disappointed, Ramma. You'll make me think you don't like me.'

Ramma blushed. 'I just wanted to tell Harry some good news. Can you ask him to telephone me? On second thought, I'll write him a note.' She picked up a pen and dashed off a note saying she had exciting news and wanted to meet Charles Carew. She handed it to Ingrid saying, 'You will remember to give it to him?' and then hurried away.

Once back in her flat, she switched on her laptop. She was the first in her department to buy a Micron laptop but she was sure, once the price came down, every student would have one. She emailed her father with the exciting news that her thesis could be groundbreaking.

*****

That morning Harry had set off to view an auction with some art glass he liked the look of, and on the way back he decided to call on his old friend William, a member of the association that specialised in Whitefriars glass and Benson lamps. Among the pieces from Carews' chest was a brass lamp with an attractive spiral attachment. Harry felt sure it was made by Benson, the first designer in England to make lamps to hold electric light bulbs. William Morris, a good friend, had nicknamed the lamp maker 'Mr Brass Benson'.

William Carew and his partners traded from a beautiful tithe barn that was a delight to visit. Their dog, Oscar, rushed up to greet Harry and danced around wagging his tail so energetically that Harry thought it would fall off. 'Wow ol' boy! Where's your master?' As he reached out his hand, William Carew appeared in the doorway, 'Hi Will, I'm always staggered at how Oscar manages to avoid breaking the glass when his tail wags at 100 miles per hour.'

'Good to see you, Harry. How's Kathy and Deco-rators?'

'As long as we stay active and don't rest on our laurels, we make a profit. I can't see me getting a holiday this year, though. I'll make sure Kathy can get away with Paul and the boys.' Harry unwrapped the lamp. 'I want to show you something.'

William was pleased because it was indeed a Benson lamp. William persuaded Harry that a swap was in order: a pair of 1930s Whitefriars lamps in pale purple glass with swirls like dark snakes entwined around them in exchange for the Benson lamp.

'Where did you find it?' asked William.

'I bought it from two academics in North Oxford. Their surname is the same as yours. The lamp probably belonged to his father, Douglas, but it could even have belonged to his grandfather, Bartholomew.'

'Bartholomew Carew! From the Lancashire Carews. Crikey! Distant but not so distant that we didn't know them. My father revelled in telling me stories about Bartholomew. Not exactly the black sheep of the family but a mysterious figure nonetheless;

he was the one they all talked about.'

William invited Harry to have a late lunch with him in the garden under a fiercely carved head that had once graced a plinth outside the Sheldonian before it was damaged by traffic pollution. William told him all he knew about his distant relative. 'Bartholomew's father owned a mill in Halifax and made a pile during the industrial revolution. He wanted to move up the social ladder and sent his son to Harrow. Bartholomew was frightfully intelligent and went on to Oxford. He read Classics but dabbled in everything. Like most adventurous young Victorians, Bartholomew wanted to see the world. His father encouraged him to enter the Indian Civil Service.'

A confused Harry replied, 'I didn't visualise him as a civil servant. The chest was full of scientific instruments, drawings of archaeological sites and photographs taken in remote places: in deserts, up mountains. Bureaucracy doesn't quite fit the image.'

'From what I was told,' continued William, 'he fell out with the ICS, not because of the paperwork, but because he disliked his colleagues. Sixty years earlier, he could have been a White Mogul with a local family but in the 1880s, he didn't fit in. Imperial attitudes had set, you know. The problem for an open-minded man like Bartholomew was that the civil service had become infected by Macaulay's disdain for Indian culture, and the ICS had become dismissive of Indians themselves.'

Harry nodded. 'I gathered as much from his correspondence. The chest was full of his papers, articles and letters. None of it is organised but I've read enough to realise he wasn't popular. In a letter to an Indian friend, he expressed disgust about the colour bar in the clubs. He talks of musical evenings with sitar music and dancing but he doesn't say where they took place.'

William surprised Harry with a family story. 'He made some dangerous enemies. He criticised the East India Company for destroying Indian-owned industries. The company put its own financial interests above everything and everyone. Bartholomew fell out with his father who profited from the Company's rotten business tactics. The Carews owned a mill so after the East India Company wrecked Indian looms and Indians were forced to buy their cloth from England, it made the Carew family a lot of money.'

Harry was horrified. 'I didn't know that. We weren't taught that in school!'

William gave a philosophical shrug of agreement and made a noise as if to say, school education, pfsst. 'Bartholomew worked for the Great Trigonometrical Survey and that was an incredible achievement. But the East India Company was like the huge multi-nationals today – only interested in money. Bartholomew's father vowed to cut him out of the inheritance if he didn't shut up, as his knowledge and standing weren't good for business. Despite the Raj, Bartholomew found some things to his liking. While working on the survey, he came across some archaeological remains that interested him. He attracted support for a dig from a wealthy aristocrat whose name I've forgotten. As children, we weren't allowed to forget that, because of his interest in science, they made him an advisor to the Viceroy.'

'In his folders, there are tables about measuring the height of mountains, but I think his passion was for archaeology and photography. How he could pursue all those interests in such depth is amazing. Quite the Renaissance man.' Harry was painfully aware of his inability to deepen his own artistry and now with Ramma, he had even less time. 'I read a report he'd written before setting out on an archaeological expedition during the hot months. He never returned from that expedition.'

William nodded. 'He disappeared and was never heard of again. Because of the enigma, *Boy's Own* used him as an inspiration for some of their adventure stories. All sorts of conspiracy theories and oriental mystery stories abounded. One was that he was eaten by the Abominable Snowman.'

Harry laughed. 'I'll have to tell Mike Wells. I sold him some of Bartholomew's mountaineering measuring devices. He'll enjoy that story. I also promised the American couple who bought his chest of drawers that I'd let them know if I learned more about him, so thanks a lot, Will.'

Harry called by at Deco-rators, to see how business had been. Ingrid said a glamorous American blonde had been looking for him.

'She looked familiar so I gave her your mobile number. Did she ring you?'

'No,' said Harry, ignoring the implication. 'Did she say what it was about?'

'Not to me, but she will come back because she's left a deposit on Kathy's French mirror.' Engrossed in wondering where she had seen the blonde customer before, Ingrid forgot to give Ramma's message to Harry. He told Ingrid about Bartholomew's story and how William was a distant relation. It prompted her to say, 'The shippers telephoned. They are coming for the chest of drawers tomorrow. You'll need to rehouse the contents!'

'Thanks for reminding me,' said Harry. 'I'll be here early tomorrow and see to it first thing. Bless you for standing in for me today. You are a star, Ingrid.'

Harry rang Jerry and Marge to tell them what he had learned. When they heard his story, Marge asked, 'Can you copy some of the papers for us?'

Harry made a photocopy of the newspaper article from *The Times of India* and put it in one of the drawers. Marge came into the shop and bought a couple of Bartholomew's scientific instruments and asked Harry if he had a photograph of him. Harry had found some and telephoned Judith Carew asking if they wanted them back but she'd said, 'No, but thank you for asking; we don't have children to pass them on to.'

There was one of Bartholomew and his wife, Dora, with their baby, Douglas, but the one he gave Marge showed him with some soldiers on a bleak mountain. Harry was surprised that he was clean-shaven. His image of Victorians, from Darwin to Dickens, was of men in badly fitting suits with beards or moustaches. Although Bartholomew's clothes were of the time they were not as formal as Harry had expected. Bartholomew had a modern demeanour. There was something that reminded Harry of the Augustus John portrait of T. E. Lawrence. It was the eyes and the determined jaw.

Handing the pictures to Marge, he said, 'Charles Carew rather resembles his grandfather but his features are somehow softer. Bartholomew looks more rugged but they have the same nose and jaw.'

Marge said her farewells and gave Harry her address in Illinois, along with a suggestion. 'If you ever come to Champaign-Urbana, you have an open invitation to stay with us. Every time I open one of these drawers, I'll remember your delightful shop.'

After she left, Harry finished emptying the chest of drawers. He stared hard at a turbaned man in one picture. 'Surely,' mused Harry, 'he's not an Indian. That's Bartholomew Carew!'

Harry rang the Pitt Rivers Museum but was disappointed. He thought he was a bearer of interesting and fresh material but discovered that they already knew about Bartholomew because he had made donations to the museum. The curator said, 'Bartholomew's gifts include Tibetan prayer wheels and books in Parsi with wooden covers and pages held together with threaded string. But the gifts we most value are his photographs from northern India. It must have been challenging to transport his equipment to those remote places.'

The museum was interested in Bartholomew's cameras but had a tiny budget for acquisitions. Harry promised that he would donate them. As he put down the phone, Harry realised he'd become hooked on Bartholomew Carew. More of his day had been spent talking about the Victorian than about the business. In the final drawer to be cleared was the enigmatic man's rosewood writing slope. Harry put that on his desk. He decided to keep it and store the best photographs in it.

He remembered something Ramma had said. 'There are days when I wonder why I am doing this. Outside the sun is shining and the blossom is on the trees yet here am I in the library ploughing through badly written articles. But then I discover a nugget of something rare, a revelation that feels like uncovering a bit of the world for the first time.' A spark of excitement had lit up her eyes as she recalled one such revelation in the British Library.

Thinking of Ramma, Harry picked up the phone to call her. There was no answer. Harry reluctantly put away the rest of the documents and photographs of Bartholomew. There was something about him, something intriguing. Harry ground his teeth. 'I must stop wasting my time. One day when I don't have to earn a living maybe I'll write about him. His story could inspire a novel.'

The idea amused him but he had to prepare for a demanding fair. Kathy had been sceptical when he'd suggested that they exhibit at prestigious interior design and antiques fairs every three months.

'We need to get our name out there, and the most cost-effective way is to exhibit at big fairs with lots of footfall,' he'd said to her. 'You know my opinion. One day the internet could become a selling tool as more and more people get online. When that happens we'll be able to contact customers from all over the world. Art Deco collectors from the US and Australia could order items we have put on the net... you never know.'

'Stop dreaming, Harry,' an amused Kathy had responded. 'Who's going to want to buy something they haven't seen and handled? And how do you propose we run the shop and a stand at the fair at the same time?'

'While your children are small, I'll run the stands and we can pay Ingrid to help you out here. What do you think? Simple?'

His plan had worked. Visitors to the fairs called in when they came to Oxford. A popular event near Birmingham was imminent. The four-day fair involved considerable effort. He needed to set up his stand on Tuesday and put decorative finishes to his display, while the stands were being vetted on Wednesday. Dealers at the show did some business between each other on the vetting day. Because his prices were competitive and he had an eye for the unusual, Harry always sold well before the fair opened to the public. By the end of those fairs, he was exhausted. While he packed his stock for the fair he thought about Marge's remarks.

'She really meant it when she invited me to Champaign-Urbana. This business may be tough but it has its advantages. New friends in America and Ramma from Mumbai. You can make good friends in this business even when the going is hard.'

Harry had a small, contented glow. Four years ago he took the plunge and left teaching to trade full-time. What would he have done if Aunt Julie hadn't thought of him in her will and enabled him to open Deco-rators? He had so much to thank her for. He was even living in her little terraced house in Canal Street, which he had bought off her when she moved into sheltered accommodation. Harry had taken out the mortgage while he was still a teacher. If he had applied for a loan after he quit teaching, the bank would have been less likely to grant it. Without Julie's inheritance, he would still be teaching. Harry smiled as he worked. His mother's ring caught on the edge of a box. 'If only Mum could see me now,' mused Harry.

CHAPTER 10: All the Fun of the Fair

Dehra Dune, November 1878

Dora posted a photograph of Douglas on his second birthday. What to do? I have a strong desire to meet the little fellow. Dora became with child at such remarkable speed. I had promised she should come to India but when she told me she was with child, I could not let her come. There are too many graves of women who died giving birth in India & I could not expose Dora to that risk. Although a healthy child surely, Douglas is still too young to risk being brought out to the tropics. The diseases here, & the heat, take out sturdy young men at a rate of knots. I cannot risk my son. Another reason why they cannot join me here.

Dora writes that we have not spent sufficient time together. Her disappointment of not being with me in India is immense. She is not mistaken; we hardly know each other. That is not unusual in Indian marriages. Couples often meet for the first time on their wedding day.

If Dora is to come to India she needs to know how I am regarded by members of the club. They rejected my proposal that Indians should be allowed membership. They are unable to accept any Indian as an equal. As a naïve and trusting youth, I departed from England awash with the belief that Indians are like children who need our moral guidance. That assumption was shattered within days of my arrival & I drew enormous pleasure from learning about Indian philosophy & mathematics. It came as a great shock when that buffoon, Jones, called me a white nigger.

They interpret Charles Darwin's On the Origin of Species's concept of survival of the fittest as proof of their superiority.

I re-read it & did not misunderstand Darwin's thesis. It concerns a particular biological meaning. It is about species adapting to their environment so they can reproduce. I was not free of these assumptions when I arrived but my experience troubles me. Why should questioning the validity of these assumptions make me a traitor?

The only other authority that can guide me on this issue is the Good Lord above. It is accepted wisdom that it is His Will that we be dominant. Those with faith do not question His Will. Why is it that I cannot stop my thoughts from going down these unwelcoming tracks? I find myself at odds with both my homeland & my faith.

There is no one with whom I can discuss my concerns or my ambitions. Except, of course, for this battered diary.

Harry had picked up a hire van after closing the shop and Kathy was helping him load the larger items for the fair when Ramma telephoned. She seemed annoyed, saying something about leaving a message.

He apologised. 'With packing for the fair, it could have got covered up by a piece of stock. Can it wait? Tell me about it in when you come to Birmingham on Sunday. Sorry, honey, but I can't talk now. Kathy has come in especially to help me load the van and has to fetch her children from nursery.'

Ramma knew that Harry wouldn't be able to introduce her to Charles Carew until after the fair. She decided to tell him her news on Sunday when, driving home, she would have his uninterrupted attention.

*****

While unloading the van at the exhibition hall near Solihull, a fellow exhibitor waved him over. 'Hi Harry. Have you heard the news? That muppet Joe Buy is filming his latest assault on the trade here. A lot of us want to take it up with the organisers. He devalues everything he touches. Hope you'll join us.'

'With pleasure, Ed, but I hope tomorrow is okay because I've a lot to do today.'

The stunning layout he'd devised was intended to promote his interior design skills. Interior design was one of those businesses where he needed one proselytizing customer to set the ball rolling. He began by crisscrossing two beams over the stand, from which he intended to suspend twenties chandeliers. The gauze ceiling he arranged with a tent effect. His days at St Martin's had not been misspent. Harry hung up a wall hanging on which he had painted the Art Deco entrance to the Savoy. He made a semi-circular step leading to it on which he placed a mannequin dressed in a spectacular Schiaparelli dress. Harry had invested a lot in the gown but now that it was on the step under the chandelier, it looked spectacular.

On the other wall, his background was a touch Italian. He hung one of Kathy's French mirrors between the stone pillars he'd painted like a stage set. The shimmering Schiaparelli dress was reflected in the mirror and glistened under the lights. It would be a pity to sell it on the first day; it would ruin the effect. In the middle of his stand he placed an art deco dining suite on a vibrant thirties circular abstract rug. He had hired two cabinets: one for Kathy's stock and one for his. The DIY skills Harry had acquired as a teenager combined with his artistic talent gave the Deco-rators stand the wow factor.

Pride of place on his eye level shelf were the tapered Keith Murray black basalt vases. Harry had done something unusual for him: he'd priced them high. In general, he went for a modest mark up and a quick turnover and had to work hard finding the stock to keep it up. But this was different. All his other stock, the furniture, the bronzes, the Whitefriars and the Susie Cooper were competitively priced but the vases was to be the star of his show and command Hollywood fees, because selling them would be like parting with a good friend.

Harry had produced a promotional brochure for his art and design work. Another member of the regional association was into reclamation, so Harry had included sketches of architectural features as background to some of the photographs. Over a hundred dealers had picked up his '*Deco-rating Interiors*' leaflet even before the fair opened.

There had been an uneasy atmosphere among the exhibitors because Joe Buy was filming at the fair. The title of LYNX TV's show, '*Buy and Sell the Buy Way,*' said it all. The novices, groomed by him, were meant to outshine everyone at the fair – even those who had been in the business for thirty years. LYNX TV liked him because his shows were cheap to produce, and they exploited his flamboyant appearance and his catchy bylines. LYNX TV... 'Cheetah' would have been more accurate! 'Follow the Goggles' referred to his huge round specs but also, cleverly, to the idea that in the antiques trade you need to develop an eye. The traders resented his presence because the celebrity had begun his career as a dealer. Pete, on the next stand, crudely expressed what others were thinking. 'He's kicked the balls that gave birth to him.'

Kathy's suggestion to buy the window model and spotlight the dress had worked. The Schiaparelli sold even before the opening. One of the vetters bought it and was happy to leave it in situ with a sold sticker until Sunday. Harry was still the proud owner of the black basalts but he had sold six other Keith Murray pieces. To crown it all, he had a potential customer for his design business. A glamorous American film star, Selene Charmer, attended the fair and admired Harry's stand. On a closer look, she recognised some of the stock.

'I bought a mirror from your shop. It's that bijou place in Walton Street, isn't it? I've bought a manor house near Abingdon and I need to furnish it.'

In one of those poignant coincidences, Harry immediately knew that it was Sutton Manor and how much she'd paid for it. For a million pounds, she had bought the house that Ingrid and her sister used to rent in the late seventies and eighties. Earlier in the year Ingrid had brought *The Oxford Times* to show him the estate agent's advert. She had struggled to control her emotions. Not bitterness, just the end of an era. Now here he was, meeting the new owner.

'The house badly needs to be completely made over! I don't think anything has been done to it for forty years. It needs to be gutted and new services installed. Then you can come and give me your opinion. I'm not promising you the whole contract, but I like your style so you can begin with the dining room. Tell me about this Art Deco suite.'

Harry didn't let on that he had lived in the manor house in his student days but knowing it so well, he made confident suggestions to suit the surroundings. He found it hard to suppress a grin when Selene said, 'I'll need fumigators too. There's a strange cat-like smell coming from under the windows.'

It felt too good to be true. Selene Charmer as his client! Paying his mortgage could prove easy after all. 'If I become her interior design consultant and am able to help furnish Sutton Manor, I might even be able to afford to take a holiday,' Harry said to Pete. 'Ingrid's a regular moviegoer at the Phoenix Picture House. I don't understand why she didn't recognise Selene when she visited Deco-rators! Do you think it's because she looks shorter and slimmer off the screen than on? Or maybe Ingrid has only seen her dolled up in plunging necklines, not in jeans and a jumper.'

Harry got on the phone to update the astonished Kathy on the identity of the mysterious American whom Ingrid had failed to recognise. 'That has to be brilliant for business. Could we suggest she use the shop as a film location?' After laughing with his mate, Harry spared a thought for Ingrid. The estate agent had been discreet because had Ingrid known who the buyer was, she would have told him.

After lunch on the final day, the fair became lethargic. Ramma arrived by train at two o'clock and agreed to look after the stand while he went for a good look around. He strolled past Joe Buy's TV stunt stand; the celebrity looked anything but cheerful. Harry stopped for a gossip with a fellow dealer in Art Deco who was close by.

'What's with the teeth and goggles?'

'Unlike yours, his stand hasn't been popular with the punters. Rumour has it that their takings would have amounted to a loss if they'd paid rent. You do know that the organisers provided him with a free space for his over-the-top glitter? They take the line that he's good publicity but most of the stand holders don't agree. Joe Buy came under the misguided belief that we'd give him a hero's welcome, so he must be disappointed.'

Harry agreed. 'He gives the impression that anyone can succeed in our business without knowing anything or putting in the hard work. If you don't care about or know anything about art and design history how can you be successful? Customers won't trust you.'

'One or two people said as much to his face. For a moment, I thought he was going to explode. You know his reputation for a foul temper and those who work with him feel the brunt of it. Knowing the TV cameras were constantly running, it was fun watching him struggle to control himself.'

'Is it true that someone actually called him by his real name?

'You heard about that, did you? That didn't go down well either. They'll have to edit that out of the film. It was Jenny, the Camden deco dealer. And he was foul-mouthed to her face, four-letter words, you can imagine.' The dealer pulled an appalled face.

'I don't mean to flaunt my youth but I don't remember that far back. What was he called?'

'When he traded in Harrogate, he was John Bald. It doesn't exactly ring bells, does it, especially as he's so proud of his ginger locks. After he was offered that *Buying Bargains* series, the name Joe Buy caught on and the big round glasses appeared. He couldn't lose with that image: unforgettable!'

'The fair's nearly over now. His long–suffering staff will get the full benefit of his good mood after six o'clock. Although I met one of them, and she was a piece of work herself. They need to be hard as nails and twice as tough to cope with him.'

On his way back to his stand, Harry met Mike Wells, the dealer in scientific instruments, taking a look around. 'I'm surprised to see you here on a Sunday. I'd have thought anything you're interested in would have sold on the first day.'

Pointing to a large carrier bag he replied, 'I've just collected some gear I'd reserved. Bainbridges gave me a call. They've picked up some interesting early photographic stuff and it's from India. Surprising, isn't it. That Bart chap – you sold me his altimeter, he was in India too, wasn't he? I've been looking into it. A lot of those guys were from wealthy families and able to afford all the latest gizmos. I'm wondering whether a trip to India could be worth my while. What do you think?'

'Why don't you give me a call next week? I've some of his equipment left, although I want to keep a couple as souvenirs. Do you know William Carew, he trades out Henley way? It turns out that he is distantly related to Bartholomew. He told me that Bartholomew became a kind of superhero. I could try ringing Charles Carew in case he has anything else that could interest you.'

'I appreciate the tip. I just passed your stand. Who's the lucky guy, then?' Harry looked embarrassed but it reminded him of the time. 'I'd better be heading back there. Good to see you. Let's have a drink and a chat when you're next in Oxford.'

Harry, by way of an appeasement for taking so much time, bought double ice creams on the way back and handed Ramma a coconut and mango sorbet.

'Hi honey, everything okay? I've bought these in case you need to cool down. Sorry I've taken so long.'

'Ha ha...actually, I have enjoyed myself. These gentlemen have been looking after me, even if you have not.'

'Surprise, surprise,' said Harry signalling to Paul the art dealer opposite. Harry admired Ramma for adapting to their banter, learning how to answer back and not taking him too seriously. He liked that a lot.

'Why don't you take a look around, honey?'

'Good idea. I want an insight into this strange world you inhabit, Harry. It is all quite new to me.'

'Business can be dire on the last day, so don't expect it to be busy. That's why it's the best day to network. See if anything catches your eye.' It was a suggestion he was to regret.

Ramma wandered up and down the aisles until she was drawn to an incredibly ugly but strangely attractive bird. She stopped to look at it. The dealer approached her. 'It was made by Robert Martin of the famous Martin Brothers, Britain's first studio potters. This piece was made in Southall.'

'I know Southall. When I get homesick, I take a trip there. Strange, but your bird reminds me of something,' replied Ramma. This bird had a touch of mischief, almost a wink. She found it hard to believe it was ceramic.

The dealer said, 'It's called a grotesque, and these feathery personalities are the most desirable Martin Brothers pieces.' The bird had its eye on Ramma and she continued looking at it while she moved away. As she stepped backwards, she bumped into Joe Buy, who was stalking the aisles, Davina Green and a cameraman in tow.

Snarling with rage, Joe Buy roughly pushed Ramma away, swearing loudly. 'Watch where you're going, you fucking Paki bitch.' Spittle sprayed.

Thrown against the stand, Ramma flung her arms out, off-balance.

As she steadied herself, he slapped her behind. 'Piss off. Get back to where you came from.'

Delivered with contempt, his words shook her to the core. He was in her face, breathing hotly, malice radiating like something physical. It seemed as if he might hit her.

An eerie silence lasted for what felt like minutes but was only seconds. The dealers within earshot froze. The camera was still rolling; surely this was staged? One look at the humiliated Ramma was enough to convince them. They darted forward and shielded her from the angry Joe Buy. In a flash, a group stood between her and her abuser.

The celebrity was hurried away by his embarrassed attendants.

'Are you alright, dear?' asked the owner of the bird.

No one had ever racially abused her before. In her protective bubble of love, with enough wealth to avoid the harsher aspects of life, Ramma had entered adulthood almost unbruised. 'Excuse me,' she whispered and dashed off.

'Who was that? Was she your customer, Mary? If so, that ghastly man has lost her for you. Did you hear what he said?'

Ramma took some time locating Harry's stand. Dazed, she lost her way in the aisles. Harry saw her at the end of his row looking confused, and waved. She didn't respond but walked hesitantly towards him; her usually glowing brown skin looked pale and devoid of blood. Her hands were shaking. Harry asked her what the matter was, quickly sat her down and brought some water. She was so quiet Harry thought she must be ill. The timing was dreadful. The announcement that the fair was closing came over the loudspeaker system. It was time to pack up. With apologies for not helping her, Harry got to work, breaking up his stand.

In any case, Ramma did not want Harry chasing after the vile abuser and neither could she repeat the words he had said. For her, to utter them would mean some kind of acknowledgement, almost a victory for that pig of a man. So she simply said, 'Harry, I feel faint. Is the air conditioning off? It has become oppressive in here.'

Harry didn't want Ramma to help with the carrying but she insisted, hoping the activity would alleviate the shock. The drive back to Oxford was unusually subdued. Ramma didn't want to talk. The excitement of her discoveries in the Bodleian had vanished, replaced by despondency. Harry turned on Classic FM. They always played soothing music on Sunday evenings but he said to Ramma, 'There's that recording of Ravi Shankar, in the dashboard, if you prefer. It has an evening raga, too.'

Ramma closed her eyes, and he could not hear what she replied. It was as if he didn't exist. Wherever Ramma was in her head, she wasn't with him.

CHAPTER 11: Disaster

On Board the Benares, June 1879

Apart from the ports of call the best thing about a long voyage is having the time to read. Disappointed in Murchison's biography of Faulkner. He seems surprised by his Indian assistants' proficiency with the theodolite & explains it as 'the intelligence, docility, & exquisite manual dexterity of the natives' when 'backed by their faith in the guiding head of the European.' Bah! I've been to the best schools & worked with the best of their alumni & I could tell Faulkner a thing or two about our guiding hands. Thereafter, I switched reading material to Indian mathematics. An explanation of their invention of the zero is the Hindu & Buddhist concept of nothingness.

Read Gibbons' Rise and Fall of the Roman Empire. The Romans were also entrenched in arrogance. They believed their empire would last forever. Gibbons interprets the world beyond the Greco-Roman Empire as 'barbarian'. How can a fair-minded person possibly describe the Ottoman, Indian and Chinese civilisations as 'barbarian'? A sense of superiority underlies most empires, it seems. The Survey is a great scientific achievement – one of the greatest of our century. I am privileged to have worked on this admirable endeavor, but I feel ill at ease when I witness the less sophisticated cartographers embellishing their maps with Indians kowtowing to their so-called British masters.

Was a sense of superiority & domination over others equally true of the Ashokan civilisation? The evidence I have collected appears otherwise. Ashoka, as Priyadasi beloved of God, did not appear to want to rule other countries but to influence them.

For now the British Empire looks invincible, but pride cometh before the fall. No one in India talks of Ashoka now. I am beginning to think that his was one of the greatest civilisations the world has ever seen. In my wildest imagination, I could never have conceived of an empire at that time which worked for all classes of people and tolerated dissent. What happened to Priyadasi's world? Why was he written out of history?

As they came off the M40 at Junction 9, the heavens opened. Even with the windscreen wipers on full speed, the road was only just visible.

'Bloody rain! Sorry for the language,' said Harry. 'I'll unload the van in the morning. Let's just have supper and crawl into bed.'

The plan had been that, for the first time, Ramma was going to stay overnight. But this wasn't the mood he had hoped for.

He tried to lighten it with a joke.

'I'm knackered and I'm looking forward to being spiced up.'

The previous day, Ramma had made Chana Massala and Chilli Paneer to heat up when they arrived back in Canal Street, tired and hungry. But Ramma said nothing nor did she show any reaction to his double meaning.

'Fair enough. I wouldn't get a comedy slot on the radio.'

Harry was worried when there was still no response from Ramma, but just ten more minutes and they'd be home. 'Hmm,' thought Harry. 'Home? It's really just my house but the word "home" came into my head. Why's that? Because Ramma's coming to stay? Because I want us to make it a home?' The thought was like a resolution to Harry. He would make things right. After a meal he could find out what had caused the sudden change in his girlfriend.

In front, there was a lorry driving carefully in the treacherous road conditions and a motorcyclist with headlights full on was coming up fast behind. Harry signalled to turn right and swore as the motorcyclist went into the middle of the road, headlights glaring, and began to overtake him.

Wagnerian lightning split the sky, the sound so penetrating that Harry's body jerked. The equally surprised motorcyclist skidded on the wet road and Harry swerved to avoid him, braking sharply.

'Bloody idiot.' The words were hardly out of his mouth when he heard an ominous crack as Ramma's head hit the windscreen.

'Ramma, Ramma, are you alright? My god, what happened to your seat belt? Ramma, speak to me. Please... speak to me.'

Thanks to Harry's quick reflexes, the motorcyclist was unhurt and sped off without apologising or seeing if they were okay.

Ramma slumped back into the chair, her head flopping forward.

Harry's mind raced. Suddenly, all tiredness vanished. He knew exactly what to do and did it with burning efficiency. He spun the van around and drove as if Ramma's life depended on it. The speed camera on the Woodstock Road flashed. Up Rawlinson Road on to the Banbury Road, another ominous flash, the last mile down the Marston Ferry Link Road. Flash! He arrived at A&E in five minutes flat. Running for help and a stretcher, he babbled like a man possessed. But when they saw Ramma, they took him seriously. The doctor took her blood pressure. It was going through the roof. Harry could see Ramma's heart beating and she was shaking uncontrollably.

'Please, please, don't let her die.'

It had been years since Harry had prayed but it was all he could do. Not since his mother was diagnosed with breast cancer had he felt so desperate, but prayer had not worked then. He felt helpless and hated it.

An hour later Ramma regained consciousness, and the

doctor concluded his examination.

'Miss Gupta, you'll be pleased to know that there should be no permanent damage. Try to rest and not return to work for at least a week and only then if your GP checks you and gives the go ahead. We prefer to keep you in overnight for observation. Is there anything in your past medical history in India that we should know about?'

Ramma seemed forgetful and so Harry suggested he phone her father.

'That sounds like a sensible idea. You should go home and leave her to us, Mr King. You look as if you could do with some sleep,' said the doctor.

*****

Harry parked the hired van, noting that he should move it before the parking wardens did their morning rounds. Once inside, he had a quick sip of brandy. And then topped up the glass before picking up the phone.

Harry found himself talking to Gangabharti for the first time. He introduced himself quickly and wasted no time explaining what had happened. Then he said, 'The hospital asked if there was anything we should know about Ramma's medical history. She did have quite a blow. They were surprised at how deep her concussion was.'

'I'll ring our doctor right away and book the first possible flight,' replied Gangabharti with urgency and anxiety in his voice.

'She'll be alright, I promise you,' said Harry. 'Knowing that you're coming will lift her spirits. Ring me when you have a flight number and I'll meet you at the airport. I'll let you have any news.'

Harry didn't think he would sleep but he did. First thing in the morning, he rang the hospital. The ward sister said, 'You can take Miss Gupta home after the doctor's round when he is likely to give the okay. She will need to make an appointment with her GP.'

Harry gulped down a coffee and rushed outside to his Volvo, passing the hired van and seeing that it had already acquired a non-resident's parking ticket.

He quietly swore. He would ring Kathy to help him unload but only after he'd visited Ramma and brought her home, and made her comfortable.

Later, sitting in his bed, Ramma looked ill. Harry fussed helplessly. Then the phone rang. He told Ramma that it must be her father but it was an aunt saying her father was on his way

'Good news. Thanks. He'll see that Ramma's going to be fine. Would you like to speak to her? Here she is.'

He handed the phone to Ramma. Ramma looked pleased after a long conversation.

'I told her there was no need for him to come as you are looking after me but she says his plane should arrive at Heathrow at 11.20. It will be good to see him and I can introduce you two.'

'I'll meet his flight. You'll be okay for a couple of hours?'

'No, I am completely helpless! I have described you to him before but I'll write a card with his name on for you to hold up.'

Harry felt relieved. Ramma's humour had returned.

CHAPTER 12: Arrivals and Departures

London, December 1880

My address to the Royal Geographical Society in Kensington was well received. There was quite a stir when Richard Burton entered the lecture theatre. I had the good fortune to meet him & his wife, Isabel, in Bombay in '76. They remained there only a short while because small pox was raging. Isabel & Dora should get on famously. They can both work themselves into a state of ferment when witnessing cruelty to animals. I would invite the Burtons to dinner but there was an insurmountable obstacle: Dora does not approve of Richard. She claims to know of unpublished papers by him relating to unsavoury practices indulged by him on his travels in Africa. According to Dora, he is unworthy of the name of a Christian gentleman & should be prosecuted under the Obscene Publications Act. She took a hackney carriage home to Bloomsbury rather than meet him.

It was very considerate of Dora's father to leave the London house to Dora. The location is convenient for me, close as it is to the British Museum. Dora spends a great deal of time at Kew. The Metropolitan Railway has transformed journeys west. A network of underground railways is under construction. I have requested access to observe techniques of tunnelling before I return to India. Methinks an underground crossing of the Hooghli could do for Calcutta what Brunel's tunnel under the Thames has achieved for London. Putting aside my irritation with the prejudice of Empire, the excitement & optimism I get from these great technological achievements knows no bounds. Thank goodness my part in the India project is with the Great Trigonometrical Survey, which must be a good thing for India & the world.

Burton took me to his club. I imbibed somewhat excessively. In the absence of the ladies Burton went into great detail about the sexual practices of the harem & his intention to translate the Kama Sutra. At such time as it will be published, he has promised me a copy. He was at Trinity College twenty years before me but any mention of him was frowned upon. His escapades were notorious.

Douglas is a fine little chap & James & I took up where we left off, as brothers can. I wish I could say the same for Dora. We had not enough time together prior to my return to India. India felt alien in '69 but now I miss it. It is more my home than is Halifax.

Terminal 3 was busy as usual. Harry joined the crowd around the arrivals exit and held up a sign saying "Harry for Mr Gupta". Harry wished he could have met Gangabharti in India. And he worried. 'He may not like me being so close to his daughter.'

Ramma had given him a photograph of her father. He was a tall man with striking carved features and long hair tied back: an ageing Indian hippy. Harry saw him coming through the gate and went to greet him, putting out his hand.

'It's great to meet you. Ramma has told me such a lot about you, sir. She'll be so happy to see you.'

'How is my daughter? I want the truth, young man.' Harry did his best to describe what happened but couldn't hide how he felt responsible for the accident.

'I am not interested in who or what was responsible. I need to know how she is and if there will be any permanent effects,' said Gangabharti.

Driving back north up the M40, Harry did his best to answer his anxious questions.

'The John Radcliffe is a good hospital, sir, and they reassured us that there should be no side effects. Ramma is usually a fount of energy but she does look tired. It may take a day or two to get over the shock.'

Leaving the motorway Harry tried changing the subject to Ramma's work. Twenty minutes later while parking his car outside his little terraced house in Canal Street, Harry noticed the hired van, heavily decorated with parking fines.

'Oh, damn,' he said aloud.

Gangabharti looked surprised.

'Sorry, Control Plus has given me another parking ticket on the hire van. I didn't get a chance to unload it. That'll be a sixty-pound fine and an extra day's rental. Fuck. Sorry about the language.'

Gangabharti did not appear impressed by either Harry's tiny terraced house or his swearing. Neither form of address was in favour; they were not off to a good start. Harry unlocked the door and a pale Ramma ran to her father.

They hugged each other long and hard as the tears welled up. Harry discreetly left them to it and went into the kitchen to put the kettle on. He loved his little cabin of a kitchen, but how it would appear through a Bollywood singer's eyes? Ramma's father was no shallow crooner; surely he would see beyond the superficial? Harry returned with a tray of tea and Susie Cooper cups (no mugs today), and some of Kathy's homemade lemon drizzle cake. Gangabharti was smiling.

'My daughter tells me you saved her life. I want to thank you; she is the most precious thing in my life.'

He went to Harry and held him in a powerful bear hug.

'Ramma tells me you painted that picture,' said Gangabharti, looking towards a canvas of a dreamy floating Radcliffe Camera. 'You and I are going to get along.'

Harry relaxed into his winning smile. He made an excuse and left the room, leaving father and daughter some catch-up time. There, piled up in the hall, were four days of mail and newspapers. He went through the post and fifteen minutes later took the newspapers into the lounge. Ramma smiled at Harry and then at her now-relaxed father.

'Oh, the famous English press. Let me take a look.' He began happily flipping through the pages occasionally reading a feature and making a witty remark. 'I see Selene Charmer is closing her sweet mouth. Sensible girl. That rascal Sean Lemon must leave a sour taste.'

Suddenly his face screwed up with rage. Ramma had never before seen such an expression on her father's face.

'Daddy-ji, what is the matter? What is wrong?'

Gangabharti threw the paper on the floor.

'There – look at that! I am taking you home – right away – no matter what it costs.'

Harry picked up the paper. He was looking at a photo of a distressed Ramma facing an angry Joe Buy and a smug Davina Green under the headline *TV Celebrity Joe Buy Accused of Racist Attack.*

An exhibitor who had witnessed the incident at the fair had let the press know about it. The celebrity's narcissism meant his TV crew was subject to his wrath when anything went wrong – especially if he was responsible. So it was hardly surprising that an employee of LYNX TV then leaked some film to the newspaper. What was gossip and hearsay became completely verifiable.

Harry was appalled. This was the first he knew of it. Of all the possible things that could have gone wrong, he'd never considered this. 'Ramma, honey, why didn't you tell me? That was why you felt faint – nothing to do with the air conditioning.'

'Sorry, Harry, but I could not bring myself to describe what happened or repeat those words.'

Harry wanted to hug her and promise to protect her in the future but the expression on Gangabharti's face stopped him in his tracks. Her father had already picked up the phone and was asking Air India to reserve two tickets on the next flight to Mumbai. He didn't give Ramma a chance to object. He also seemed to be blaming himself.

'What kind of father am I? Why did I let you come here alone, forcing my dream on you? Forgive me, Beti. There you were in hospital without a loving family around you, abused by a man who should know better. Your image disrespectfully in a tawdry newspaper... We shall put an end to this. Your aunties and cousins will help you put these unpleasant experiences behind you.'

Ramma began to protest. 'Daddy-ji, it was my dream too and everything was going well until...' but the shock and the accident did not help her powers of persuasion. Sad relief swept over her; at least the homesickness would be over.

Harry drove them to Ramma's flat to collect her things. He wanted to talk to Ramma alone but there was no opportunity.

'She'll tell Gangabharti that she wants to stay,' thought Harry. 'If she wants to leave me, then I bloody well won't plead for her to stay, not in front of her father.'

Ramma moved as if to take his hand and he immediately regretted his anger. She looked exhausted and ill.

'You will come back to Oxford, won't you?' he asked, a touch of despair in his voice.

'Of course I shall, Harry. I have to finish my doctorate and the Carew papers you gave me this morning will help. Thank you for everything. Can I have one of your sketches to take with me, Harry? When I see it, it will remind me of you.'

'You can have all of them, you do know that, don't you?' said Harry.

'Do you remember you sketched my hand? Can I have one of yours?'

'I'll fetch my book and do another one while you pack.' Harry took his sketchbook out of the car and set to work. When he was finished, he cut out the page, rolled it up and held it out for Ramma. As she took it, she accidentally knocked the sketchbook, which fell open on the floor. A picture of herself her face and shoulders, her body half turned to him, lay looking up at her. Harry scooped up his sketchbook without a word. Ramma was not certain how to react. Harry had sketched more than her hand but when and where had he done that? She visualised all his other "models". Was that all she was to him?

When their taxi arrived, Gangabharti said goodbye to Harry kindly enough but without the warmth he experienced before he had seen the sensational picture of Ramma in the paper. Having been in Oxford for less than half a day, Gangabharti was heading back to Heathrow, his daughter beside him. Harry watched the taxi drive off, hoping that something would happen. Ramma throwing open the car door when it slowed for the red light and running back to him. The taxi circling the block so that she could give him a long, passionate kiss. Neither happened. He would have settled for a turn of her head and locked eyes. Or even a raised hand and a blown kiss. Really anything, he'd have settled for.

He had let himself love again and now Ramma had left him. Why did everyone he loved die or leave him? Did Ramma even know how he felt about her? They hadn't seemed to need words. Harry got up and paced up and down the room. Why was he such an idiot? He had just stood by and let her walk out of his life, without putting up a fight. He didn't blame Gangabharti, in fact he felt responsible for what had happened. After all it was he, Harry, who had suggested Ramma visit the fair – it was he, Harry, who had suggested she take a look around. But how could he have predicted what would happen? He could not imagine anyone wanting to treat such a lovely person with anything other than respect.

His anguish was interrupted by the sound of his new Nokia ringing. He fumbled for it, still unused to having a phone on his own body. It was Kathy. 'Harry, I am at the shop and see you haven't returned the stock from the fair...'

'I'll be there ASAP.' He drove to Deco-rators and unloaded. He returned the van to the hire company and paid the excess. He explained about the parking tickets. The man on reception raised his eyebrows.

'I hope you're loaded, mate. We'll have to pass your details on to Control Plus. Thanks for telling us.' Harry nodded resignedly. What a day.

Two days later, a subdued Ramma phoned him from Mumbai. He should not worry. She would be fine and would always remember him and that first visit to Deco-rators. 'The deco bronze is in my study. It looks wonderful. I shall see it every time I work at my computer and it will remind me of all the fun times we spent together. I'll frame the hand sketches and hang them side by side.'

Harry knew he should grasp that moment to tell her how much he loved her but somehow, being worlds apart and on the telephone, the right words didn't come.

'Are you sure you're telling me everything – you really are better? I... I... I could not bear it if I thought...'

'Really. I am fine, just tired and confused. Yes auntie, I'm coming.' Ramma had described life in an Indian home; how lovely it could be for children. There was always someone to respond to them. Friends and relations constantly called unannounced.

Harry found himself saying somewhat formally, 'Give my regards to your father.' As he put down the phone, he despaired of himself. 'Did I really say that as if Gangabharti was a customer?

CHAPTER 13: The Aftermath

The Suez Canal, March 1881

Dora chose not to see me off. She is angry with me for not arranging for her & Douglas to come to India. Dora is an intelligent woman & is finding her life frustrating. She said she married me to share in my adventurous life, & if she had known she was to be abandoned she would have chosen another suitor. I do rather feel that she has a point. Therefore, I am resolved that my procrastination must end. My concern for their health is genuine but, in truth, Simla would be a safe enough location for them.

I must be honest with myself. Father gave me this diary as a place wherein I can do that; a secret place to wrestle with my soul. Despite its beauty, I have come to detest the life in Simla & I stay away from the upper town as much as I can. Is it really my concern for Dora & Douglas's well-being or my ambivalence about the Raj & that, through Dora, my family could come to know about it? They would regard my siding with Indian ambitions for deliverance from the British as not only unpatriotic but also as treasonous.

It was hard saying my farewells to Douglas. My father is looking none too well. He thinks that my interest in geology & archaeology will soon fade, like a child's passing fancy. I should tell him, I am over thirty now, not just a grown man but solidly middle-aged. This is who I am. Yes, that is what I should say. But then we would have a blasted row & I don't want to leave England with recriminations. Better to be reticent. Besides, I am ashamed to admit it but I am still dependent on his financing my trips. The ICS, unfortunately, is generous to me no longer, & I have found no other backer for my explorations. The public appetite to fund private adventuring apart from the polar regions & Egypt seems to be diminishing. This leaves me dependent on his good will. Nonetheless, I should be filled with remorse about leaving him & Dora & Douglas. Thank the heavens for James. Any regrets are eclipsed by the excitement that I feel about this assignment. I spared no expense on the new camera. The rapid development of gelatine dry plates will make field photography an easier procedure. The cartographers in Himachel Pradesh will be impressed.

The phone rang with friends and customers who'd seen the pictures in the newspapers. Once reporters knew of Harry's connection to Ramma, they kept asking to interview him. Harry was unsure how to deal with it. He wanted to expose Joe Buy but Gangabharti was determined to preserve his daughter's privacy. Impotent, angry at Joe Buy and aching for Ramma, Harry retreated inside himself. Kathy took charge, politely but firmly turning away the press. The takings from the fair had been excellent, whereas sales in the shop were falling. At first, she thought it was a seasonal blip and nothing to do with Harry's mood, but selling is a strange business. Kathy knew when you felt upbeat and confident, sales increased. A self-employed life style didn't come with holiday pay, sick pay and pensions; somehow she and Harry had to provide that for themselves. And the bills for the shop overheads came in regardless of Kathy and Harry performing under par.

Ingrid had introduced them at the Jam Factory, the affectionate name for the old Coopers Oxford Marmalade factory where Kathy had rented space. In those days Harry was an art teacher and had on his arm Helen, a pretty lawyer who worked in the City. They'd become friends and when Kathy and Paul married, they'd invited both of them to the wedding.

The spark of their business association began with a conversation over lunch in the Jam Factory's café, The Marmalade Cat. This was where he first talked to Kathy about his idea of starting a business devoted to good design from the past and the present.

'Not everything old is good and not everything new is ephemeral.'

After Kathy asked him what triggered his passion for good design, Harry gave a typical Harry answer. 'Have you heard of Buckminster Fuller?' Kathy thought the name familiar but couldn't place him. From anyone else, the subsequent lecture could have sounded pompous but when Harry was passionate about an idea, he was engaging.

'Buckminster Fuller was way ahead of his time. Even in the 1920s, he was talking about the problem of finite resources. *The Operating Manual for Spaceship Earth* was his solution. What a great concept and it didn't involve a hair shirt. Rather than reduce our standard of living, he said we needed design efficiency to make more with less. Ever since I read his book I knew for certain that when design and function are perfectly married, the product is beautiful too.'

It was unusual for a man to talk to Kathy as one human being to another with no gender stereotypes. She was lucky because her husband, Paul, was the only man she wanted and he enjoyed Harry's company too. 'Harry thinks outside the box; he's open to new ideas. You know how some people feel threatened by anything a bit different. Harry is the opposite; he embraces diversity and he has a sense of humour too. We all need that.' Kathy still agreed.

She remembered when Harry had brought his mother for lunch at the Marmalade Cat. She'd witnessed the strong bond between them. His mother had died tragically young; fifty-five was no age nowadays. Kathy and Paul had gone to the funeral with Ingrid Lindberg, Mike Wells and William Carew. Kathy knew how devastating it had been for Harry and was gutted that she hadn't known how to help him.

Since then, Harry had become important in her life. Her first baby had turned her life upside down. The second didn't help any. Although she loved her sons to bits, her life disappeared under the pressure of feeding and nappy changing. Her trading seemed to be going nowhere fast at a time when she most needed the income. Then Harry's Aunt Julie remembered him in her will. His inheritance came with a note saying that he should use it to follow his dreams. Kathy would never forget the day when Harry invited her to share Deco-rators.

'Harry, are you sure? You know my answer is yes! Say it's true. And knowing you, you've done all the risk assessments and returns on investment. This means I can develop my business with you and still have time for my family.'

An Indian summer evening blessed the opening party at Deco-rators. It was one of the most memorable nights of Kathy's life. Picturing it gave her a warm glow. She recalled the excitement as the guests poured in admiring Harry's quirky signage and discovering the dazzlingly elegant interior. There was no clutter. It had a Scandinavian lightness with added warmth and personality. Cool but not bland. Harry made sure the glasses sparkled with prosecco while she welcomed the guests.

A friend of a friend, who shared her passion for the 20s and 30s, bought seven pieces of her vintage jewellery and that gave Kathy the confidence that Deco-rators could be a success. She recalled showing her customer around.

'Here's my Pottery Ladies display. Doesn't the colour blow you away? That cabinet belongs to Harry. He's a devotee of Keith Murray, you know, the architect who designed for Wedgwood in the 30s? His ceramics are a bit plain for me. Harry sometimes turns his hand to sculpture and prefers the elegance of simple shapes. Didn't you know that Harry is an artist? Let me show you some of his work.'

Kathy pointed to Harry's amusing paintings. 'He painted this one in Cornwall. I love the beach sandals on the stairs and the floating grandfather clock.'

Her companion nodded in agreement. 'I'll buy that, Kathy. It'll be such fun looking at it over breakfast. It's kind of mischievous but beautiful too.' Beaming, Kathy put a red dot on *The Sandals of Time.*

'Have you really finished teaching, Harry?' another customer asked, as Harry wrapped up one of Kathy's Charlotte Rhead chargers.

'I'll miss the kids but there was never time to be creative. Even here, much of my time will be taken with running the business. But look,' Harry enthusiastically opened a door on a small studio, 'at quiet times I can work in here and the bell will let me know when I'm needed.' Some of the well-watered guests demanded a speech.

'This is bittersweet moment. My biggest supporter was my mother. Many of you here tonight knew her and would know how proud she would be of Deco-rators. None of this would have been possible without her sister, my Aunt Julie. Please raise a glass to the memory of both of them. Thank you all for coming and supporting us. Kathy and I hope this won't be the last time you walk through that door. We need to do some business to pay the rent! But whether you buy or not, you can be sure of a warm welcome and a cup of tea!'

'Since when all this devotion to tea? Remember the beer drinking bet we had at college?' called out an old student friend. 'Or was that the cause of your conversion?' The company enjoyed the interruption.

'Trust Justin to remind me of past errors! You're revelling in the past and I,' and he pointed towards their stock, 'in past glories.'

As they all toasted each other, Ingrid and Kathy turned

towards each other smiling with pleasure at the cheers of approval. Harry went over to Ingrid and kissed her on both cheeks. The seventy-two-year old blushed like a schoolgirl but beamed with pride.

'This is your fault, Ingrid! All those trips in your battered Volvo – it was you who led me astray. I'll know who to blame if it all goes wrong,' he teased.

The night was still balmy as the guests began to leave, when Mike Wells, a large bearded Welshman, loomed over Harry. 'Where's that lovely girl of yours, Harry? Thought she'd be here tonight.' Harry's mood deflated for the first time that evening.

'The bank offered Helen a permanent contract in New York, so she's not coming back.'

'Sorry to hear it. Keep cheerful, Harry, old fellow. Think of all those gorgeous students who'll come through this door.'

Kathy remembered how Harry had struggled to smile.

Those had been optimistic times but now Kathy believed she was fighting for the survival of Deco-rators. Harry was in danger of a serious depression. His gloom infected the whole shop. Kathy wasn't just worried about her livelihood. She was more worried about Harry. About what would happen if he didn't pull out of this funk of his. He showed absolutely no interest in customers when they came through the door. He barely made eye contact, as if that was too much effort. Sales were plummeting. When Helen had left, Harry had carried on. But it was different with Ramma. Their backgrounds could not be more different but there was something poignant about Harry and Ramma together. Harry told her that he and Ramma had lost their mothers in the same way and didn't need words to understand how they felt. Kathy knew what that meant to them and had imagined them moving in together quite soon.

'Everything's unravelling,' concluded Kathy to Ingrid on the phone. 'I'm thinking of ways we can help.' And she ran an idea past Ingrid. 'Let's organise an exhibition in the shop and have a jolly preview evening and invite all our friends and favourite customers like we did when we launched Deco-rators.'

'Remember how excited Harry was at buying those black basalt vases? What about a joint Keith Murray and Clarice Cliff exhibition? Call it *Psychedelic Colour meets Minimalist Shape*? Could that arouse his enthusiasm?'

They made some plans and checked dates and then confronted Harry with the idea.

'It can be a kind of anniversary exhibition,' said Kathy.

Harry agreed for their sakes. When they set about organising it, he seemed to be going through the motions but his heart was not in it.

'Have you been in touch with Ramma? How is she?' Kathy asked him.

'Yes, I emailed. Amazing tool, isn't it? She replied only an hour later. I'm grateful to Tim Berners Lee.'

'Who on earth is he?' asked Kathy.

'The Englishman who invented the internet. Or at least, one of them. He was a student here in Oxford. I heard that he was banned from using the lab computer and made his own.' Harry hesitated. 'But it may be weeks before we can email again. Ramma wrote that she was leaving for Ujjain in Madhya Pradesh. Her father suggested she join an archaeological survey organised by Delhi University. They're investigating some Buddhist sites. Her Oxford tutor knows and is happy with the arrangement. This must be Gangabharti's way of keeping her far from the clutches of the press until this Joe Buy thing dies down.'

'But after that, she'll come back here?'

'She'll come back to present her thesis and have her viva but I don't think her father will want her to settle here.'

'When will she need to finish her DPhil?'

'No idea. She said she couldn't get online while in the field but promised me a snail mail letter. But that was two weeks ago and since then, nothing...'

Harry bit his lips. That was how it began with Helen, the gaps between calls getting longer and longer until nothing and then that letter.

Kathy was quick to pick up on Harry's body language and said, 'See here, partner. If Ramma doesn't stay, she isn't the last and only woman out there. But if she is the one for you then Carpe Diem. Do something! Post her an invitation to the preview evening. Pity there's no chance of her coming but at least it will keep her in the loop.'

Harry liked the idea and it gave him more energy too. He'd write to her about it and have something they could share on line. He wanted to fight for her but didn't know how unless he closed the business and went to India. His capital was small. His business ran on turnover and a bankrupt suitor was unlikely to appeal to Ramma's father.

CHAPTER 14: The End of Deco-rators?

Calcutta, July 1881

My Indian team continued excavating the sites of the pillars & recording the rock edicts even after the money I left with them had been exhausted. They are as engaged with this discovery as I am. The cantonment, however, pours scorn on the project. Someone reported on my strange attire. The accusation of going native has resurfaced. Fieldwork with the cartographers is just what I need to get away from the malicious gossip.

What occupies my mind, however, is the vexing issue of funding. Lord C's money will soon run out. Have I sufficient resources to continue my search for Ashokan inscriptions? I believe that I am uncovering a lost civilisation but am I deluding myself about the importance of this Buddhist-inspired government? Indeed, one is forced to delve into metaphysical issues that befuddled me at Oxford: Do we ever learn from the past? Buddha taught that one should release oneself from these fears; that a man cannot be free to pursue his true path until he frees himself from his worries & concerns. So I shall take this worthy advice. I simply must stop procrastinating & decide what to do about Dora & Douglas. I do indeed long for my own family. The work fully taxes my abilities day & night, but there is a longing that goes unanswered. Bringing my family over would solve that problem & make Dora happy in the process. I have forfeited much for this career path: my faith, my compatriots, & now the tenderness of a wife's embrace. As well, if Dora were here, she would grant me respectability.

The cost however is a life beyond the cantonments. I would be captured & contained & I am not good at meaningless dinner party small talk. And I could not take Dora with me. Few British women are prepared to befriend Indian women as equals & despite her intelligence, Dora is a snob.

Accepting Viceroy Ripon's request that I advise on the routes of railways given my experience on the Survey could help solidify my position here but the privileges of the Raj which come with it feel to me a loathsome burden that I must carry in order to continue my studies.

Harry and Kathy set about re-arranging the shop ready for the show. Harry threw himself into a grand tidy-up and while sorting through a pile of receipts, his heart jumped. The handwriting in front of him was Ramma's. It was an enthusiastic note about, of all people, Bartholomew Carew. It must have been the message she had tried to tell him about before the disasters happened one after the other so quickly.

'What's the matter?' asked Kathy.

'I've been such an idiot. Ramma was excited about something the day before the fair and I didn't listen, did I? Look she left a note.' Harry waved it.

Now he understood why she had sounded annoyed on the phone. She believed that Bartholomew Carew was the original lead she had been seeking and wanted him to put her in touch with Charles and Judith Carew.

Clenching his fists, he banged them on the desk. Even the sound was painful. Harry tried but couldn't keep still. He began to pace up and down the shop.

'Oh, Harry, I hate leaving you like this but I must fetch Rory from the nursery. I haven't forgotten Selene Charmer's visit this afternoon. A friend is having Rory to play. I'll get back just as soon as I can, I promise. I'll definitely be back to look after the store while you show your designs off to Selene.'

As Kathy hurried out of the door, the postman called a cheery hello and dropped off their mail. Harry opened three letters from the Thames Valley Police and swore bitterly. There laid out in front of him was not one but three speeding fines incurred when he had rushed Ramma to hospital! Weeks had passed so why only now? Then he remembered the police would have contacted the hire company first. These notices meant not just the fines but more seriously, the points on his license! He would be banned from driving for a year! How could he run his business without a car? How could anyone survive in business without a car? How could he pay his mortgage without a regular income? He'd need to take a job as a supply teacher in order to keep up the payments. How could he tell Kathy? He threw the letters at the wall, and then swung his arm across the desk, scattering the files.

Feeling utterly sick, he turned the key in the lock as if it was for the last time and made his way to his local, aptly named Jude the Obscure. He felt like a character in a Hardy novel: he'd be the miserable git. The novelist understood how it felt to love and dream only to see everything spiral out of control. As he sat down alone with his pint he drank to Ramma. What a lucky escape for her! What kind of husband or father would he make? Unreliable, just like his own father.

While he was out, Selene Charmer, his first film-star customer arrived. Selene had an appointment to discuss her dining room makeover. She tried the door of Deco-rators.

When Harry had told Kathy about the prospect of a film-star customer, she'd danced around the shop. 'You do realise what this could mean? Once the gossip gets around that Selene shops here her fans will follow. If her friends like your work on her house, the orders will come rolling in. This could put us on a secure financial footing. You'll be able to take a holiday, Harry.' This was the big day when the foreseeable future of Deco-rators could be assured.

Outside the shop, Selene Charmer looked at her watch. Two

o'clock. She was on time, a few minutes early, even.

She turned sharply on her heels and snapped at her driver, 'If he can't be bothered to be here, he doesn't deserve my money. We're leaving. Now!'

Kathy, on her way to the shop so Harry could give time to Selene, waved merrily when her car whizzed by. But Selene looked annoyed and didn't wave back.

The shop sign said "Open" but as she tried the door, Kathy realised it was locked.

'Oh Harry, what have you done?'

Fifteen minutes later Harry returned to find an upset Kathy. Paper was strewn all over the floor and she was on her hands and knees picking it up. But when she saw Harry's expression, her anger disappeared and she gave him a warm hug. He told her the whole miserable story.

'Leave Selene Charmer to me,' she said. 'Go home and call Mike Wells – he's in town. Go out for a drink with him – NOT on your own!'

Kathy dialled Sutton Manor and related to Selene the whole sad tale of the dash to hospital, the incident in Birmingham and Ramma's rushed return to India and now the likely driving ban.

'In normal circumstances, Harry is so reliable and hard working. You'll love his ideas, I know you will.'

Selene listened. She was a kind woman and said that, despite what had happened, she would continue to patronise Decorators but, from what Kathy had said, Harry couldn't work for her at the manor – not without a car. But she agreed to come to the exhibition preview to show that she forgave him.

Next, Kathy rang Harry and persuaded him to appeal the points on his license, after all there were extenuating circumstances. Harry took her advice and sure enough a month later the length of the ban was reduced from twelve to three months. But the judge said to Harry, 'There *is* a reason why we run an ambulance service, Mr King. I can't let you off altogether.'

CHAPTER 15: Meanwhile in India

Letter to Edwin Howard, September 1885

> I have received a report from Bahadurgarh. Surveying a sparsely populated area near the Nepalese border, Major J. stumbled across 'an unexpected monument' but no evidence of any other structures or remains. Could they have stumbled on an Ashokan pillar? Questions are filling my head, far more than I have the wherewithal to answer so I must desist from posing too many. I have devised a systematic exploration of the area but the Viceroy has foisted me with a project which could take up to four months to complete. Alas, my friend, our trip north will have to wait. Have you any suggestions for the meaning of the last line of this rock edict ...

Seated on a canvas-covered stool beneath a banyan tree twenty miles outside Ujjain, Ramma was enjoying the break in the middle of the day. Most physical work was done in the morning and early evening to avoid the hottest parts of the day. Ramma had been reading a letter from Bartholomew Carew to a fellow Indo-enthusiast, Edwin Howard. She had been going through the Victorian letters that Harry had thrust in her hands as they made their goodbyes. 'These are more use to you than to me,' he'd said.

Since the dramatic events of her final week in Oxford she had concentrated on living each day as it came but suddenly she was filled with regret. 'I let Daddy-ji take me home without saying anything. What must Harry think? Could it help things seem normal if I write to him about what I am learning about Bartholomew from the letters and papers Harry gave me?'

She began to write to him.

Hi my King,

I have an idea where Bartholomew was heading when he disappeared. In correspondence with Edwin he mentioned a trip north and discussed searching for the birthplace of the Buddha.

I am sorry, Harry, but I cannot email for a while. I have the opportunity to join the national archaeological team on a dig in Madhya Pradesh, near Ujjain. Ashoka was governor of the city during his father's reign. After that we move on to Sanchi, which is not far from Bhopal, the state capital. (You may have heard of it, because of the disaster, in 1984, when the Union Carbide pesticide plant leaked noxious gas.) Hope to get on-line again between digs but if not, I promise to write you an old-fashioned letter. I will try to make it as engaging as the letters I am reading. Accha.

But then Ramma stopped. She really didn't have anything else to say. Her father had forwarded her post to Ujjain and she'd received the invitation to the opening of an exhibition of work by Keith Murray and Clarice Cliff at Deco-rators. Another chance to show off the black basalt vases! Harry was getting on with his life. She could still feel his enthusiasm and hear his voice when he'd told her about Murray.

'Keith came here as an early aviator, trained as an architect and designed the Wedgwood factory at Barleston. There was this gleaming new factory using moulds from the nineteenth century! He set about creating pared-down contemporary shapes. Look at these. Don't you just love them?'

Ramma guessed that Kathy would be exhibiting her Clarice Cliff. Thanks to Kathy and Harry, Ramma had no choice but to know that Keith Murray and Clarice were contemporaries, yet their ceramics couldn't have been more different. 'Clarice Cliff is more to my taste,' Ramma had told Harry. 'How could a homesick Indian in Oxford not be attracted to her colours?

They're more Indian than English.'

Now, sipping her cool drink, Ramma mused, 'Harry and I are as different as Clarice Cliff and Keith Murray.' She imagined a grey sky over Walton Street and that was how she suddenly felt: ashen. Had she lost Harry? He was part of that world while she was here, digging into Bartholomew Carew's world. Had Bartholomew ever felt as isolated as she was feeling at this moment?

Ramma still regretted her criticism of Harry for not risking a career as an artist. But he had hit a nerve about archaeology. She was working on a site but wasn't being paid. She really didn't have to work at all at anything. Daddy-ji had made that clear. But Harry didn't have that choice. She felt bad about the way everything had ended without warning. When Harry had phoned her in Mumbai, there were other people around her in the house. Harry had sounded sad on the phone but had not said, 'I love you'.

That rational section of her brain kept poking her soft bits. 'He could just be missing his model.' There was no doubting her strong desire to achieve something that wasn't tied to her father's name or her mother's beauty. But her heart had acquired an irrational beat. Ramma, like Harry, resorted at times of dilemma to asking her mother. What would Rani have done about Ramma's irrational heart? Back then, marriages were completely arranged by parents. After Rani's funeral, Ramma's aunt Sushma told her things about her parents' marriage that were news to her.

'You know your mother loved your father long before they married,' said Sushma Massi.

'How could she?' asked Ramma.

'Silly girl, just think about it. Your father was well known in Mumbai. Even as a young man before he was famous, he sang at your grandparents' house. Your grandfather heard Gangabharti-ji at a reception for a trade delegation concerning the export of chemical dyes. While they ate, they were entertained by your father. Grandfather was moved by his ghazals and asked him to entertain a group of businessmen he had invited home. Rani was only twelve and was too young to be present but she saw Gangabharti arrive. She heard his voice from her room and told me she fell in love with it.'

'But how was she able to marry him?' asked Ramma.

'Your mother was the first woman in our family to go to university but your grandparents started looking for potential suitors while she was still a student. Rani knew what was going on. It was not a secret. She did something that is not special now but was unusual then. She confided in her parents that she was attracted to your father and asked whether they could consider him. In traditional families, he would have been regarded as lower caste and unsuitable but Gangabharti's music had already become popular so he had acquired enough money to make him rather desirable on the marriage market. Besides, your grandfather was a modern man and admired Gangabharti. He didn't promise anything but made discreet enquiries. Once satisfied, her parents approached Gangabharti's father through a matchmaker. So a meeting was arranged.

'Your grandparents told your mother to always look down and never at the suitor, and to appear demure and modest. They had to insist on it because your Mummy-ji was no shrinking violet! But she was curious to see the man whose voice had the sweetness of honey and her curiosity got the better of her. Contrary to her instructions, she looked directly into his eyes, from beneath her eyelashes. According to your Daddy-ji, he fell instantly in love with her right then.

'And the rest you know. Rani had a mind of her own. Ramma beti, I miss her so much...' Her aunt Sushma hugged her and her tears soaked her dupatta.

Ramma remembered her mother singing to her and teasing her. She pictured herself as a little girl, taking her mother's words seriously and falling into her traps. Like that wide-eyed child, she needed help.

'What would you do, mother, seriously please? Actually, I do know what you would do. You would be decisive.'

Ramma took up her pen and began to write.

CHAPTER 16: Harry Gets a Surprise

Calcutta, November 1881

What an honour! I spent the whole evening with none other than the Director General of the Archaeological Survey, the legendary Alexander Cunningham.

He is now a venerable 66 & there are moves to encourage him to resign. He gave me much excellent advice & an introduction to R.G. Bhandarkar who, he says, is second to none for advice on Sanskrit inscriptions. I left with a signed copy of The Stupa of Bharat inscribed to me in Brahmi!

His anecdotes were as memorable as his work & warnings. He says the Asiatic Society of Bengal has been taken over by 'Naturalists'. He recently visited the museum where he had deposited a Buddhist statue he had excavated in Sravasti. He eventually found it 'in the midst of a herd of stuffed deer & antelopes which completely hid its inscribed pedestal from view.' We shared a bitter, knowing laugh.

Our conversation spread wide and deep. I discussed my ideas of possible areas to search for Ashokan stupa and rock edicts near the Nepalese border. We discussed the Mughals too, regretting their iconoclasm & destruction of temples & defacement of so many irreplaceable statues, removing heads & faces. We concluded that the ruination was even worse than during the Protestant Reformation. The Mughal legacy is stunning architecture and we compared the purpose of Ashokan monuments with the Mughal mausoleums & tombs.

Why, we asked, are Ashokan monuments intended as education for the living & Ancient Egyptian & Mughal monuments seemingly for the dead? We regretted not being able to visit Xian but expressed our admiration for the translations of the detailed diaries of the Tang dynasty Chinese Pilgrims without which some of his search would often have been for a needle in a haystack.

I broached my confusions over Buddha's teachings of freeing oneself from the world. How did Ashoka accept this and be a ruler of an empire? Did he reconcile himself to that contradiction by using his rule to spread on Buddhist beliefs? Cunningham shrugged & told me that only Ashoka could give an answer as it was of course a private matter. I took the message not to discuss it again.

On the night of the exhibition preview, Deco-rators looked beautiful. The door was kept open as people came and went. Inside the shop was buzzing, champagne corks were popping, Indian snacks were rapidly consumed and money flowed. But when Kathy asked everyone to raise a glass to Harry and to absent friends, Harry's smile vanished.

Kathy looked straight at him and said, 'Right Harry, all your friends have decided that we have seen enough of your miserable face for a while. We have something for you.'

She handed him an envelope. With a poorly disguised grimace, Harry took the plain white envelope and turned it over to slit it open. But he fumbled opening it, finally ripping the edge of the envelope. An airline ticket to Mumbai floated to the floor.

'What the hell! I don't know what to say. Are you offering to manage the shop while I take a holiday?'

Ingrid interrupted. 'Who said anything about a holiday? You are going for twelve weeks. I'm going to help Kathy run the shop. You needn't worry. I won't clutter it with my bric-a-brac. Kathy says she won't speak to me again if I do.'

Harry gave Ingrid a big hug.

'Ingrid, you're amazing. Kathy, you're a partner in a million for organising this. I wish I had the words to thank you properly. If only I could take you up on it. You know that I'd like nothing better. But I can't afford to go for that long. Even if the business brought in enough to pay the overheads without me, I'd get behind with the mortgage payments on the house. I wouldn't want to return to find a repossession order on the doormat.'

Kathy coughed and said, 'I phoned the university accommodation agency and they are desperate for short-term accommodation in the centre of the city for visiting professors. Guess what? You have the choice of three couples who have three month sabbaticals in Oxford starting in one month's time. The rent should cover your mortgage and household bills and a bit more besides. That means you've no excuse, buddy. I took the liberty of telling them about your plans. You only need to ring them to confirm.'

'You better get your skates on, Harry,' shouted Mike Wells. 'Take one of Carew's cameras and imitate some of his great photos.'

All the guests cheered and said, 'Until next year, Harry.'

With nothing prepared he looked haplessly at his friends. His face lit up as he grinned. 'How amazing is that? I can leave and see Ramma again without worrying about losing my home. Since that ghastly incident in Birmingham, I have been the most lousy business partner you can imagine. Thank you for all the letters of support. I'm sorry I didn't reply. Selene, what can I say? I can't think of many customers as generous as you for forgiving my appalling behaviour. Kathy may even have saved our business tonight. Please everyone. Three cheers for Kathy, the best business partner a guy could have.'

Mike Wells hooted and shouted over Harry's voice. 'And don't forget: Never did faint heart win fair lady!'

Harry joined in the laughter. 'I'm beginning to think there's something in this karma idea.'

Selene was one of the last to go. She handed Harry two

cheques, one for a Deco rug and one of his paintings followed by a second, substantially larger.

'But what's this for?' gasped Harry.

'I've decided I'd like an Indian style conservatory. I want you to furnish it for me while you're there. Come over before you leave, take a taxi from Abingdon and we can discuss it. Seek out some talented Indian artists worth investing in. I trust your judgment and we'll discuss what I like. This cheque should cover your expenses in India after paying for everything you buy for me.'

Harry was dumbstruck. His luck had changed but what kind of reception would he get in India? He loved Ramma and this would be his one and only opportunity to prove it. He wanted to share his life with her. He could think of nothing else and now he owed it to his friends as well as to himself to be determined. But if, after all their efforts, he met with rejection while away from home and from them, how would he cope?

CHAPTER 17: The Carews, Past and Present

Delhi, January 1882

Father has died. He has left the company to James but did not cut me out, for which I will remain forever grateful. I wish I had been a better son. My fortune is enough for me to now live by independent means. Having the ear of the Viceroy is needful for the prospects of projects close to my heart; hence, I shall continue to undertake occasional work for him & enjoy being consulted. It was with some regret that I ceased my employment with the Survey but my newfound freedom will allow me the opportunity to undertake archaeological explorations. I shall concentrate on discovering relics of the Buddhist period, as discussed with Alexander Cunningham, with a view to writing a history of Ashoka's unification of India &, inspired by the Buddha's teachings, the secular manner in which he spread his edicts.

Father's legacy provides me with the necessary financial resources to be free of an entity he loved: the British Empire. But that is life's way of playing jests.

He needed to take a trip to London to arrange his visa, go to the manor house to see Selene Charmer and get the house ready for the tenants. But first Harry booked a hotel in Mumbai and sent Ramma an email telling her the good news. For a brief moment his confidence waned. Would she be pleased? Would she even receive it? And what about Gangabharti? Clearly, he'd have to woo the father as well as the daughter. Like he knew how to do either.

And then he realised that he did. Batholomew Carew led to

Ramma's heart and Ashoka led to Gangabharti's long-denied passion. And Harry knew how to get to Batholomew Carew. He wondered about making a phone call and finally decided it was better to write a letter.

In his letter, he told the stories of Ramma and her father and the reason Gangabharti had sent his daughter to Oxford. Harry discreetly avoided details about Ramma's sudden departure; he simply said she hadn't been well but 'Ramma was so excited when she realised your grandfather had corresponded about the Emperor Ashoka. If there is anything more you can tell me I'd be so grateful.'

He was hardly back in the shop after putting the letter through their door when the phone rang. It was Professor Carew sounding amazed.

'I have just read your extraordinary letter. The coincidence... I can't believe it. I'll explain. Come here tomorrow night at about 7.30.'

Harry arrived at Leckford Road that evening with flowers, a pocket tape recorder and a notebook. Judith answered the door, looking neat and business-like wearing a blue blouse and navy knee-length skirt. As she led Harry towards the library he noticed her grey hair was arranged in a French pleat, in contrast to her husband's more tousled look. There was evidence of packing. Charles came in holding out his hand and saying, 'Can I get you a drink?'

Once sitting down with a glass of red, Charles looked at him with a penetrating gaze and came straight to the point.

'You have no idea what a surprise your letter contained. They say real life is stranger than fiction! If you consider that India has a population of nine hundred million and yet I met one of the people mentioned in your letter. I didn't know his name but I know the bookshop. I visited it in 1962 and remember it well. It was a popular and convenient meeting place for foreigners.'

He walked over to a glass-fronted bookcase, unlocked it,

and took out a book. 'I bought this from your friend's father. He was not much more than a boy then. You can see here the stamp that he put in the front of the book with the name of the shop and the price.'

Harry didn't recognise the language. 'It's Brahmi, the ancient language from the time of Prince Gautama, the Buddha,' Charles Carew explained.

Harry blinked in surprise. 'Impressive that you can read this,' he murmured.

'Oh I can't. Not at all. But I can recall with almost perfect clarity the conversation around this book. It's one of the blessings of old age. I can remember like it was yesterday, conversations from a half century ago.' And then with a sad smile, 'It's remembering what I did yesterday that's a challenge.'

'If you can't read this language, why did you buy the book?'

'I was browsing in the store checking out the history section. Having a passion for books is a hazard of my profession. And this book tumbled to the floor. I must have knocked it over. There was a cloud of dust and I coughed and coughed. It was hot and I was irritated from the heat. And your friend's father scampered over to help. And then he started to talk to me about how old this book was. The boy's enthusiasm for his own history delighted me. He told me it was about the welfare state based on Buddhist beliefs of pacifism and diversity. Ashoka apparently tried to ban capital punishment. Quite extraordinary, if it's true. So I bought the book.'

'And he became my friend's father.'

'He won't remember me. I was just another foreigner in a bookstore dominated by foreigners. But it feels right that it is going back to him.'

'This will be a wonderful gift for him. But please, tell me more about Bartholomew Carew if you can.'

'When it comes to my own family history, I've been reluctant to talk about it. That's because of my reservations about

Bartholomew.' He paused for a moment, sipped some wine then continued.

'Grandfather Bartholomew was admired for his enquiring mind and his sense of adventure but my father didn't really know his father. Douglas was born in Yorkshire, near Halifax. Bartholomew was in India working on the Great Trigonometrical Survey when he was born. The idea was that my grandmother Dora and their son would follow. Instead he returned to England for nine months to meet his son but Douglas was too young to remember that. Three years passed and since Bartholomew still hadn't sent for them, Dora made up her mind to follow him whether he liked it or not.'

'It was Dora who bought the chest of drawers,' added Judith.

'She filled it with personal belongings and set off on the three week journey by sea to India. When they arrived in Bombay, Bartholomew was not even on the quayside to greet them. He was in Ceylon looking for Ashokan stupas. Dora had to make her own way to Simla.'

'Crikey, that must have been tough,' said Harry. 'I wonder where she got the gumption to do that.'

'It would have been completely acceptable in those days to stay at home and wait for her husband to return,' Charles agreed. 'One of the secret pleasures of a historian is asking those kind of questions, knowing that we'll never find the answers. What was the tipping point that induced Dora to leave for India? And then leave India to return to England?'

'All we know from the family is that Dora found it all hard to forgive. Douglas remembered his father returning from that trip and teaching him to play cricket. He knew Bartholomew must have been around at other times because there were photographs of them together but he had few recollections of those occasions. He remembered that his mother often went to Delhi leaving him with his ayah.'

'Didn't your mother say that Douglas's happiest memories

of India were of a loving ayah and running wild in the garden and beyond with the servants' children? That's how he learned Punjabi,' said Judith.

'The house was in Simla, Harry. I expect you know that it was the summer capital of the Raj. The administration moved there when the temperatures soared in the plains.'

'My father told me that Bartholomew handed in his resignation to the Great Trigonometrical Survey when he inherited money from his father, although he accepted the role of scientific advisor to the Viceroy – not an arduous post. Douglas said his father was nearly always away exploring somewhere or other and if Dora needed to see him she had to go to Calcutta to coincide with meetings with the Viceroy in the capital. Delhi didn't become the capital until Lutyens finished the building of New Delhi in 1931.

'Then in 1889, he went north searching for an Ashokan pillar near where he thought the Buddha could have been born. What was clear was that the stone came from East India and yet these huge pillars had been transported all over India and even as far away as Sri Lanka and Afghanistan.'

'A Stonehenge kind of enigma! How was it done? Why was it done?' asked Harry.

'Exactly. Bartholomew was more interested in proving they were Ashokan and translating the inscriptions than in his own son. That is what Douglas came to think. Dora may have encouraged him to think like that and you can understand why she decided to return to England. Anyway, Bartholomew went in search of archaeological remains, which he hoped would prove that Lumbini was Buddha's birthplace. A few months later he disappeared, never to be seen again. Before he set off on that last trip he shipped the chest of drawers and its contents to England saying it was for Douglas from his father.'

Judith carried on with the story while Harry listened with complete astonishment.

'Douglas couldn't grieve much because he didn't know his father well. Once Bartholomew was legally declared dead, Dora remarried an enterprising industrialist. In a class sense, she was marrying beneath her but her second husband ran a successful business, so financially they were fine. Douglas was sent to Westminster School. Dora had two children by the new husband and although we have no reason to believe that he wasn't a good stepfather, Douglas didn't warm to him.'

'That's right,' said Charles. 'The love he remembered throughout his life was his ayah's and my mother's. Douglas read Classics at Cambridge, including Sanskrit, and returned to teach at Westminster School. After he married my mother, he asked if she would go with him to India to establish a school in Mussoorie. The chest of drawers you bought from us went to India on a second journey, this time with my parents.'

'You called it the well-travelled chest of drawers and that's obviously an accurate description,' said Harry. 'Did I tell you that it has gone to Illinois?'

Charles laughed before continuing with his story. 'The reason it came back to Oxford was because my mother didn't want me to go to boarding school in England and my father didn't like the idea of being both my parent and my headmaster. I was seven when we returned, in 1931. My father often told me adventure stories set in India, hoping I'd want to return there sometime. He loved India.

'The war intervened and I joined the army so I wasn't able to go to university until 1949. I was lucky to go to Princeton for my Ph.D. and came back here having been offered a post at Oxford. It wasn't until the 60s that I had the chance to explore the country of my birth, and that was how I came to be in the book shop.'

Surely Gangabharti would love this story, welcome him and forgive him for exposing his beloved daughter to a revolting racist? But Harry kept those thoughts to himself.

'That is incredible, Professor. I can't wait to tell Gangabharti – Mr Gupta. I'm going to Mumbai in three weeks' time. I understand your reservations about Bartholomew. It sounds like he was not a man to be tied down by marriage and respectability, but the way you describe Dora, she sounds intrepid and could have been a great companion on his adventures if he'd just let her.'

Judith smiled sadly. 'I'm just speculating, but being open-minded in some ways does not mean he was open-minded in all ways. He was, ultimately, a Victorian and there were few men who willingly embraced a woman as a true equal. They regarded us as the weaker sex. Like so many families, we should have asked more questions when we could. Douglas was killed during the war and although Charles's mother died only twelve years ago, she had rarely met Douglas's mother. Dora had a second family in Lancashire and although we have some letters she wrote to Douglas, they were rather formal. She died in 1937 aged 82. Charles can't remember his grandmother. Dora didn't see her son after they came back from India – perhaps she didn't want to be reminded of Bartholomew. You see, all the men in the family have a strong physical resemblance. Douglas had many of his father's features. And Charles too has the same nose and jaw.'

Judith went to a cabinet and took out an album of photographs. Flicking through it Harry had to agree. The resemblance was striking.

'Charles was close to his mother, weren't you darling? She had such a warm and cheerful personality whereas, by all accounts, Dora could be cold and distant. We didn't have many conversations about the grandparents. So many other things seemed more important.'

'So all that you know about your grandfather was from the contents of the chest of drawers?' asked Harry.

'They have some of Bartholomew's photographs at the Pitt Rivers and more in the V&A. He was a keen photographer and his photographs of India are much admired. I suppose I should've followed them up but I developed an interest in American history instead and apart from that one trip, I haven't travelled in India. Out of curiosity, I followed in some of Bartholomew's footsteps during those three months and bought a collection of books including this one in Brahmi but didn't, in the end, use them for serious research.

'Your friend is working on an important and often neglected part of Indian history, one that was lost when Buddhism declined in India. From what I have read of Ashoka, his ideas of good governance for all people and non-violence were in advance of his time. He created a kind of Buddhist empire, an oxymoronic concept if ever I heard one. I wish your friend every success and please give my regards to her father.'

Harry stood up and went to thank Judith and Charles.

'You have been so kind. I do appreciate you taking me into your confidence. I feel touched and I'm sure Gangabharti will be as delighted and surprised as I am.'

They began moving towards the door, when Charles turned and picked up the book in Brahmi. He held it out saying, 'Give this to your friend as a gift from me. She'll make better use of it. Tell her she can take her pick from my Indian book collection when she returns to Oxford. By then, we should be settled in Bagley Wood Road. Here's the address.' Charles handed Harry a card with his new address and waved his hand saying, 'this house is going to be turned into a language school. As you know, we have to clear a lot of furniture and effects but our books are coming with us.'

Harry choked. He'd not expected such a welcome from the professors. He had previously thought Charles to be somewhat stiff and now he felt guilty about his preconceptions. Harry clutched the book to his heart. This gift was so precious. He knew there was nothing that he could take with him to Mumbai that would be better appreciated. He tried putting his thanks into words and left more optimistic than he had felt since before Ramma had flown to Mumbai.

When he reached home, he carefully put the book on his desk next to Bartholomew's writing slope, which he had kept to store some of Bartholomew's intriguing photographs under the lid. He opened it and slid the book inside under the pen tray. It fitted nicely in its emptiness, filling it entirely. Harry remembered his surprise that it had been empty given that every other nook and cranny of the old chest of drawers had been stuffed full.

He looked at it more closely. Harry knew that writing slopes were often made to order. The book so completely filled the space that it looked a little ludicrous, like a cat that had managed to fill a box far too small for itself. Harry took a step back and examined it from all sides and then blinked in surprised. Aloud he said, 'What an idiot I've been!'

He lifted out the pen tray and moved his fingers around the edge, carefully feeling and pressing. The speed of the opening of the secret drawer took Harry by surprise. He pulled it fully open. With the assured delicacy of an antiques dealer, he removed a soft leather-bound book. Stored so well that its pages lay flat and were not infected by insect or mould, it felt like it had been secreted away yesterday, rather than over a century ago. Harry turned the cover over. The first page was an inscription.

To my son, Bartholomew Carew, on the advent of his journey to India representing the best of the British Empire. From his father. Discere Faciendo 1868.

Knowing what he was about to see but almost overcome with emotion, he turned the first page. And there it was. A younger scrawl. Less tidy but still legible.

My attentions have long been diverted by the attractions of the Natural History Museum, so my 1st in Classics was astounding.

Father's pride & delight provided me with an opportunity to broach my suggestion. When he sent me to Harrow & Oxford, it was with the intention that I should go into politics; reading Classics was to prepare me for the Commons. I did not utter the truth that such a career is not my vocation...

Page after page. Year after year. The maturing script of a man privately grappling with his burdens and beliefs.

Harry inhaled deeply, pulling the air to the depth of his lungs and holding it there, his heart racing and his blood pumping. He closed his eyes and let the buzz of the discovery light up his insides.

Charles had given him a book for Gangabharti. And now he could present Bartholomew's diary to Ramma. Would this historical gem open a way into her heart?

Part 2: *India*

CHAPTER 1: Bombay Dreams

Ceylon, May 1882

What a surprising discovery for me (but not for the Ceylonese)! Ashoka's eldest daughter, Sangamitra, came here to spread the teachings of Buddha at the request of King Devanampiya Tissa. It appears that Ashoka's initial reluctance to send his daughter on an overseas mission was overcome on the insistence of Sangamitra herself. She founded the nun-lineage of Bhikkhunis & they are still in existence. Why didn't I know this before? Their aim is to achieve the highest attainment in Buddhism as men. Extraordinary, simply extraordinary. If John Stuart Mill knew about this, it would add fuel to the fire of his determination for women's rights, an issue that I have long regarded with scepticism. This discovery is making me reconsider my position on the Second Reform Bill.

I have been guilty of underestimating Dora. She too is a determined woman. Dora & Douglas are on their way. They should reach Port Said next week. I must find a way to reach Bombay for when their ship docks. The early monsoon has wreaked havoc. The floods & landslides are devastating. No one wants to travel. It has taken thrice the expected time to reach Colombo. It is proving to be extremely difficult to find a ship willing to take me to Mumbai. Pinning my hopes on a clipper returning from Hong Kong.

When the well-travelled chest of drawers was shipped to Mumbai it was called by the British name Bombay and the journey to India through the Suez Canal took three weeks.

Harry's was a lightning journey in comparison: a flight of nine hours.

He emerged from the air-conditioned jet and stepped onto the tarmac at Shivaji Airport and the heat took his breath away. Although he wished the arms of the Hindu god could stir up the Mumbai air, the artist in him was conscious of the vast sky and the dazzling light. He had booked into a medium-priced hotel not far from Marine Drive in the knowledge that Gangabharti's apartment was nearby, a mile from Chowpatty Beach. He wanted to settle in and acclimatise before calling Gangabharti. At least that is how he rationalised the delay. His procrastination was really because Harry had no idea how Gangabharti would react to his unexpected arrival. Ramma had not replied to his emails. Was all the effort to be a wasted journey?

He unpacked his sketchbook and opened at a drawing of Ramma. Was she still in Madhya Pradesh? How would she react to him pursuing her to India?

After tea and a rest, he took a stroll onto Chowpatty dreaming that Ramma might be in Mumbai and had decided to do the same thing. His eyes swept over the crowds, taking in the vibrant colour. The beach framed a vast panoply of life: yogis, families out for a stroll, ragged children, hawkers, tourists, fishermen and office workers heading for the stalls of bhelpuri. Despite the unreasonableness of the expectation, he was hit by a wave of disappointment because Ramma was not part of this Indian picture.

He joined a queue of workers at a food stall. Ten minutes later he sat on the sand admiring the artistry of the paper dosa before taking a bite from the mouth-watering stuffed South Indian pancake. Made from fermented rice and lentil flour it was shaped like an elegant fan. Harry savoured the aromatic sensation. Was this experience really his for less than fifty pence?

The food stalls made the temptation to eat hard to resist.

The aloo tikka chaat garnished with coriander and tamarind sauce and the yoghurt looked healthy as well as desirable. Waiting for his salad to be assembled, Harry's attention was distracted from the variety of life on display around him by the sound of children shouting.

A crowd of ragged boys exclaimed excitedly as they splashed into the sea. It was different from Europe – of course – there were no adults in the water, except fishermen bringing in their catch. The boys alone were having fun in the water – swimming, or, at least, trying to. Women in saris and small children dipped their toes in the ripples on the shore but did not swim. Most had bare midriffs, which must have been blissfully comfortable in the heat, and they giggled whenever they delicately lifted their hems so the waves could caress their ankles.

Harry pulled out his sketchbook and drew them like colourful ghosts on the shoreline, their brightly-coloured saris blowing in the sea breeze. In England, with the sun low in the often-cloudy sky, the vermilions and tangerines would appear garish but here they radiated brilliance. On a grey winter's day in Oxford, he wanted to be able to close his eyes and experience this moment again. It crept up on him, the most romantic sunset he had ever seen. Ribbons of green, brown, red and grey shimmered on the water as the languorous dying sun throbbed just above the horizon. There was all this beauty around him but no sign of Ramma. Harry's senses yearned for her. Why hadn't he felt this certain in England? Emotionally exhausted, he headed back to his hotel, showered and slept.

After breakfast, he plucked up the courage to phone. A manservant answered, so Harry gave his name and asked for Gangabharti. Ramma's father received his call, sounding full of bonhomie.

'Harry, so you are here. Where are you staying? We have a guest room, you must come here, no? This morning I must be in the studio. Why do you not join me? Would you like that?'

Harry breathed a deep sigh of relief. He tempered his excitement at what he was hearing with a desire to be tactful: not to rush things, not to ask if Ramma was there too.

'That is so generous of you, sir. I don't want to put you out but I'd love to take you up on both your offers, if I won't be in the way.'

'Not at all, young man. My driver will pick you up at 10.30 and drop your luggage off here before taking you to the studio. We can catch up with our news this evening.'

*****

'Gupta Sahib is presently in a meeting. He is an important man, is the Sahib. He honours you. My name is Subhash and no worries. I am a careful driver,' explained Gangabharti's chauffeur on the drive to Miramma Studios.

Subhash sounded his horn as a fragile looking scooter-taxi tried to overtake on the outside and a moped carrying a family of four – minus helmets – weaved its way in and out of the traffic. They became stuck behind a lorry belching dirty diesel fumes. As it cleared, Harry was staring at an evil eye painted on the back.

'Crikey, what does that mean?' asked Harry.

Subhash hesitated. 'Dangerous things happen. Lorries, they turn over and we drivers, we worry. Bad karma.'

The chauffeur hurriedly changed the subject and told Harry that he was invited to join Gangabharti at a recording session.

'It begins at 12:30 maybe, maybe not.' The driver handed Harry a pass to get him through security. Arriving at the information desk, he presented it as he introduced himself.

'My name's Harry King. I am a guest of Gangabharti Gupta. Studio 3.'

'Sign here. Take a left down the orange corridor, second right after and left across the courtyard then right again, theek hai?'

The corridor was buzzing with activity, young people with

files weaving their way past porters with trolleys of props and costumes. Harry tried to remember the directions and once across the courtyard hovered by a hanger-like building. He thought this must be it.

A man with a clipboard approached him saying, 'You are late. Filming has begun. Jaldi, jaldi. Sit inside on the right and wait. Vikki will come.'

Harry followed the instructions. Entering the studio he was surprised to see a backdrop of Big Ben. Forty energetic dancers were performing a rhythmic bhangra and miming to piped music. He recognised the actress in front from one of the films he had watched with Ramma. As the crowd parted, the director said to her, 'Amita, sweetheart, I have no desire to spoil your good looks but remember you are playing an ill woman.'

'Yaa, but what kind of ill? Fever, coughing, nausea?' Amita asked.

'You know, filmi ill,' as he waved an arm across his brow and sighed.

Harry noticed a young woman beckoning him and followed her out just as the director was saying something about an advertisement. Vikki ushered him into a dressing room. He started to say something about Gangabharti but the flustered young woman ignored him and said, 'Challo challo, Shiv Shankar Sahib said, "three minutes".'

'There must be some mistake…' started Harry but she wasn't listening and a moment later he had acquired red cheeks and a pencil moustache.

Vikki said, 'Jaldi, sahib,' and she pointed to the opposite door. Harry was about to protest when a bowler hat was placed firmly on his head and an umbrella thrust into his hand and before he knew it, he was beneath the bright lights in front of a camera. The next thing he knew Shiv Shankar was yelling at him, pointing to the autocue.

'Can you not read?'

Harry thought it best to oblige. 'At times like these, what you need is one of these.'

Shiv Shankar waved his arms looking extremely annoyed. 'You play an Englishman so talk like an Englishman, blockhead!'

Harry caught his breath and muttered, 'Um, I am an Englishman but I... ' Harry was not able to finish his sentence before Shiv Shankar marched onto the stage.

'No, no, let me show you. Imagine a plum at the back of your mouth. Then say it.'

'There may have been a mistake,' ventured Harry.

'You are telling me there has been a mistake? Of course there's been a mistake! Starting with your English! Do it again! Where is that idiot of a casting director?'

A nervous little man approached from the wings, a print-out of an actor's head shot clutched in his hands, eyes darting from the photo to Harry in some confusion. 'Sahib, Ravi Arora was highly recommended. I wouldn't have cast him otherwise.' And he threw Harry a look of sheer desperation.

All eyes flicked to Harry. Then back to Shiv Shankar and the casting director. The photo of a light-skinned Indian man looked nothing at all like Harry. 'I'm Harry King from Oxford. I've come to meet Gangabharti Gupta and was directed here. I'm sorry to be the cause of such ...' In his head Harry conjured "chaos".

In the split second of silence after Harry spoke, the casting director seized the moment and silently eased himself out of the room.

Gangabharti's name had the magic of abracadabra: the atmosphere changed instantly to one of respect.

'Why didn't you say so?' said Shiv Shankar..

Harry protested but half-heartedly. 'Perhaps someone can direct me to him?'

CHAPTER 2: **Getting to know Gangabharti**

Simla, July 1882

I am an utter failure both as a husband & a father. I do not blame Dora for not speaking to me. To arrive in India & have to cope alone with Douglas in such circumstances. She is a capable woman & she made their way to Simla by train. While it was fortunate that some friends she had made on the voyage were also heading to Simla, it must have caused her huge embarrassment when I was not at the dock to meet The Ravenna. The Cutty Sark made good time from Colombo but not good enough. Despite its speed, the days of this elegant clipper are numbered. The steel ship carrying Dora & Douglas arrived in Bombay early & The Cutty Sark was delayed.

Douglas must have drunk water that had not been boiled & filtered. Thank the Almighty that he is now recovering well. On one thing alone I did not fail & that was the appointment of his ayah. I shall always be grateful to Niraj for his recommendation. Kesarai is unusual for a woman in her position. She is literate in Hindi & knows some English. Douglas took to her immediately. She is teaching him Hindi & her English is improving every day, thanks to Douglas.

I must try to repair things with Dora. She cannot disguise her delight for Simla nor her lack of delight for me. I must bite my lip & introduce her to the club. I had vowed never to cross its threshold again but that is one thing I must do if Dora & I are to have any future together.

Ripon gives me hope. The Vernacular Press Act will give new freedom to the Indian people. At last their voice will be heard. Ripon wants to establish local self-government &

the Factory Act is curbing the worst abuses. The number of hours children can work will be limited by law. He feels like a new broom. I'll put my project on indefinite hold & do what I can to assist this Viceroy. Such work could even help me mend fences with my wife.

Gangabharti was amused by the scene Harry had caused. On the drive home he laughed infectiously.

'These directors see themselves as little gods. No one challenges them. The sycophants hang on their every word and obey each command without question. Did he really tell you to talk like an Englishman?' Harry half-nodded as Gangabharti continued.

'This will be the talk of Mumbai. In the scene you walked into, the heroine of 'Salaam London' is sent to the damp city to film an advert for cough sweets. A bowler-hatted city gent takes one from his pocket and hands it to her. Bollywood produces films at a galloping pace and is lazy about stereotypes. Little attention is paid to the script, also. Hollywood is bad enough but it is ten times worse here. It is not unusual for actors to see the script for the first time – if there is one – when they arrive in the studio to film; hence the autocue.'

'Thank you, Laxmi.' Gangabharti nodded towards a model of the goddess of good fortune swinging in the windscreen. 'I am fortunate to work with fine composers and songwriters but I am not immune to the antics going on around me. I shall enjoy telling your story.' The final words were said while playfully slapping Harry on his shoulder. Harry smiled but felt subdued; there was still no mention of Ramma. What little confidence he had when he flew to India was ebbing away. The brief interlude at the Miramma Studios had made Harry conscious of the extraordinary status of his companion. Even in England, Harry had become aware of Gangabharti's fame but the reaction in the studio underlined the respect he commanded at different levels of Indian society. The silly incident had helped the initial communication between him and Ramma's father, but Gangabharti didn't know the real reason for Harry's visit to India. How would he react if he knew that sitting beside him was an upstart trader from a poor background with limited prospects, who had come to India to ask to marry his only daughter?

He wanted to find the right words to express his feelings in a way that wouldn't alarm Gangabharti. But if he restrained his emotions would he appear like that stereotypical image of an uptight Englishman? Doubt led to procrastination.

'At least I don't own a bowler hat,' grinned Harry recalling the Bollywood scene.

'You would look quite the prince in a turban, Harry King. You are in the wrong business. Having dipped a toe in Bollywood, you may like to take a splash.' With gratitude Harry relaxed in the humour of Gangabharti's welcome.

Harry was not surprised by the elegance of the apartment. It was in a quiet location with a view of the sea from the balcony. A work of art had brought him and Ramma together. Now he found himself admiring the paintings and sculptures that had been the background to her childhood. Harry examined an exquisite Chola bronze of Krishna dancing and said, 'These ninth century figures are so tactile.'

'You have good taste, my friend. You have spotted the finest work in my collection. A friend of mine from Khajuraho helped me buy it twenty years ago. I could not afford it now. That kind of Indian art was crushed under the Mughals, when they segregated the sexes, and the British Raj was rather prudish, also. You may have noticed that in today's India our young are beginning to shed some of those inhibitions. Did you enjoy the energy of the dancing today?'

'Ramma showed me some of the films you sang over. She likes the older ones best.'

'That must be my fault. I encouraged her to be interested in the past and she often seems happier there than in the present.'

'Sir, how is Ramma? Where is she? I haven't heard from her for some time and after all that happened, I've been anxious. Does she know I'm here?'

'I persuaded her to take part in a project near to her heart. She has joined an archaeological dig near Sanchi. They're trying to discover how the Ashokan pillars were transported all over India. But email communications have not been possible so she arranged a phone call last week. The team will be leaving soon. She said that despite some interesting finds they are no nearer to discovering how they did it with only the limited tools available in 250 BCE. Ramma plans to stay on until Friday with her porter – she said something about following up an idea that came from that fellow you introduced her to. Bartholomew Carew? By the way, you can call me GeeBee. I appreciate your adapting to Indian ways but I prefer to be informal. My parents gave me a heavy burden when they named me after India and its sacred river – one is bad enough but two! It was not ideal in school. But I should not complain: it has been useful in my career.'

'Thank you, S... GeeBee. Talking of someone else with a long name, Bartholomew Carew, I have a gift for you and Ramma.' Harry fetched the book and as he handed it to GeeBee he asked, 'Do you recognise this?'

Gangabharti looked hard at the ancient cover and the astonishment on his face was worthy of a Bollywood Oscar.

'How did you come by that?' gasped Ganghabharti as he examined the stamp on the inside cover. Harry told him the amazing story of how Bartholomew Carew's grandson, Charles, was the Englishman Gangabharti had encountered in the bookshop all those years ago. That same Charles had sold Harry the chest of drawers filled with memories of his grandfather and given him the book to return to India to its previous owner.

Gangabharti's eyes glazed over, visualising himself as a

teenage boy enveloped in clouds of dust when that book fell to the floor of his father's shop. Coming out of his momentary trance he asked for Charles's phone number. Harry was sure his hand was shaking as he dialled but his voice was steady and melodious as ever as he thanked the Carews. Putting down the phone, he spread his arms out as if enveloping his guest.

'We have arranged to meet next time I am in England,' said a beaming Gangabharti.

Feeling more positive, Harry replied, 'Sir, er... GeeBee, before I gave you Charles's book, you were saying that you are expecting Ramma at the weekend?'

'Not here, no. I suggested a break could be good for both of us. We are booked into a small hotel in Khajuraho for a long weekend. It is not a glitzy American place. The Harmony Guest House is owned and run by the wife of my friend Rabindranath. He is a proficient yogi who was a great support to me when Rani died – that was a difficult time.'

Harry understood. 'That was one of the things that connected Ramma and me. I also lost my mother. We... it's difficult for both of us. People say you should move on but it was good to be able to talk about our mothers.'

Gangabharti observed Harry's haunted look. 'If you want to come with me, Harry, I'll ask my secretary to book you on the flight and I will ring Mrs Srinivasan to arrange for an extra room.'

If Gangabharti didn't know before, Harry's flash of pure joy dispelled any doubt about his attachment to his daughter.

'Thank you. I don't know what to say. You've been so kind to me.'

'Not at all, I shall enjoy your company. I want to hear more about Charles and the contents of that chest of drawers. My daughter started to tell me about this character, Bartholomew, but we were interrupted.'

'Just before I left, I discovered Bartholomew's diaries in a secret drawer in his writing slope. I started reading them on the plane. Which reminds me, I must email Charles Carew. Some stories passed down in their family are probably one-sided.'

The name of Bartholomew augured well. Harry was beginning to feel that his fate was linked to that of the Victorian explorer.

Gangabharti continued, 'I shall be out of town for two days. You must explore Mumbai. Is there anywhere in particular you want to see?'

Harry talked about Selene's commission to furnish her Victorian conservatory. Gangabharti had seen some of her films and had a shrewd idea what she would like. He explained that the destructive climate, the invasions and plundering had robbed India of many of its ancient treasures.

'That's why the government has banned the export of anything older than one hundred years. Art Deco was popular in Mumbai in the thirties. You could concentrate on that period and the work of traditional craftsmen and modern artists, no?'

Harry's broad grin was answer enough but he said, 'My shop is called Deco-rators for a reason. If you can point me in the direction of dealers in Deco that would be perfect.'

In bed that night Harry took a while to fall asleep. The film of the day kept replaying. A warm glow spread through his veins as he remembered how Kathy and his friends had conspired to make this trip possible and now he would have the opportunity to put things right with Ramma. He might even be able to repay their generosity because there was a good chance that with Gangabharti's help he could find something stunning for Selene.

*****

The excitement Harry felt at the prospect of an antiques hunt was blasted out of him when he hit the streets of the city the next morning. Harry hailed a scooter taxi and showed the driver the address of a shop called Cornucopia. When he pulled out into the noisy Mumbai traffic, Harry jumped out of his seat at the urgent sound from the decorated lorry behind. The cacophony of horns was deafening – The Mumbai Symphony Orchestra rehearsing on the streets.

The scooter taxi ran on a motor no larger than a sewing machine. It parked in a tiny space near the shop located a few streets behind the Taj Palace Hotel where Gangabharti had suggested he go for dinner.

'Stick to bottled water and avoid ice except at places like the Taj Palace Hotel but nothing refreshes more than fresh coconut water or chilled soda with a twist of lime. You can buy those drinks quite safely even at the roadside. Freshly fried street food is fine also,' said his host as they parted after breakfast.

The shop was friendly, if a little dusty from the constant traffic outside, and Harry spotted some possible purchases, the coloured glass lampshades, for instance, and the carved screens. He discussed his ideas for conservatory furniture with the polite owner who said he could produce some photographs for Harry to send to his client.

'It is possible to attach photographs to email messages. Perhaps, you should learn to do it, sahib, if your client can receive them?'

Harry emerged from the shop, an hour later, feeling pleased with his first experience of business in India. He wandered down towards the harbour and was struck by the way architecture that could be in England was somehow Indianised.

He walked through India Gate built by the British for the 1911 Durbar celebrating the coronation of King George V. This symbol of the British Raj and the grand hotel behind would not have been out of place in London but the hotel was the creation of an Indian entrepreneur. The atmosphere around India Gate had changed. Ramma had told him about it.

'The last of the British army left through that archway but we Indians have not destroyed or vandalised the Raj monuments.

Some decay gracefully but we have adopted India Gate. It has become our gateway to the world.'

With the ugly white supremacist attitudes seen off, Ramma had said that Indians cherish some legacies of the Empire.

'The English language, the railways, British law and some ideas of the Enlightenment. But it is hard to forgive the way it ended. Not preparing for or policing Partition has poisoned relations between India and Pakistan ever since.'

Harry felt agitated.

'I need to calm my mind. Everything I see reminds me of Ramma and things she told me.'

He wandered towards the beach to try a coconut drink as Gangabharti had suggested. The customer in front of him was a well-dressed businessman with a pencil thin moustache. He seemed to be haranguing the poor coconut seller. He grabbed the coconut with straws in the hole the vendor had pierced for him. He took it roughly, without touching the poor man's fingers, and threw a few rupees on the ground to make him scrabble in the dirt and left without a thank you. The seller was about sixteen. Harry felt disgusted by the scene he had just witnessed and tried to speak kindly to the young man, who looked up at him suspiciously. Harry asked, 'How much?'

'Thirty rupees, Sahib.'

Harry deliberately placed fifty directly in his hand. 'This looks great. I need this. Cheers.' The young man didn't really follow Harry's English but smiled in response. His smile grew even wider when Harry refused the change.

When the sun reached its zenith, Harry returned to the flat for a siesta. That evening, acting on Gangabharti's advice, he went to the Taj Palace Hotel. Once past the handsome doorman, his first stop was the bookshop. He bought a copy of a just-released novel called *The God of Small Things* by Arundati Roy, whose nose, in the photograph on the back, reminded him a little of Ramma's.

Ambling into the courtyard garden, the tranquility seemed a gift after the throng of the street. Harry sat in the shade of a potted palm, to read and order a drink before dinner. His peace was disturbed when a young and excited couple asked to join him. They leaned back in the comfortable rattan chairs and talked about England. Harry glanced to see if he was wearing a label saying, "I'm English."

The young woman introduced herself as Shubika, and her companion as Krishan.

'Where are you from?' asked Harry.

'We are from Kolkata. Here for the cricket, ya.'

He gazed at Harry's face, waiting for the admiration and amazement.

'You have tickets?' asked Harry assuming that was what Krishan wanted to hear. His judgement proved spot on as Krishan winked at Shubika.

'I have her to thank. Shubi's brother is married to Preity whose family lives here in Mumbai. Preity really is pretty and pretty useful too because her father's friend knew someone who knew someone in the book office.'

Harry invited them to have dinner with him. As the array of dazzling dishes was brought to the table Harry developed a voracious appetite. He was starting to appreciate the spice that was life in India, sometimes delicate while at other times, exploding in his mouth. As they dug in, Harry tried to change the subject but somehow Krishan always found a metaphor to return to batting and bowling.

'You English – you do not know how to support your team. You clap like ladies at a village match. How do you expect them to win?'

Shubika laughed shyly before asking Harry, 'And what has brought you to India?'

'A friend. I hope to see her at the weekend.'

'Who is this miss?' chuckled Krishan shaking his head slowly from side to side. Harry was not sure what Krishan meant.

'She's a historian working on an archaeological site near Sanchi.'

'What is her good name?' smiled Shubi.

'Ramma.'

A serious shadow spread over Krishan's face. 'She is your would-be?'

'If you mean is she my girlfriend, the answer is I hope so.'

'She is British or Indian origin?'

'Indian. She's the real thing.' Krishan's smile tightened into a flat line. He politely thanked Harry for the meal, exchanged more pleasantries, and explained that they had an early start in the morning. As they left, Harry missed the expression of deep disapproval on Krishan's face.

CHAPTER 3: Harmony and Disharmony

Simla, September 1882

Douglas is a fine little fellow. He was shy with me at first. My lack of experience with small children is all too apparent. Dora has not yet forgiven me for my absence in Bombay but her anger has abated because she approves of Simla & enjoys the life here. Who could not like its location framed by the grandeur of the Himalayas? The oddity of the situation never ceases to amaze me. For six months of the year one fifth of the population of the world is ruled from this hard-to-reach town. Dora & her friends could just as well be in Cheltenham, albeit a Cheltenham with an idyllic climate. The Indian town is separated from us down the hill. It's all white up here, apart from the servants & some token civil servants.

Dora runs the house with military precision & pursues her botanical studies with vigour. She approves of my interest in photography. I am teaching her to photograph the flora using the latest gels. The results are not as good as her watercolour sketches but it is helping to bridge the divide between us.

I have had greater success with taking pictures of Douglas's attempts to wield a cricket bat. Jane, the governess, travelled with Dora from England. She is attracting the attention of young officers. I wonder how long we will keep her given the shortage of white women here. I suggested we have an Indian tutor to teach Douglas arithmetic but Dora rejected it outright. Amazing how the bullock carts managed to carry Dora's enormous chest of drawers up the mountain. They packed the contents of the drawers in separate containers & carried them on a separate cart. Dora thought the contents mixed up & was not at all happy.

The flight to Khajuraho in Madhya Pradesh was short but on the journey Gangabharti told him about where they were heading. 'We are flying to a village of just seven thousand people.'

Harry looked surprised.

'"Why does a village have an airport?" You must be wondering, ha?' Then Gangabharti answered his own question.

'Khajuraho was the capital of the Chandela kings from the 9th to the 13th centuries and they built eighty-five temples in the city, can you imagine so many? Then, the area was rich and fertile supporting a large population. Water became a problem and drove the Chandelas eastwards and Khajuraho was abandoned to its fate.

'The site was sufficiently remote for the Mughal conquerors to ignore. Spared destruction, it was forgotten until an Englishman named Captain Burt stumbled on it like the prince discovering a sleeping beauty. You saw plenty of dancing when you came to the studio but, in Khajuraho, the stones dance.'

'Bartholomew Carew mentioned Khajuraho in his diary. Something to do with the *Kama Sutra*?' asked Harry.

Harry was only half listening as Gangabharti told him more about the art of the temples because his mind was on Ramma. Would she be pleased to see him? His situation thousands of feet above her prevented him from pacing up and down. Gangabharti read his thoughts.

'I have been going on? No wonder my daughter is a serious academic. Many of her school friends are not interested in careers, only in clothes and jewellery. No, that is harsh; they are kind and loving girls but Ramma is different. She grew up fast when Rani died. From what she told me of you, Harry, you make her laugh and take her out of herself and that is good. Ramma is overly serious – concerned with forging a place for herself in the world and she needs to relax and trust herself. That way it will come. She will be pleased to see you and we shall have some fun. Ask my friend, Rabindranath, to talk about the tourist reactions to the temples – he has some hilarious stories to tell. The airport, being only two miles from the village, means that we will not have long to wait to see Ramma. She is coming by road from Bhopal, the nearest city to Sanchi, and should have arrived four hours before us. What luck, no?'

As the plane touched down Harry tried to smile in anticipation while his intestines writhed uncomfortably.

Arriving at the Harmony Guesthouse, Harry glanced around for a sight of Ramma while Gangabharti greeted his friends warmly. With a wink towards Harry he asked, 'So, my friend, where are you hiding that daughter of mine? I thought she would be waiting in your courtyard, ready to greet me. These young people have no respect for their elders, no?'

His smile disappeared when Rabindranath told him she hadn't yet arrived.

'She hasn't telephoned?' GeeBee asked.

A sad shake of the head. Rabindranath suggested they have tea and discuss what could be done. He led them into the cool garden courtyard. Gangabharti's smooth voice cracked with emotion. 'My friend, please, I must use your phone.'

He spent what seemed like hours making calls but when Harry looked at his watch, a mere twenty minutes had passed. After he finally put down the receiver he said, 'Ramma's colleagues have confirmed that she intended to leave on Friday. But all of them had left the site before her so they couldn't say with certainty that she had actually left. I must leave right away for Sanchi. I must find my daughter.'

Rabindranath tried to calm him.

'My good friend, it will be dark in two hours. The roads between here and Bhopal have no lighting and are riddled with potholes and other dangers. Drive off in haste and you are likely to have an accident. And Ramma could still be on her way.'

'I'm not sure,' said Gangabharti.

'Let me order a vehicle and a driver familiar with these roads to come at 4am. If Ramma arrives before then we can cancel the booking,' urged Rabindranath.

'A driver who knows the way and the road conditions, yes, but let us find someone who will drive overnight.'

'If your vehicles pass in the dark, will you see each other?' asked Rabindranath. 'Even with a four-wheel drive there is a strong likelihood that, driving at night, you do not see a broken down lorry or come off the road and turn over. Frustrating yes, but leave just before dawn and you are more likely to make it to Sanchi and make it there quicker too. Trust me.'

Gangabharti looked thoughtful and turned to Harry. 'My friend's advice is wise but hard to take. He is right – it is possible that she may have been held up and not been able to get to a phone.'

If not for the concern of both Gangabharti and Rabindranath, Harry might have been more relaxed. Ramma might have decided to stay an extra day but Gangabharti was insistent that this was out of character.

'Ramma said she would be here to greet me that meant she intended to be here to greet me.'

Gangabharti's normal baritone was off-tune and squeaky. It was agreed that if no news came of Ramma's whereabouts, they would leave for Bhopal just before sunrise where they would look for someone to guide them to the site in Sanchi.

Harry paced up and down. Gangabharti sat down and laced his hands and then looked sympathetically at Harry. 'If you keep pacing up and down like that, Harry, the hotel visitors will be disturbed. We are caught up in our worries and have forgotten that my friends have a business to run. We shall go for a walk. The western temples are only 200 yards from the hotel. We shall try to distract ourselves. If there is a phone call or any news Rabindranath will send a messenger to us without delay.'

Rabindranath nodded in agreement. As they went out of the door, Gangabharti said to Harry, 'There could be a simple explanation but what is it about my daughter? She attracts trouble.'

It didn't seem to need a response. Before long they had reached the temples. The last thing Harry wanted was to go sightseeing but he sympathised with Gangabharti's thinking. He saw for himself that Khajoraho was indeed a village, though a village with twenty-two surviving temples. The biggest were so close to the hotel that they could receive a message in minutes.

The artist in Harry automatically took in the craftsmanship and the beauty, but the subject matter intensified his feelings for Ramma. This was India at its most voluptuous and flamboyant. The temples were like mountains covered with thousands of sculptures, celestial nymphs, gods and goddesses, bold serpents and leonine beasts above couples sharing love and lust: the *Kama Sutra* in stone.

In his mind, he could hear Ramma quietly explain why the human body is a temple and why temples are sculptures. He imagined it as the most erotic lecture he'd ever experience. He looked over his shoulder half-expecting her to walk around a corner. The tour was frenetic. GeeBee was grinding his teeth; his explanations patchy and confusing. The explicit images, seen with the father of the girl he loved added to his unease.

The walk back to the hotel saw the singer's pace become graceless, even clumsy.

A glance at Rabindranath was enough to know that there was no news. They retired to their rooms in silence. From his bedroom window, Harry looked across to a roof café where Western tourists were laughing and drinking. If Ramma were beside him, they might have sat there enjoying the cool red sunset. He sat down then stood up. He picked up a guidebook and threw it across the room. His imagination was taking him down dark roads, which he was loath to travel. Was Ramma's disappearance accidental or something more sinister?

'Where was this archaeological site, anyway?' Harry

looked it up in his guidebooks to India and almost wished he hadn't. Sanchi was in Bihar, the poorest, most corrupt and most backward state in India. It was close to Uttar Pradesh, another of the four poorer states where kidnapping was not uncommon. Harry had read stories in the Indian papers of professional gangs targeting the children of well-known people. Ramma could be a sitting target in such a remote area.

'This is a bad dream,' he told himself. His attention was drawn to a tiny movement. Climbing slowly and gracefully up the window was a tiny black spider. Things hidden in other cultures, both beauty and ugliness were on display in India. To the eye of the beholder, the spider could be either.

Since meeting Ramma, Harry had struggled to wrap his brain around the scope of the sub-continent. Its mountain range was the highest in the world while magnificent rivers flowed through flower-bedecked foothills. The tiger, the white rhino, the Indian elephant, the Asian lion were not products of the imagination; they were flesh and blood. Harry had read about the diversity of India's people from stone-age tribes in the Andamans to space-age researchers in the institutes of technology. States like Kerala had 96% literacy, but Uttar Pradesh had less than half that for girls.

Questions and yet more questions swirled around his aching brain. Where in this vast sub-continent was Ramma and what unimaginable things were happening to her at that moment?

*****

They awoke, or more accurately, went down stairs, at four o'clock. Mrs Srinivasan handed them a hamper filled with food to sustain them and they set off without any further delay, on the dangerous roads. Much of the time Gangabharti and Harry remained silent, keeping their anxious thoughts to themselves. As they passed an overturned lorry, Harry imagined

Ramma as one of the thousands killed and injured every day on Indian roads. Perhaps they should start their search with the hospitals? Harry nearly said something but Gangabharti had a determined expression. If anyone knew how to start, it was he.

It was past midday when they found the home of the porter Ramma had employed in Sanchi. Harry saw a look of anger, for the first time, on Gangabharti's face but his expression mellowed as the man explained.

'Sahib, I hope I have done no wrong. The memsahib sent me home day before yesterday. She said she is leaving for Khajuraho in the morning. The memsahib gave me leave to return with some of the team on Thursday afternoon because my wife, she is sick.'

'Mela Ram, ab dekhai. My daughter is a determined woman but I would like you to get ready to leave immediately. Where was it that you left her? Take us there.'

'Sahib, please, I fetch my sister-in-law for my wife and children. Some way we go in the Land Rover, Sahib. Then we must go on foot.'

As a small business owner, Harry spent a jaw-dropping amount of time problem solving: logistics, accounting, sudden bouts of last-minute research, it was all in a day's work. And there was no point in delegating that work; he hadn't the staff. So he did it, without discussion and absolutely no drama. Harry's mind started problem solving.

Harry said, 'We passed a motor cycle hire company. Do you think those last miles could be crossed on a motor bike?'

'Possibly, Sahib-ji, but with difficulty. The memsahib tent is in the jungle. I carried it there for her and must collect it. The memsahib planned to follow a short trail before leaving for Khajuraho. She said something about an Englishman, Barty? I hope, sahib, I did no wrong?'

'No, Mela Ram, but I shall change my mind if you do not get a move on. Jaldi, jaldi man.'

While Mela Ram fetched his sister-in-law, Harry sprinted

down the road, to the astonishment of the shoppers at the street stalls, dodging in and out until he reached the company selling and hiring motor bikes he had seen half a mile from the orderly's home. He paid over the odds with a huge deposit to speed up the process. Gangabharti was getting impatient when Harry returned riding a Royal Enfield Bullet saying, 'I can reach her more quickly on this.'

Harry tailed them until the road came to an end and Mela Ram pointed to Ramma's Land Rover. As best he could, he described the way to the camp. For the first time since his arrival in India, Harry had come to a place devoid of people. He revved up the Enfield and set off down the rough track. The track ended in small rocky outcrops and gave way to areas of spindly trees, then taller trees with denser undergrowth, then more rocks and gullies.

Most of the time, he found ways to skirt the rocks, but at others he dragged the bike over, as Mela Ram had predicted, with difficulty. Sweating in the heat, his arms aching, Harry gritted his teeth and pressed on. He wasn't sure if he was even on the right path anymore. And he wasn't sure what he'd find at the end.

Then he saw it, a small tent with the remnants of a fire outside. The last half-mile seemed to last forever until he flung open the tent to see Ramma lying there, still and silent. He had come too late.

'Oh Ramma,' he breathed. 'Oh no, please honey, please speak to me.'

Harry flung himself over her. She had a contusion and gash to her head, in almost exactly the same spot as had happened in the car accident in Oxford. He gently lifted her up. Her lips were parched, the blood dried where they had cracked and split. But he felt a faint breath. Then her eyelids began to flicker and she looked at him.

'Harry, Harry is that you. I am going mad – my brain is playing tricks on me.'

'Ramma, my angel, there is nothing wrong with your brain. Drink this water and then tell me what happened. We were waiting for you in Khajuraho.' He kissed her again and again, holding her tightly to him.

'Aagh, Harry. Hurt.'

Harry gently laid her down, apologising. She seemed hesitant as if searching for a memory.

'I remember lighting the fire and putting potatoes in it, the way you do in camp fires in England. Then ...'

'Carry on... keep talking. Don't stop,' said Harry, 'while I clean your wound.'

'The potatoes were cooking, I went to pick berries. I must have passed out. I stumbled back here and drank some water but felt dizzy and was sick... At noon it was so hot, too hot to walk to my Land Rover. It was later when I set off again but I saw double and kept tripping. My head throbbed. I thought I should try to get some sleep and hope I'd feel better this morning. Oh, Harry, how good is it to see you... I have not any energy. I am not sure I can get there without you.'

'You don't need to. I'm here now. Thank God, I found you. You'll be fine. You will be fine, I promise. GeeBee, I mean your father, is on his way. We must leave... right now, honey please. But you should drink some more water before we set off.' Harry held the cup to her lips.

'Oh, Harry, that's so good but my head feels like a drum.'

'Have you any Paracetamol or Aspirin in your bag?' Ramma nodded and while he looked for it he asked her.

'Can you ride with me on the motor bike?'

'Harry, you are here and that is all that matters. Anything you suggest.'

Harry could see that Ramma had packed her rucksack. While she swallowed the tablets, he stowed the last things inside in seconds and put it on his back. He helped her stand and walk unsteadily to the bike, supporting and helping her onto the saddle. Every step felt like agony to him. Harry knew he must get her to a hospital right away but couldn't rush her.

'Can you hold on to the bars and I'll put my arms around you?' he asked. He was worried she would fall off. She was still quite concussed. He sat her in front of him and drove cautiously until he came to the first rocky outcrop. He carried Ramma over and then pulled the bike up after them, put Ramma back on the bike and carried on. After a mile and a half they saw her father and Mela Ram approaching. Gangabharti ran towards them and took Ramma in his arms and with tears in his eyes said, 'What have I done to deserve such a wayward daughter?'

She smiled and he hugged her and held her close for a long time until Harry interrupted asking, 'Where is the nearest hospital? Ramma must be seen quickly.'

Gangabharti agreed and between them they helped her on the rest of the way to the car, partly walking, partly riding the Enfield, and then they drove to the hospital in Bhopal.

There were queues of people in casualty. Harry waited with Ramma while Gangabharti went to fill in the forms. Although his face was not shown on the movies, it was sometimes used on the sleeves of his recordings. The nurse on duty took down Ramma's name and then stared hard at Gangabharti. 'Gupta,' she paused over the name.

'You are Gangabharti Gupta?'

As he nodded she said, 'My mother has all your records.'

The news that the voice of Bollywood was in the building spread like wildfire. Everyone wanted to help. They cleaned and stitched Ramma's wound and the young doctor said Ramma should be kept in overnight for observation as she had concussion.

Harry explained that a similar thing had happened in Oxford less than four months ago so he was concerned. The doctor squeezed his lips and then shook his head. Harry was hopeless at interpreting the gesture. In India, it seemed to mean both no and yes.

'What do you think Doctor, sahib?' asked Gangabharti.

The doctor suggested they return to Mumbai the next day where Ramma could have a brain scan. Harry didn't want to leave her side but the staff eventually sent him away warning him that she needed rest. As he crept into his hotel bed that night, Harry felt like pinching himself. It was as if he had been swept up by a whirlwind and tossed from one disaster to another. A sense of uncertainty threatened to overwhelm him. He reflected that his life had become as unpredictable as India since he'd met Ramma.

*****

In the morning, Ramma looked much better and although weak, she was fit to travel. The doctor called them in.

'Her chances of making a full recovery are excellent. She is young and healthy and her memory does not appear to be affected. I recommend that you return to Mumbai by rail rather than flying. It is a low risk, but there can be effects of the pressurised cabin on the brain. Why take any risk, however small?'

Harry returned the Enfield and had a large penalty to pay. The paintwork had been scratched hauling it over the rocks. But he paid it gladly; the bike had performed well for him. Gangabharti was in a fine mood and insisted on taking a photo of him on it before he handed it back.

'Look serious, as if you are playing the part of Lawrence of Arabia.'

The simile was not lost on Harry. He had seen pictures of the adventurous hero on his beloved black and silver motor bike, which he'd named Boanerges or Sons of Thunder. Harry thought he should honour his hired Enfield with a name before he finally said his goodbyes. Gangabharti suggested, 'It sped to Ramma – so how about Shakti?'

Harry had no idea what that meant but was not in a mood to disagree. From then on the picture was labelled 'Harry on Shakti.' Only later when able to look it up, did he realise it meant 'the power of the goddess.' Harry liked that because he found the macho image of himself on the Enfield confusing. He had spent his teenage years fighting with society's idea of masculinity – which in Harry's mind was the image of his father. His thoughts were interrupted by Gangabharti.

'Did you notice the distinctive pud-pud of the Enfield engine? That's why it earned the title, The Thumper.'

That deflated the masculine hero's steed but in any case Harry preferred Gangabharti's female symbol of Shakti. It helped put his struggle with what it meant to be male safely under lock and key at the back of his mind. But before that key was turned Harry remembered the photograph of Bartholomew Carew in the 19th century looking like Lawrence of Arabia. Harry couldn't imagine a hero like Bartholomew suffering from any doubts about what it meant to be a man.

*****

Gangabharti booked tickets on the Punjab Mail leaving that evening. Harry's first experience of Indian Railways lasted thirteen hours. The station was not exactly a restful experience but Harry would have enjoyed it if he had not been worried about Ramma. Passengers were running after porters, who were trying to locate particular carriages. The sound of traders shouting their wares must have been commonplace at one time in London and it was still in full voice on Bhopal station: "mineral water", "oranges, mangoes", "newspapers". Gangabharti pointed out the bhaji wallas and poori bhaji wallas.

'No McDonald's here, Harry.'

'Thank heavens for that! The food looks mouth-watering to me. Just the aroma attracts like forbidden fruit. Shall we buy some for the journey?'

'I have first class tickets and this train has a dining car.'

At first, Harry thought they would be alone in their compartment. The engine had started up when, through the window, he glimpsed latecomers carrying enormous amounts of luggage heading for their carriage. GeeBee read his thoughts.

'We Indians are not renowned for travelling light. But the amount some carry defies belief.'

Harry believed it when a couple arrived with their porter who tried his best to stow their luggage on the over-head racks. First class or no first class, it looked at as if there would not be legroom. At least, there were no passengers clinging precariously to doors or perched on the roof, as he had noticed on some rush hour trains in Mumbai.

The train gathered speed and so did the chatter. The middle-aged couple talked away to them as if they were old friends.

'Where are you from? Where are you going? What for? Where have you been to?'

This was followed by advice on spectacular train journeys on the toy train to Darjeeling and up the mountain railway to Ooty in the south. By the time they arrived at the first station, Harry knew that this couple were heading for a wedding in Mumbai. Harry felt rather overwhelmed by their description of the event that awaited them. Ramma glanced at him, a confirmation that her tales of massive Indian weddings with noisy bands, white horses and massive marquees were no exaggeration.

White-suited waiters could bring food to you but Harry felt like a bit of exercise and wanted to get away from his fellow travellers. Friendly and well-meaning though they were, he needed a brief escape.

'You can stretch your legs at most stations. You will see that most people get off the train for five minutes or so,' commented Gangabharti.

A few hours later the conversation had turned to cricket

and it was not so different to the one he'd had in The Taj Palace Hotel. Harry longed for them to be alone. He wanted Ramma all to himself but there was no chance of that. Then he turned to her and said rather bluntly, 'Do you think you should try sleeping?'

It took a few more remarks like that before their fellow passengers got the message and Ramma drifted off to the sound of the rhythm of the wheels on the track. Harry was surprised when Gangabharti shook him awake when their breakfast arrived.

Once back in Mumbai Ramma's father rang a state-of-the-art private hospital. He made an appointment for a brain scan for the following morning. An hour after the scan the consultant rang with the good news that there was no permanent damage. But he said, 'Miss Gupta has received a serious blow to the head twice in a relatively short time She should take it seriously and rest for two weeks, at least.'

CHAPTER 4: Hope

Calcutta, November 1882

The deaths from starvation in Bengal are horrific beyond calculation. Life in Simla continues, oblivious as the social merry-go-round defines the seasons. It is better if Douglas stays there & does not witness the suffering here. There is no shortage of food in the Punjab. Dora does not seem to notice my absence. I can hardly blame her.

Florence Nightingale's analysis of the problem of the recent famines implies that they are fundamentally man-made. She records two contributory factors: the grain famine compounded by the money famine. Money drained from the peasant to the landlord makes it impossible for the peasant to procure food, & money intended for the producers of food via public works projects was diverted to paying for the military effort in Afghanistan.

In these tragic times my interest in Ashoka seems perverse. The Emperor's policies of social welfare should be relevant but in caste-ridden India, reform appears unlikely. I took up Cunningham's advice & met Bhandarkar. He is a formidable campaigner against the evils of the caste system & Brahminical orthodoxy but it is hard to change ingrained attitudes. We too fail to learn from the past; absentee landlords compounded the effects of the Irish Potato Famine. At least the Irish were able to escape on ships to the New World. In Bengal, for young peasants with any strength, enrolling in the army is their only means of survival.

As I feared, Dora is now all too aware of how I am regarded. Her opinion of me is only redeemed when she observes that my knowledge of the country & my experience with the Survey is of occasional use to the Viceroy. What has happened to that energetic young man who arrived here in 1869? Even the enthusiastic response of the students to my lecture at the Bengal Engineering College failed to lift my spirits.

My only escape, my only means of rising above this appalling situation, is the Indian practice of meditation. The yogic teacher I have hired spends far too much time on my breathing, which is one of the few attributes I rather thought I had already mastered. Apparently not, & I am to relearn a physical function that comes to one entirely naturally. I might prove too sceptical a student.

The consultant warned Ramma against physical activity, excessive reading and watching TV, but the situation Harry found himself in was far from boring. Overwhelmed by the daunting array of relatives who descended on the Guptas, he struggled to remember even a fraction of their names. Introduced by Ramma to Ankita Massi, Seema Massi, Sushma Massi and on and on, two thirds of the female well-wishers appeared to be a "Massi" or "auntie". They came bearing gifts, usually boxes of Indian sugary treats. Dulal, their house servant, took them to the kitchen where the pile grew ever higher. Harry became prey to subversive humour. On one of the rare moments when he and Ramma were left momentarily alone in the room, he amused her with his vision.

'I had a dream, a dream of battalions of aunties massed together armed with Ladoos.' And he described a chaotic scene where the aunties leaned out of the windows and threw the sweetmeats at the passers-by. 'You and I ran out onto the street and ran away with the crowd while we were bombarded with orange raindrops.'

'Harry, you've described what happens here every year, at

Holi. If you dare venture out you wear old clothes during the festival because everyone who walks the streets is pelted with diluted coloured paints. Yes really,' laughed Ramma.

'In England, I'd say you were teasing me but here I believe anything is possible.'

'The title "uncle" and "auntie" can be honorific. We address Mama and Daddy-ji's close friends and cousins that way because they are older than us. Once you are seen regularly, the little nieces and nephews will call you "uncle", also. If you are not happy to be their "uncle" you will be viewed as a sad man in India, my English friend.'

*****

As the week passed, Harry felt he had dipped a finger in a pool and as the ripples spread so did Ramma's family grow. Cousins, second cousins and their spouses all had instant access, no telephoning to see if a visit were convenient. Gangabharti presented him to everyone as "Ramma's colleague from Oxford". That was it, no hint of anything closer than Harry having introduced her to Bartholomew Carew – the now linchpin of her doctorate. To lonesome Harry it was comforting being swept up and accepted in their kind-hearted embrace, but it was frustrating when he realised that he and Ramma could get no privacy. They were rarely alone together for more than a minute.

When the visitors became loud and excitable, Harry stared hard at Ramma, concerned that it was probably better if she stayed calm and quiet. But he had no concerns about the food. Dulal's meals were not only delicious but healthy too. He was pleased that nearly three weeks had passed without a single bout of "Delhi Belly". Taste buds he hadn't known he'd possessed were roused like Rip van Winkle after his long sleep. The rice was not just rice, but flavoured with lemon and ginger or saffron. The tang of the herbs seemed intense compared to those he bought in Oxford and the homemade pickles and relishes were to die for.

Ramma was not just getting better but bantered with him again. That distant unconnected feeling after Birmingham had evaporated in the Indian sun.

'Harry, go for a jog on the beach before you burst out of those trousers. Dulal is frying pakoras and you are too weak to resist.'

Harry didn't get the chance to reply as another family arrived to see Ramma. He was constantly surprised by the number of guests eating with them. It seemed infinitely flexible and no invitation was necessary. Twelve people seemed the norm rather than the exception. Harry felt the waves of warmth. There was no shyness, everyone was welcomed, children were cuddled by family, friends and servants alike. While the food was memorable, the conversation was forgettable: weddings, weather, the Mumbai traffic, the latest gismo, the best shop for this and that, prospective and past visits.

When he felt bored, he joined Dulal in the kitchen and learned lessons in spice combinations. He adored the colours and made a watercolour of Dulal with his spice box, painting the spices in pyramids. He tore the picture out of the sketchbook and gave it to the servant. Dulal's face filled with emotion.

'Is this for me, Harry−ji?'

'Of course it's for you.'

'It will be my treasure.'

From then on, he had at least one devoted friend in the Gupta household. Dulal helped him have his first proper time alone with Ramma. He pretended she was asleep and turned a couple of guests away at a time when Gangabharti was working.

So Harry began their time together by asking, 'What made you stay on after the others left?'

'I was the new girl on this dig and did as I was asked but I wanted to follow up a Bartholomew lead.'

'Tell me about it,' asked Harry sensing that Ramma was

returning to her enthusiastic self.

'Bartholomew commented that stupas are usually raised so they can radiate to all four points of the compass. The base on which the stupa is erected represents the universe. When Bartholomew visited Sanchi the Buddhist site was in ruins. The team leader read the notes I had copied at the Bodleian. He did not dismiss Bartholomew's ideas but said they had more than enough to get on with. But he was happy for me to search the area Bartholomew believed could be the site of a small stupa once we had packed up.'

'You mean he was happy to leave you there alone?' fumed Harry.

'Harry, don't blame Sunil, it was my fault. When he agreed, he left me with Mela Ram. It was foolish of me to send him home but his wife was unwell and that night it seemed unfair to make him work an extra day. My attitude was, what could go wrong in half a day? Silly question!'

They laughed and laughed again because they could. Ramma held out her hand and laid it on his and continued.

'I used a compass and tried to follow Bartholomew's directions and I may have located it. There are shrubs growing over it now and their roots have disturbed the shape but he could be right. I took photographs and measurements and hope I can convince the team to follow it up. I must have become overtired. I cannot get over seeing you and I did dream about you, Harry.'

But Harry was sceptical.

'As a historian who searches after truth, would I lie?'

Dulal was instructed that Ramma needed to sleep in the early afternoon. He was to allow no visitors, not even Harry, and he reluctantly ended their time alone together. Harry was consumed with frustration. What had he been thinking of? Their first proper conversation and they had talked not about themselves but about Bartholomew Carew! The idea of spending another late afternoon and evening lazing about talking about nothing in particular with Ramma's aunts, cousins and neighbours was doing his head in. He wasn't used to being so idle. He needed to find a shipping agent to collect the purchases he had made for Selene so he went out and didn't return until late that evening.

*****

At the check-up the following day, the consultant pronounced Ramma well enough to return to work. But she was in no hurry. First, she would be Harry's guide to her favourite places in and around Mumbai. She would begin with Elephanta Island. They would be alone together for a whole day. As they approached the cave temple, Harry asked Ramma why she hadn't written to him. She looked shocked.

'But of course I wrote. I promised you in my email. I wrote a long letter when I was working in Ujjain. When you didn't reply I thought you had forgotten me and found a new girlfriend.'

'But Ramma, I didn't get your letter and I thought you had abandoned me!'

They looked directly at each other before darting behind a huge statue of Shiva, whose magnificent parts had been removed by offended Portuguese invaders. Despite their ease with the image of Shiva's symbolic penis, Indians disapprove of kissing in public so the art provided a suitable barrier. When they finally broke away from each other, they felt overwhelmed. Born worlds apart, it was as if they were unfinished and the discovery of a missing part had made them complete. The feeling was so intense that Harry felt he could pose the question he had wanted to ask for the past three months. They strolled up the hill above the caves away from the crowds of tourists and found a quiet place to sit unseen.

'Ramma, I love you. Please don't leave me ever again. Say you'll marry me.'

She answered him with a warm and passionate kiss but her words contained a warning. 'Harry please, you must accept the person that I am. I feel the same as you but my father is dear to me and I am Indian. You must ask him. In India, that is not a perfunctory thing. If he says "No", I shall be heart-broken because I am not sure that I could marry you and never see him again. You do understand? Please say you understand. Oh Parvati! Why is life so complicated?'

He felt his cheeks wet with her tears.

'Ramma, honey, what is the matter?'

'The tears are relief and joy and sadness all mixed together. I was drawn to you from our first meeting but I tried so hard not to fall in love with you. How could I be a part of your world? Your friends are lovely but I knew little about the art they talk about. I felt an outsider but despite my better judgment, you became a part of my life. I dismissed the feeling as loneliness and homesickness. But when I came home, I missed you so much.' Ramma sighed and said, 'I knew you cared for me, Harry, but in India, it has to be marriage or nothing. I cannot live with you unwed and I convinced myself that you would not want to marry. You said nothing that hinted at a long-term commitment and I was too proud also to do the asking.'

Harry pulled her tightly to him as if he would never let her go.

'I'm so sorry. I didn't trust myself or you, honey. Then, when your father flew you back to India, I learned what love really feels like. I thought I'd lost you for good. I tried to understand my emotions. With Helen I'd felt betrayed. But when you left I felt bereft, almost as if I'd lost the will to live. The emotions were different – one was anger and the other despair.' Harry could not believe that he had just said that. It was the longest expression of his feelings he had ever articulated.

Back at the flat, Harry showered and dressed as smartly as he could and paced up and down. In all his life he could not have imagined this situation, a formal interview with a prospective father-in-law. He liked Gangabharti and believed Gangabharti liked him but he imagined how easy it could be to make a colossal faux pas. Harry suggested that Ramma come with him to speak to her father. Harry stood nervously in front of him like a young Victorian. Ramma suggested that on this occasion he should address him not as GeeBee but formally.

So he began with a respectful, 'Gangabharti-ji, you will not be surprised by how I feel about Ramma. I believe I have loved her since first I saw her face. I came here because I can't imagine life without her. Sir, I would like your permission to marry your daughter.'

Gangabharti didn't answer but instead turned to Ramma. 'Is this what you want?'

'Yes, Daddy-ji, I would be so happy if you could come to love Harry as a dear son.'

The silence seemed like an eternity to Harry but then he heard Gangabharti saying in his magical voice, 'It is hard to refuse the man who has rescued you twice.' Turning to Harry he continued, 'Ramma is the most precious person in my life. How can I be certain that you will have a life-long commitment to her, Harry?'

Harry breathed deeply before replying. 'You have my word.'

Harry wasn't sure what to make of Gangabharti's doubtful smile and his reply confused him even more. 'Harry, I accept your good intentions and Ramma has been brought up to have a mind of her own. If you can make her happy, I shall not stand in your way but I have a request to make, a suggestion. Let us go and eat and discuss it over dinner. I'll tell Dulal to turn away visitors saying that we are out.'

Harry was nervous as they sat down with their thalis. Despite the mouth-watering aroma, his appetite had disappeared. He presumed Gangabharti wanted to talk conditions.

'Harry, I expect Ramma has talked to you about Indian family life. Marriage in India is approached in a different way to the

West. We Indians are pragmatic about it. We see it as somewhat more than the passion of youth. It is about two families coming together also. When everything is as it should be, it is an ideal scene for bringing up children to experience the love of many people. It is a means of supporting each other, through good times and bad. How do you feel about being part of an extended family?'

Harry hesitated before replying.

'I must confess that it will be a new experience for me. You see, my father walked out when I was fourteen and never contacted us again. His brother lives in Australia and occasionally sends a Christmas card. Family to me was matriarchal: Mum and Aunt Julie. They did all they could to encourage me but...'

Ramma hugged him. Strengthened, he looked at Gangabharti. 'So you see that I've had no close encounters with an extended family until, that is, I met yours. And from what I've seen, it feels a bit like my friends are my family, in the way that all the aunts and uncles are in your family. My friends enabled me to come here. But I do love Ramma and want more than anything to make her happy. Will your family accept me as I am? Could you consider my friends as the other family?'

'I can promise you that, but life can play cruel tricks on the nicest of people. You are in love but romantic love is short-lived. You need a love that can last through all life's vicissitudes. Harry, I can imagine how you are feeling. You will not like what I have to say. But I hope that, when you have a chance to reflect, you will see that my request is for the best.'

Gangabharti paused and looked the stricken Harry in the eye. 'Where are you going to live?'

Surprised by the unexpectedly prosaic nature of the question, Harry's anxiety abated a little. He glanced towards Ramma. 'Probably Oxford?'

'I have told you, Harry,' said Ramma. 'I do not think there will be many opportunities for me to carry on with both my history and archaeology in Oxford. I am sure I shall go to lots of conferences in the UK, but there is much more work to be done here.'

If he was honest with himself, Harry had assumed she'd change her mind once they were together. In a spasm of bitterness, he catalogued all the reasons for Ramma returning to England. Surely her career opportunities in Oxford would be better than in India? But what could he offer her, what exactly? A terraced house with a small back garden, financial uncertainty, and no extended family! His rescue came from an unlikely source – Gangabharti.

'You, Harry, have two months left on your visa and you, Ramma, are nearing the end of your research. Ramma tells me the writings of Bartholomew Carew have given her exciting ideas for her thesis that could provide the foundation of a promising career. And Harry, you appear interested in his story also. My suggestion to you both is to walk in his footsteps. Follow the Buddhist trail as both Ashoka and Bartholomew previously followed it. Ramma, you do not need me to remind you how important it is to complete your thesis and this way you will do that.'

A confused Harry had no idea where this was leading when Gangabharti surprised him.

'You will be together day and night. I do not want you to tell me what you plan to do or not do. Learn to know each other – to really know each other. This is your first time in India, Harry. On your travels be sensible; this *is* India. You know what I mean, Ramma. Relationships outside of caste are disapproved of in many quarters.' Then he looked Harry in the eye and said, 'This land is part of Ramma's soul. I challenge you to love it, warts and all. If you cannot do that, I do not believe that this marriage will work. You have to be able to live here and earn a living here.' He looked from Harry to Ramma and then back again.

'You will have plenty of time to talk. I want you to look at life in its entirety and see how you are going to fit your *lives* as well as your hearts together. Discuss where you are going to live and how you are going to live. Do you understand?'

A bewildered Harry heard the emphasis on the word, "live".

'Are you saying you will give your approval if I can adapt to life in India?' he asked.

'In a way – yes. If, when you return, you both still want to marry and know where you will live together and how you will earn your living, I shall arrange the wedding. I do not doubt that you are attracted to each other. When you are young, desire rules the head and that is why some marriages do not last despite everyone's goodwill. Pragmatism writ large, as you say in England, is what this is about.'

Pragmatic? This wasn't pragmatic at all. A two-month holiday with the most beautiful woman in the world wasn't going to tell him how to find work here or whether or not he could love India. Having already established himself in two careers, Harry knew something about getting a new job – and it didn't involve going on holiday. Harry carefully schooled his face so that his expression didn't betray him. 'I'll know Ramma better and she'll know me,' Harry thought to himself. 'But to decide the rest of my life on this?' Harry almost shook his head in despair. 'I don't even know how to begin to make that decision.'

'For now, I propose we say nothing to the family.' GeeBee was continuing and Harry, to his surprise, found himself nodding sagely in agreement. 'You could find your minds being changed on this journey. If you say nothing to your friends in Oxford and Ramma keeps quiet also, nothing is lost. On your return you will both have to persuade me that you have understood and Harry has met my challenge. What do you say?'

CHAPTER 5: The Road to the Himalayas

Darjeeling, February 1883

Had an affecting reunion with Kishen Singh. He & Chhumbel arrived in Darjeeling in November in a condition bordering on destitution, their funds exhausted, their clothes in rags & their bodies emaciated. He is still painfully thin. What excuse do I have for my low spirits? He arrived home to find his only son dead & his house broken. The Survey must provide him with a generous pension. The Tibetans have put a price of £500 on his head. There can be no question of him continuing the survey of Eastern Tibet. He has mapped over 4800 miles, more than any other man, white or brown.

He described to me the crossing of the Himalayas via the Ata Kang La glacial pass. At 15,300 feet in such poor physical condition, it is amazing that they survived all the hardships & deprivations. His knowledge of Tibetan & Mongolian was essential to the success of his mission — no European could possibly have done it.

The achievement of the Great Trigonometrical Survey is an example to the world. Many good men of all races have sacrificed their lives in the process. That is a legacy that the Raj can claim with pride. Whatever the future of India, it will be better with the knowledge & expertise that the Survey has provided. I am proud to have worked alongside so many inspiring men.

What could he say? In the bubble of his wishful thinking, Harry had visualised himself and Ramma back home in Oxford at a reception party dancing as one, to the delight of his friends. In contrast, Ramma had imagined herself living with her new husband in the apartment above her father's in Mumbai. Those dreams were dismissed and instead they were to be transported, like Alice in Wonderland, to the bizarre and unpredictable adventure of a field research road trip.

Harry knew his resolve was being tested but he was able to ignore it as realities intruded. He finalised Selene's shipment while Ramma arranged her notes and planned the itinerary. As the days ticked by, Harry forgot the challenge of leaving behind the life he loved in Oxford and risking a new beginning in Mumbai. He was in love with Ramma but also, all he could think about was that, if he had understood correctly, for the next month he and Ramma could be sleeping together every night. And every time he thought of that, a smile curled around the corners of his mouth.

He rang his friends to explain that they'd be travelling for at least three weeks and he'd find it difficult to phone or email. They were excited that he'd found Ramma and that she was well again and asked all kinds of questions. Harry began responding enthusiastically but had to stop short of telling them what his heart was bursting to reveal. He'd made a promise and intended to keep it.

Kathy and Ingrid were in the shop together the day he called and looked at each other, somewhat disappointed. Harry sounded stiff, and overly distant. When they'd organised Harry's trip, it had felt so romantic. They both believed that Harry and Ramma would meet again, and it would be happily ever after. They had not anticipated this unfruitful phone call.

'Are we to understand that you're helping Ramma finish her DPhil? That you have gone all that way just to find out more about Bartholomew Carew?' asked an exasperated Kathy. Then Ingrid grabbed the phone.

'Enjoy your travels, dear Harry, but don't forget your friends in this world. Enjoy those huge Indian skies and think of us shrouded in November mists. Give our love to that lovely girl of yours. We want to see her again soon.'

As he put the receiver down, Harry was pleased it would be hard to contact them. Ramma loved him. It became a private mantra. Ramma loved him, Ramma loved him and it was difficult keeping that news to himself. Gangabharti had placed him in the role of the prince in a Grimm's fairytale or the hero in a Hindi movie having to overcome great obstacles to claim his bride. Despite his passion for Ramma, Harry didn't feel at all heroic. His teenage years had been scarred by the lack of a male role model and his passions were not regarded as macho. He wasn't into competitive sport. He loved walking and cycling and he was fit but most of his generation saw those pursuits as a bit old-fashioned. He had struggled against the idea that there had to be a dominant partner and that role had to be filled by a traditionally-defined man.

He asked himself, 'Are we like a couple in a Bollywood film faced with the opposition of an authoritarian father?' But Gangabharti didn't fit the stereotype. Bewildered, Harry had no idea how he could fulfil his challenge but didn't want to consider the possibility of failure, and Gangabharti seemed to lack confidence in him. Glancing towards Ramma, he approved of the determined look on her face as she spread out a map of India. At least Ramma seemed to know what this was all about. She explained what she had in mind.

'Our first call is Bodhgaya, the site of Buddha's enlightenment and hopefully ours too,' she said with a smile. 'After that we shall visit Sarnath north of Varanasi where he preached his first sermons. Next up, Sravasti, where Buddha stayed for twelve rainy seasons before heading for his birthplace in Nepal. During the time of Buddha and Ashoka, Lumbini was in India. It is a bit odd not starting at the place of his birth but Bodhgaya is a convenient place to begin and we need enlightenment, don't we, Harry?'

She laughed, buoyant for the first time in a long time. 'What do you think? After that, we go wherever our research takes us, probably to the university at Nalanda. Bartholomew was last seen further east and we don't know if he was heading east, west or north towards Bhutan. I wish the notes he'd left were in chronological order. I need to read the diary you brought. That may make sense of everything.'

But Harry's mind wasn't on Bartholomew Carew or on Ramma's thesis. 'It's hard for me to concentrate on anything or anyone but you. Since your mind will be on Bartholomew in search of Ashoka in search of the Buddha, I face daunting competition. If you don't want me to feel left out, give me something to do.'

Ramma suppressed a smile and pointed to photocopies of the papers and letters from the Bodleian. 'I wanted to show you them that day I called in Deco-rators and left the note with Kathy. I'm sorry about that day. I thought you had ignored it, and me. Then everything spiralled out of control. I waited for you to say something but when you didn't, I thought Daddy-ji was right to want to take me home.'

A hangdog look came over Harry. 'I felt so guilty about what happened with Joe Buy. You didn't tell me but I saw that you were upset and I should have known. It was my fault exposing you to him and I felt a failure. Then the accident and it was me who was driving. I couldn't believe that you could love such an idiot. Promise me you won't keep things secret from me ever again.'

Their conversation came to a quick end as Dulal ushered in three aunts who had somehow got wind of the Buddhist tour. Ramma made sure they saw her pass Harry a pile of papers.

'Twice you have dashed to my rescue. In return, let this grateful tutor suggest that her artist student read these. How about an essay in 2000 words on Bartholomew's view of Indian Art? Have it ready for a seminar in Varanasi or Sarnath but our first stop is Bodhgaya.'

After thirty tedious, if kind, minutes with the aunts, Harry needed to get out and be active. He made an excuse that he needed to meet an artist who may interest his film-star customer.

*****

On the plane north Harry stretched out his hand to grasp Ramma's. She looked pleased but embarrassed.

'Sorry, Harry,' she whispered as she folded her hands together, 'but we have to be patient.' Harry could hear her father's warning about how to behave in India. No kissing in public.

'Let me take your mind off your frustrations and tell you how I became interested in Ashoka. When I was little, father told me stories about him and his world lost in the mists of time. He made some things up but I came to see it as the greatest period in Indian history and that made it an obvious choice for my thesis.

'What is so great about Ashoka that you and Bartholomew Carew share this passion to learn about him?'

'Ashoka began as just a warlord, one among many. After yet another bloody battle, he was filled with remorse and invited some Buddhist scholars to teach him. We call them Buddhist because they followed the Buddha's teaching, but you need to know that Buddha was a guru who attracted a huge following in the states nowadays called Bihar and Uttar Pradesh. Even after his death, there was no religion called Buddhism. Ashoka was responsible for that, rather like St Paul creating Christianity. He united India and sent emissaries all over Asia, although he ruled in a secular way but with Buddhist ethics. That is how Buddhism spread to Burma, China, Sri Lanka, Thailand and Japan. This was the nearest thing that India ever had to having an empire, but Ashoka achieved it without violence. He did it through ideas and trade.'

'A kind of soft power compared to the hard power of a

military invasion?' asked Harry.

'Oh, Harry you get it. You see why Ashoka is so relevant,' enthused Ramma.

'I told an old college friend, Ravi, about your thesis and he knew hardly anything about Ashoka. Why's that?'

'The Brahmins, who had been knocked off their perch at the top rung of the ladder, wanted him and his ideas to be forgotten. So they clawed back power. The civilisation that he had developed weakened slowly from 400 to 700 CE. The devastating destruction wrought during the Mughal invasions from the 12th century wiped away most of the monuments from his time. Nearly all the temples in the North, both what we would call Hindu as well as Buddhist, were destroyed. The languages of his time were no longer spoken so even the memory of him faded.'

*****

They checked into The Ashok Travellers Lodge and set out for the Buddhist Mecca. Ramma noticed Harry was carrying a wooden box.

'What is in that box?' she asked.

'My watercolours. Most of my art school friends think I'm mad still working in oils and watercolours when they've gone in search of sensation and conceptual art. Don't get me wrong, I'm not against conceptual art – artists like Antony Gormley and Anish Kapoor are doing amazing things. Their work has presence. But it's sad, isn't it, that at thirty-two, I'm regarded as an old fogey because I love painting and drawing.'

'I loved your sketches of Oxford, Harry. It's as if they have prana,' said Ramma.

'What's that?'

'It's the Vedic idea of the breath of life. It's the essence of life.'

A smile spread softly over his face.

'I love that way of putting it. I've always kept a visual diary. For me, sketches catch the atmosphere and the essence of personalities better than photographs. Now you've explained why. They have prana and it comes from the combination of hand, eye and spirit.'

Ramma nodded with a grin. 'I loved that book of sketches you made when you lived with Ingrid, although there were too many cats for my liking.' Harry had gone quiet. Talking about art made him introspective.

'Have I upset you, Harry?'

'It's my dilemma. More than anything I want to be an artist and for it to define me. But I need to earn a living. From my background, I knew that would be a struggle. When I discovered art and antique dealing, it seemed the way to keep the wolf from the door while keeping my eye active and allowing me to paint. Just selling my pictures can't pay the bills. Traditional art isn't commercial anymore.'

It was Ramma's turn to be silent as if she was learning something new about Harry. Compared to Harry, she was fortunate. She didn't want to live off her father but he did give her financial security. She was learning about Harry's passion for art but was unsure that she really understood him.

'I want to explore the essence of being human but at the same time I have to manage a business. Having to make money doesn't leave time for the contemplation and daily practice needed to have a chance of success as an artist.'

What Harry carefully did not say, because he was worried that it might come out as a criticism, is that now that Ramma's father wanted him to focus on India he had to figure out how he could earn a living here. He could manage it in England; he doubted he could in India.

Suddenly, none of it was a problem. He saw at once that he must paint Bodhgaya. Set amid woods near the Niranjana River, the entrance was through a carved torana. The high temple was crowned by a bell–like stupa. The colonnades surrounding the temple supported four smaller turrets shaped like a majestic heart.

Harry had an impression of calm and balance that fitted his sense of the Buddhist religion. Behind the temple was the descendant of the bodhi tree under which the Buddha found Enlightenment. Ramma explained that all the trees planted there had come from saplings of the first. There was something magical about the shadows of those trees speckled with drops of sunlight. Beside the spot where Buddha once sat and contemplated Nirvana, chanting in deep bass sounds, was a group of saffron-robed Thai monks.

Harry sat down a short distance away and took out his watercolours and what he saw was serenity itself after hectic Mumbai. Ramma left him for a while. She took photographs of the few examples of Brahmi and then sat cross-legged beside him making notes.

'What are you writing about?' asked Harry as he tried to do justice to the azure skies.

'I was thinking about what they say about converts,' said Ramma. 'Converts are meant to be the most zealous. You know, the zeal of a neophyte. Ashoka became a complete devotee but Bartholomew discovered this Ashokan inscription:

I act in the same manner with respect to all.
I am concerned with all classes.
I have honoured all religious sects with various ceremonies.
I consider it my religious duty to visit the people personally.

There was nothing fanatical about him. And how unusual is this? He even believed in kindness to prisoners.'

'I'll second that,' joked Harry wanting to change the subject. 'I'm completely in your power. If my jailor doesn't take good care of her prisoner, he may try to escape.'

'I've gone on far too long,' laughed Ramma. 'That is enough of a lecture for my unruly pupil for one day. Shall we exercise the body as well as the mind?'

Harry had waited and waited for her to say that. He hastily packed up his paints but as they walked to their hotel, he realised that Ramma's thoughts were not entirely on him. She seemed to have had her own enlightenment moment under the bohdi tree.

'Harry, how about this for the title of my thesis and the book that will come from it: *The Re-Incarnation of Ashoka*? Before 1839, when James Prinsep translated Brahmi, Ashoka was just a name in a list of kings. Some quite remarkable Englishmen came to India and were interested enough to uncover his story. I want your advice on how to make those Englishmen involved in the story come alive.'

'I thought I was the one and only Englishman in your life. I'm jealous.' Harry made a theatrical gesture.

Ramma smiled. 'I need to know why these Englishmen were different from most of their contemporaries. Their efforts to uncover the past are in wonderful contrast to the prejudice of the Raj. Men like William Jones, Prinsep, and Alexander Cunningham dedicated their lives to the task and are well known but no one has written about Bartholomew and that is what I want to do. Can you help me reincarnate Bartholomew Carew's personality?'

'You reincarnate Ashoka for me and I'll try to bring Bartholomew to life. I began to read his diary on the plane here but I wasn't concentrating. I got the impression he was a bit tragic. But my mind was on you and not him and it still is.'

Ramma turned to him. He wanted to kiss her but she made a gesture of warning. Restraint was proving hard for Harry. He had waited so long that he felt like a dog straining at a lead. They left via the garlanded gateway through which they had entered. As Ramma walked beneath the flowers he couldn't help thinking of how seductive she looked when she was enthusiastic.

When they arrived back at their room, Harry eased the door shut behind them. His pent-up emotions were set free and judging from her expression, Ramma and he were at one in their desire for each other. Harry stroked Ramma's hair and gently kissed her, then all of her, letting contentment wash over him.

'Today has been so special. I love the thoughts of the Buddha but I know I can't become a Buddhist, Ramma my angel. How can I renounce desire with you lying beside me? I have desired you since the day you walked into Deco-rators.'

And she responded with an intense moan of pleasure that seemed to come from deep within.

*****

After the energy of their love making, they emerged slowly. Harry had little desire to get out of bed. He couldn't stop touching Ramma, nuzzling and stroking her, enjoying the way she curved into his touch as her eyes consumed him and glazed over, satisfied. He knew once they left the room, they'd have to stop touching and now that they'd been intimate, it would be even harder. He wanted to crow to the world, 'She's mine and I love her and she loves me.'

So it was evening when they returned to the temple. After the relentless heat of the day the sky was shrouded in a golden glow spreading long shadows of dusk. The last rays felt like a tenderness.

The complex glittered with tiny yellow lamps and Ramma explained why. 'The temple is managed jointly by Hindus and Buddhists. That must be something hard to imagine in the West? That is why I am a Hindu but think much like a Buddhist.'

As they drew nearer, the sound of drums and cymbals was hypnotic in the gentle but warm night air. Monks paraded into the temple chanting their litanies. He asked Ramma if she knew the meaning of the litany. He hoped it could express his happiness.

'If you will worship in the noblest way bring flowers in thy hand. Their names are Contentment, Peace and... I forget the rest,' she sighed.

Harry relaxed into the peace of the night and the contentment of his mind and body and forgot the purpose of their journey.

CHAPTER 6: Sex and Sadhus

Simla, April 1884

We have to consider Douglas's education. Dora wants us to return to England.

I've been taught a new word, or to be pedantic, the new meaning of an old word. I've been accused of indulging in introspection. In Latin 'introspectus' means to examine or observe attentively. This new concept concerns looking within, searching one's feelings or thoughts; it has a rather negative connotation. This strikes me as peculiar as it was Socrates himself who said that an unexamined life is not worth living. I cannot help but feel that it is convenient for the Raj to insist that anyone who interrogates himself & his conscience is engaging in an unhealthy pre-occupation. This is what my diary is for: I am able to unburden myself in it & then, having closed its cover, return to duties.

I must, nonetheless, extricate myself from the slough of despond in which I have allowed myself to wallow. My life has been driven by a desire to explore the richness of this world. I have disciplined myself to increase my knowledge & then to employ it. When inactive, the frustration is hard to bear. Bearing witness to Dora's unhappiness & the violence underpinning the Raj I despair at my selfish preoccupations. I am determined to change. It is one thing to have a change of heart but quite another to effect that change. I continually question how Ashoka succeeded in not only transforming himself but India too. I find no difficulty understanding the change of heart of this warlord on surveying the dead after the bloody battle of Kalinga. Remorse after battle is not uncommon but what is unfathomable is how he was able to alter his thinking completely & create a new civilization that renounced violence. Unbelievable today let alone in 300 BC. I am cut in two. I owe it to Dora & Douglas to try to be a good husband & father to them. I am indeed remorseful, yet the Buddha left his wife & child. And Jesus encouraged the disciples to leave their families to follow him.

The next morning started slowly. Luxuriating in the joy of touch, they ignored the alarm clock and put off leaving the cocoon around themselves. Harry found himself wishing that this universe consisting of just him and Ramma could last forever. But they eventually emerged for a late and leisurely breakfast. Harry ordered omelette and toast because he didn't feel like curry first thing. The omelette looked fabulously fresh and appetising with finely chopped herbs and vegetables coloured as brightly as his artist's palette. Just looking at it made him feel hungry and he began by taking more than he should. Ramma laughed as he choked. The omelette was sprinkled with the tiniest but fiercest chillies Harry had ever eaten.

'Lights, camera, action, as my hero rushes into the furnace. Here's some water to hose down the flames!'

Harry adopted a mock Bollywood look of disappointment. 'Have you no sympathy for your burning lover?' he asked while making a resolution to avoid chilli before lunchtime.

Harry suggested they head back to their bedroom but cooled his ardour when Ramma said, 'I want to enjoy you all my life, Harry, but I have to concentrate on my thesis also. I need to start writing it up in less than two months' time.'

For a moment, Harry doubted himself. Had he failed as a lover? He looked longingly at Ramma. She grasped his hand and whispered in his ear, 'This is so hard. After last night I want ... I want you to love me forever and ever. For that to be possible, this is what I have to do.'

Harry decided that his best bet in the circumstances was to distract himself by helping her. He set about organising Bartholomew Carew's notes and letters.

*****

In the afternoon they boarded the train for the four-hour journey to Varanasi. Harry took out the copy of the 1966 classic, *Slowly Down the Ganges* he'd bought in the Taj Palace Hotel. Harry had seen film of the ghats and pilgrims bathing in the Ganges but that was all he knew about the city of divine light.

'Have you heard of the Kumbla Mela?' asked Ramma.

'Who is he?' asked Harry.

'Not who, silly,' laughed Ramma. 'What. It is the biggest religious gathering anywhere in the world. It began in the Vedic period and celebrates the creation myth about Lord Vishnu and takes place at four locations along the Ganges. Last year it was at Haridwar, which is the closest of the four to the Himalayan source of the Ganges. Ten million people attended.

'You're exaggerating but I like it.'

'There were that many people and the next one will be bigger still. In 2001, it will be at Prayag, near Allahabad and that will be a Mela that takes place only once in 144 years. Believe me, you do not want to get lost in a Mela. The government is planning for 40 million pilgrims.'

'Is there a Mela on in Varanasi now?'

'For us, it will not be that crowded. They will make way for the King.'

'Ha ha, two of us can play at that. Since your mother was "Rani" from now on you can be "Princess".'

'Sorry, Harry, not that, please. That would be torture. I promise no more jokes about your name.'

Harry loved the way Ramma had learned to banter. She was

at heart a serious person but Harry felt it wasn't good to take oneself too seriously. He returned to his book but after a few minutes decided that his personal guide was more interesting.

'So honey, tell me why we're heading to Varanasi if it's a place of Hindu pilgrimage. We're in search of Bartholomew who was in search of Ashoka who went in search of the Buddha.'

'Varanasi is one of the oldest cities on earth,' replied Ramma. 'The city is so ancient that it was already old when the Buddha went there, around 500 BCE. It is contemporaneous with Thebes and Babylon but unlike them, it is still a vibrant and alive metropolis.'

'The buildings survived that long?'

'No, the temples were destroyed during the Mughal invasion, but much has been rebuilt and rumour has it that there are over two thousand temples. It was a struggle to be Hindu when some of the Mughal emperors imposed the Jezya tax on non-Muslims.'

'So all the Hindus paid the tax and stayed Hindu. Is that how Varanasi stayed Hindu?'

'A lot of people converted to Islam but the Brahmins kept Vedic ideas alive. You could say the same about the Brahmins living in Varanasi during the time of Ashoka. The Buddha was against caste but the Brahmins never let go of the idea of caste and the power it gave them.'

In his short time in India Harry had witnessed the influence of caste and had read about the failed attempts to rid India of the corrosive inequality. Ramma failed to read his thoughts as she said, 'You will be able to see the world of Siva worship, yogis and priests, castes and ascetics. But Sarnath, where Buddha preached, is only eight miles from Varanasi and is the cradle of the Buddhist faith. This area is the beating heart of India, a bit like Jerusalem is to the Abrahamic faiths.'

Although they arrived in the dark, Ramma suggested he get his first glimpse of the Ganges before going to bed. It was a full moon and they arrived at the Raja Ghat in time to watch an Arti, an ancient Hindu ceremony in full swing. The priest chanted to the sound of drums, cymbals, and bells while burning torches illuminated the scene. Harry felt he had travelled in a time machine that had transported him to antiquity. Late as it was, large crowds had gathered by the river to watch the Arti. At the end many of the pilgrims bought for a few rupees little boats made from lotus leaves filled with marigolds in which they lit small candles and floated them on the current joining an armada of lights drifting away into the distance.

On his way down crowded streets to the river, Harry had been distressed by the poverty, decay and dirt all around. Could this really be a holy place? Coming to terms with poverty in some parts of India was going to be one of the obstacles Gangabharti had placed in his way. There was no way they could live a modern life in Varanasi. He had to be persuasive and change Ramma's mind about life together in Oxford.

Once they were by the river Harry sensed the magic. He saw that in this place the poor were not cowed but part of the noisy and colourful life of this city. Their little offerings floated like hopeful dreams in the fragrant evening breeze. He allowed himself to hope, even when the sights and sounds of India assaulted every sense and threatened to overwhelm him.

Ramma woke early and Harry, exhausted by their midnight love making, mumbled, 'Where are you going?'

'To do some yoga on the ghats,' waved Ramma.

Harry's limbs didn't want to move. His body seemed numb.

'Wait for me... I'll come too.'

As he walked to the miles of steps beside the river, he realised it was only 5:30. In England, he was regularly on the road at that time so it wasn't usually a problem for him but the world around him couldn't have been more different. He was just one of thousands making their way silently down the narrow streets towards the Ganges. The vast river looked ethereal when bathed in the sun's first rays.

Harry had learned some yoga and though he failed to sit comfortably in the lotus position, he felt at peace until he was shaken from that calm. A man brushed roughly past him, completely naked. His grey skin appeared plastered with some kind of ash and his only covering was his long, matted hair hanging below his waist. Yet no one seemed to take any notice. Walking back to the hotel for breakfast, he asked Ramma about him.

'Did you see that mad man?'

Ramma laughed. 'Harry, he's not mad, you have had your first encounter with a Sadhu, an ascetic. He has renounced all worldly wealth including clothes. Sadhus believe that through renunciation they get in touch with their spiritual being. All the clans of Sadhus gather for the Kumbla Mela. Do you remember, I told you about it? As a child I saw them rush to bathe into the Ganges at first light. It is etched on my memory for ever.'

Intrigued as he was, Harry once again felt out of his comfort zone and, given his desire to assimilate, that presented another challenge. After breakfast, they decided to read for a while. As promised, Harry took out the file containing Bartholomew's letters. He found one in which Bartholomew described the change in British attitudes after 1853, which the Empire named the 'Indian Mutiny'. Bartholomew's letter was to a Matthew Alwright, the son of an East India Company man. It took a while for Harry to understand the context because Matthew was asking Bartholomew if he would be better off living in England. It suddenly dawned on Harry that Matthew was neither British nor Indian: he was Anglo-Indian. Harry noted that Bartholomew thought most of these mixed marriages were successful. Their children usually stayed in India but apparently, Matthew had the option to go to England. Carew had written to him:

It is sad to note how attitudes have changed since Her Majesty was made Empress. It is unlikely that your situation will be better in

England & the climate is damp. If my project in Calcutta comes off, then I might be able to find you work suited to your ability.

Harry looked for other letters on the subject and found one to an Oxford professor of Sanskrit.

The Indians made it easy for the British to rule India. The Raj simply created a new ruling caste of British administrators. One caste feeling superior to others & not even wanting to touch people at the bottom is what the idea of caste feeds on. The Indian Civil Service is small for such a huge country so the Raj uses the Anglo-Indians to virtually run the railways and other engineering projects. But they are looked down on by both the British & the Indians. I am fortunate in having many Anglo-Indian friends but they do not really know where they belong. They feel British, as most speak English as their first & sometimes their only language, but they are barred from the clubs. The narrowness & prejudice I have witnessed is disgraceful.

On rereading Bartholomew's letter, a shiver of anxiety went down Harry's spine as any children born of him and Ramma would be Anglo-Indian. The issue of caste, like the issue of race, had not gone away. Their children would be mixed in more ways than one. In a world awash with prejudices, they'd be vulnerable.

*****

Harry needed exercise. 'I need a break from reading,' he said as he left Ramma busily writing. As he headed for the Ganges, his eyes were drawn to the smoke rising from the burning ghats: the reality of death was undisguised in India. Harry guessed that the Raj establishment would have protected their wives from sights of erotic sculptures, naked Sadhus and burning pyres.

Harry had mused, 'Oh the irony. Those conservative pillars

of the establishment would turn in their graves if they knew that the majority of Brits had been won over by Hindu ideas and now cremate their own dead.'

He pictured his mother's cremation and the little plaque where her ashes were buried at the crematorium in Barton. He knew that Indians scatter ashes in the Ganges so there is nowhere apart from the river to commune with the dead. But his mother, how could he leave her in Oxford? He had promised he would always talk to her. It seemed like every step forward in his attempt to adjust to India was followed by a step back towards the city of his birth.

In the afternoon and evening they abandoned their studies and had eyes just for each other. 'I know your father told us to be pragmatic, but honestly my angel, it's hard for me to think of anything but our love.' Ramma smiled in agreement. So they conveniently forgot Gangbharti's challenge.

*****

At breakfast the next morning, Ramma asked Harry about the results of his research. Harry felt pleased with himself because he had an answer ready.

'Bartholomew was intrigued by Indian art. Did you see his sketches from Khajuraho? I wish my mind could have been on them... Perhaps we can go back there together?'

'Accha. You read Bartholomew's correspondence with Ernest Harvell?' asked Ramma.

'The young Harvell wrote to Bartholomew as an undergraduate even before he headed for India. Due to his support for Indian art, good old Ernest had a right ding-dong with the establishment at The London Asiatic Society. With some notable exceptions, Indian art was regarded as ritualized and a monstrous representation of gods.'

'Most human beings react badly to anything different from

the culture they are taught as children. If it is at all challenging they interpret it as threatening. Prejudice invokes a reflex action,' said Ramma.

'Too true. The Impressionists were regarded with disgust by the establishment. And Picasso! Quelle horreur! Too many people are threatened by the new and different, although fortunately not everyone. Rodin was probably the first Western artist to recognise how sublime Indian sculpture is.

'I loved how, at Khajuraho, the sculpture exaggerates and enhances to sensual effect. Think of Rodin's "The Kiss" and you can see how he was influenced. But the Royal Asiatic Society was not amused! Victorian Britain was shocked by eroticism, at least in public. Did you know that Jacob Epstein's work was vandalised?'

Harry drew a quick sketch on his notepad of Epstein's work. In no way did his drawing do the artist any justice. He couldn't lug a library of books around India to show off pictures to Ramma; it would have been so useful to have a portable library of images and information on which he could just look things up.

'I've been wondering about Bartholomew and Dora. Do you think the estrangement between them was caused by that attitude? Victorian women were not expected to enjoy sex. The very idea was shocking. I get the impression that Bartholomew had no patience with prudery,' said Harry.

Harry read out aloud extracts from a letter to Bartholomew's friend, Harvell, where the explorer regretted not beating Richard Burton to translating the *Kama Sutra*.

'Perhaps Dora was like Burton's wife?' suggested Harry. 'Isabel Burton was adventurous, intrepid but also a bit prudish. Isabel was proud of her husband's bravery and his exploration of the Nile but after his death, she burnt all his research on the *Kama Sutra* and other erotic Indian art, boxes and boxes full of it – all absolutely irreplaceable.'

Ramma smiled. 'It would make sense of their marriage or

their lack of it. But Harry, our purpose is to follow Bartholomew's journey recording Ashokan stupas and not to speculate on the more exotic aspects of his life. Shall we move on and book a driver to take us to his next destination, Sarnath? It is only eight miles away so we can return to this hotel tonight. We shall be moving between Hindu and Buddhist worlds.'

CHAPTER 7: Sarnath and the Pillars of Dhamma

Simla, March 1885

Dora found my copy of Burton's translation of the Kama Sutra after too vigorous a cleaning of the library. Because of the Obscene Publications Act, there was no possibility of Richard publishing it for general readership; instead his Hindu Kama Shastra Society sent me a copy last year. What was I thinking, not concealing it better? Thank the heavens for this writing slope with its secret drawer. Sadly, it is only just big enough for this diary.

Dora is not at fault. Our society is riddled with hypocrisy. Before the Mughal invasion there were few inhibitions about sexual encounters in Hindu society, & men & women mixed freely. No one is quite sure of the date when Vatsyayana wrote the Kama Sutra but it is thought to be between 400 BC-100 AD given the style of Sanskrit in which it is written. Reading it I struggled to appreciate that the author was a celibate scholar! His teaching was that if we practice pleasure we should do so properly & a man should know how to satisfy a woman's desires. He observed that women have stronger passions than men. If he is correct in his assertion then it follows that in our society women are indeed repressed. Dora made no attempt to hide her disgust. What little married life we have enjoyed together is, as far as she is concerned, at an end.

How has our society become so prudish? I struggle with my faith but if God designed the means by which we must procreate, then why should we be appalled by it? And if Mr Darwin is correct, & it wasn't God at all but natural selection, then there is even less need for the severe modesty that governs our bodily functions.

Alexander Cunningham has described to me the temples of Khajuraho. He says they are covered with scenes from everyday life, which includes yogic erotic art. I have yet to see them myself, Madhya Pradesh being one of the few parts of India I have not yet visited. Most of my fellow countrymen do not try to understand Hinduism. As an Abrahamic religion, Islam is easier for them to appreciate.

Harry felt an overwhelming sense that this journey was special. He was grateful to Gangabharti for suggesting it. He hoped it could resolve his annoying doubts and questions about what he should do with his life. If he stayed in England, everything was clearer. He had a company that he himself had built from scratch, which paid him something and might pay him considerably more if he stuck with it. But he didn't have time to inhale, much less do what he really wanted to do: paint. And persuading Ramma to join him in Oxford was turning out to be tougher than he'd thought. On the other hand, he really hadn't a clue about how to live here, what to do. And the idea of being unable to sit quietly without a tsunami of relatives exhausted him. On the other hand, Ramma was here. And he could paint!

Sarnath was where the Buddha had preached his first sermon about the road to Nirvana. Harry resolved that this journey must be the road to his own nirvana whatever form it would take.

In the taxi, Ramma explained, 'At Sarnath, the Buddha talked of his Middle Way, the golden path between indulgence and asceticism. Harry, my Harry, you are becoming a seasoned India traveller. You have been to Bollywood and Khajoraho. You have seen Mumbai and the Varanasi Ghats. You have an idea of the extremes. And in Sarnath, you will be exposed to the sublime.'

Harry was startled by his first encounter with an impressive stupa. Its broad base was carved repeatedly with a symbol familiar from his childhood. He hunkered down to examine them more closely and then stood in disbelief.

'They are not Nazi swastikas, Harry. The Nazis subverted this ancient Indian symbol and used it to represent their perverted idea of Aryanism. The Nazi swastika is a mirror image of the Indian version. We have used it for 4000 years. For us it is auspicious, a sign of good fortune.'

They examined the carvings to the sound of a group of Tibetan Buddhists entering the park chanting, 'Om mani padme hum.'

'This was a deer park when the Buddha came here,' said Ramma. 'We may not exactly be pilgrims but look over there; plenty of Buddhists come here now. It is a sacred place for them.'

'I feel a painting coming on. Something about the secular and sacred dripping into each other and flowing like a river of watercolour.'

'Add the effects of time, Harry. See over there? Ashoka erected two pillars with the lion symbol on the top but those foundations are all that remains of them. The first was knocked down by the Mughals and the rubble used as building materials in the 18th century. The British damaged the other one. When they were dismantling it, relics were also found inside but they threw them in the Ganges. Passing time had eroded the knowledge of what they were and left indifference. Why is it people feel they can destroy the past without a moment's hesitation, Harry? Can you paint that?'

'A brush with human nature?' joked Harry. But seeing Ramma's serious expression he added, 'These emotions hold just as true today. Greed and carelessness lead to that kind of destruction. I remember once going to Tunisia with...' Harry had gone there with Helen.

Ramma sensed his embarrassment and broke the awkward silence.

'Don't worry, Harry. Helen is a part of your history. You cannot write her out of your life. As long as you love me, it will be okay. I was trying to point out that, because of the destruction and pillaging, there would have been little to see but forest when Alexander Cunningham came here. He must have been thrilled when he excavated and discovered the stupa. He bored a shaft from the top through the centre.'

'How did he know this was where Buddha delivered his first sermon?'

'Cunningham found a stone tablet with an inscription with the word "Dhamekha", which has that meaning. Let's go to the museum to see the Ashokan lion capital that Cunningham uncovered. That is special; it's the national emblem of India.'

Harry was impressed by the story of its miraculous survival when it fell forty-five feet from the top of the pillar. They walked around the beautifully preserved remains and came to a small alcove temple.

'What is it about the finest images of Buddha? They exude serenity. My mind is crowded out with questions about you and me – not to mention Bartholomew – but looking at that somehow brings peace to my mind,' commented Harry. But Ramma wasn't listening. She pointed ahead.

'Look, Harry. Here is one of Ashoka's edicts.'

Ramma focused on it with intense concentration and started to take photographs but Harry began to feel he had had enough of Ashoka for one day. He looked at Ramma and found it hard to take his mind off his desire to make love to her. In Khajoraho, he would have been stuck on the bottom level of the temple, unable to rise above it.

*****

Back at the hotel after dinner, Ramma showed Harry a modern copy of a book written by a Chinese Buddhist, Hiuen

Tsang, who toured India in the 7th century CE. She explained, 'Bartholomew would have known him as Xuanzang; Mandarin translation was different then. He came in search of the Buddha's footsteps but he recorded the Hindu temples he saw on the way also. His is one of the best descriptions of a Kumbla Mela. It is strange but we know more about what life in India was like at that time from him than from Indian records. Look at this: he recorded 1500 priests in daily attendance around the Banyan tree close to the Vihara Temple. Buddha probably spent many years in meditation here. He has left his aura.'

'So 2000 years ago, there was already a hippy trail in India.' They both laughed.

'The next person to copy Hiuen Tsang was Alexander Cunningham. By which time only a fraction of the sights that would have greeted Hiuen Tsang remained. Sarnath was virtually abandoned until Alexander Cunningham excavated the stone on which Dhamma is written. Alexander had spent over thirty years travelling and recording what he saw but he was not an artist. Havell and Carew were rare in appreciating the merit of Hindu art. Did you read that letter where Bartholomew wrote warmly about their meeting?'

While working through Bartholomew's articles and the letters that Ramma had copied at the Bodleian, Harry had read an angry tirade Bartholomew had written to *The Times*. A British engineer in Allahabad had knocked down the remaining Ashokan pillar and used it as a road roller. Carew described it as, "*...the work of vandals of which the British government should be ashamed. How would we react if Stonehenge were used for building material or Nelson's column used as a road roller?*" He went on to say that a department should be set up to preserve the monuments and most important buildings of ancient India. It was not only men who destroyed them but the climate too. "*Without conservation they will turn to dust. Unlike the ancient Chinese who meticulously recorded everything, the history of India* *is mostly found in literature and architecture."*

'It wasn't until 1899, long after Bartholomew's disappearance, that Curzon started to conserve Indian monuments. But maybe Carew planted the seed and Curzon had listened to him. Bartholomew was right, Indian records were not kept as meticulously as the Chinese. Thank goodness for the stupas.'

'What are they about?' asked Harry.

'The stupas were carved with Ashoka's edicts – obedience to parents was one of them. No worry there then. We are obeying my father. Concern for friends and relatives was another. I care about you, Harry. So far, I am not doing too badly, am I? Good treatment of the poor and servants is another,' added Ramma.

Recalling the incident with the coconut seller on one of his first days in India, Harry said with uncharacteristic sharpness, 'That one needs repeating!'

'Without modern media, their means of communication were limited. Carved pillars and rock edicts were his means of spreading his ideas. Ashoka's inscriptions interpreted his idea of Dhamma. The enigma that no one has worked out is how they were transported over 500 miles.'

'It sounds similar to the mystery of how Stonehenge was built.'

'You are right. In this case we know why it was built but not how. A certain artist from Oxford is uncovering India's past and appreciating it a lot more than most of my fellow countrymen.'

Harry was not sure. His love was art and design but their history? Not so much. Maybe he should try to become passionate about their origins. Fake it 'til he made it. But he kept that to himself.

*****

They decided to return the next day, so Ramma could visit the museum again and study in the Mahabodhi library. Harry left

Ramma searching for details of Cunningham's excavations and Bartholomew's visit to Sarnath in 1886. For a while he worked on his own visual diary and realised Ramma was right; he felt at home sketching in the tranquillity of the restored ancient sites. It was in the bustle of modern India that he felt foreign.

'If you want to stay in the library, I'll return to Varanasi and tap into some ordinary life. I'll see you back at the hotel this evening. Okay?' asked Harry.

Ramma felt pleased. She wanted to give Harry a kiss but they were in a sacred place so he had to make do with a smile. As he left, Ramma thought, 'This is proof that our relationship is working. I shall be able to tell Daddy-ji that we share an interest in each other's work but do not need to be together all the time, even when travelling. We respect how our work is important to our identities. Is not that what Daddy-ji wants us to confirm?'

*****

Back in the city, Harry headed into the maze of alleys away from the ghats and observed Indian life at close quarters: the betel nut sellers, the shoe shiners, nose hair trimmers, the spice markets and the vegetable markets that were brighter than any of his oil paintings and yet sensuous with aromas and texture too. Harry had learned to avoid public loos but was amazed when gorgeous Indian women, dressed like queens, sallied into those most vile places, seemingly oblivious to the filth. He aimed for a busy restaurant, which had reasonable and much needed facilities.

Once inside, he was soon chatting with another customer over tea and samosas. It was easy to talk to people in India. No one took offence if you struck up a conversation. Harry imagined the reaction he would get in London. His fellow countrymen usually needed the ambience of a pub or a club and the help of a little alcohol to be as approachable and open. His neighbour looked up from his copy of *The Hindustan Times* and asked, 'Hello. What part of the world are you coming from?'

'I'm from Oxford, England. And you?'

'All my life, I lived it in Varanasi.'

'Can you tell me why so many people are queuing next door?'

'Indeed. They are consulting their genealogy.'

'Why so much interest in their family trees?'

'Many reasons: they record births and deaths but most want to know for marriage, yes?' Harry looked confused. The old man may have lived in Varanasi all his life but he had a cultured air, one of awareness of the wider world. 'But of course, you do not understand the ways of Indian marriage. Parents arrange marriages here. Professional matchmakers are well known but mostly families use their own networks. The boy or girl's family is investigated. Their families want to know they are well suited and their background reliable. You get what I am meaning?'

Unfortunately, Harry did. At least he had been honest with Gangabharti about his father. He thanked his companion and made his way languorously through the incense-filled lanes. If he could have seen himself from behind – a solitary young man framed in the shadow of the narrow archways – he could have imagined himself to be a lost soul. Emerging onto a main road, he hailed a taxi back to the hotel.

They decided to have dinner in the hotel. Ramma changed out of her jeans into a shimmering sari. In her jewels she could have stepped out of a fashion magazine but he dared not say so. Harry gestured her to lead the way to the restaurant and savoured the pleasure of walking behind her, watching her effortlessly graceful movement. Alcohol was rare in Varanasi, but Harry wasn't missing it. He was getting all the stimulation he wanted and was becoming addicted to Indian food (apart from breakfast). The waiters seemed concerned and pointed out the milder dishes but his confidence had grown. When he ordered a Madras fish dish, he knew the waiter would ask, 'Is it not too spicy for you?' and answered as if he'd been in India for years.

After ordering, Harry described his day in Varanasi and recounted what he had learned to Ramma. 'My genealogy may disappoint your father but at least I can say that my taste in food has adapted.'

Over their mango dessert, the colour of a sunset, they discussed where to go next. 'How about Lumbini?' said Ramma. 'When Bartholomew was alive no one was sure where Buddha was born. In his diary Bartholomew suggested it was Lumbini long before that became accepted. Judging by his last letter to young Harvell, Bartholomew must have been there not long before he disappeared.' Ramma suggested they hire a car and driver for what could be the last leg of their journey, which would take them into Nepal. At the hotel reception they arranged to check out on Monday morning before venturing out for a walk in the cool night air.

Wandering aimlessly through the narrow streets of Varanasi at dusk, they came across a bizarre troop. Harry tried estimating the number of people in the party but proved unequal to the task. 100, maybe as many as 200? But then more appeared from around the corner walking between ribbons of moving fluorescent tubes. As one man held up the electric strip light, a wire dangled from it to the battery carried by another man and so the light-and-power-men alternated, lining both sides of the road. Ramma explained that autumn was the start of the wedding season and this was a groom's party on their way to be garlanded by the bride's family. The crowd was joyful and raucous, singing and clapping their hands. They weren't waiting until the wedding to start partying.

She pointed as the groom came into sight wearing a red turban and riding a white horse.

'How would you feel on your white horse like that Indian bridegroom, Harry?'

'The wedding looks fun but aren't we meant to be discussing

our life afterwards?'

'Could you make a life here, Harry?'

'I wanted to talk to you about that, honey. I know you said that you want us to live here but there's nowhere better for an academic or writing career than Oxford. And it's not just the old Uni either. Oxford Brookes's history department is well regarded and London is only a short coach ride away with more great libraries, the British Museum and world-class academic institutions. Things are changing fast in India, I can see that. But it will be a long time before your universities catch up with Oxford.'

Ramma looked angry. 'You really don't know what difference this makes, do you?' Ramma pointed to her face. 'I have brown skin. How could I not be aware that in England there is a glass ceiling for academics of colour? It may change but will that change before India changes? Here I can be a groundbreaker and I don't start with any disadvantages.'

They walked in silence, their tempers cooling as the evening cooled.

'Sorry, Harry. I did not mean to sound angry. But if I produce good work, a sabbatical in Oxford would be on the cards. Breaking into academia in England is harder than you think. Academics are treated better and paid better across the Atlantic. India is starting to copy the USA more than our old colonial masters.'

The noise of the raucous wedding band drowned Harry's half-hearted response. Ramma turned to a red-faced Harry and asked quietly, 'What will happen first: a colour-blind Britain or Indian development?'

Harry sighed as he acknowledged his failure to answer it. They arrived back at the hotel and their attempts to resolve their dilemma had failed miserably. Ramma looked disappointed. Lying on the bed beside her, Harry closed her eyes and gently kissed them.

*****

The following day, while Ramma continued her research at the museum in Sarnath, Harry chose to stay in Varanasi. He wanted to mull over their discussion. Ramma was intelligent and ambitious and the amazing thing was that she loved him. His problem was that he couldn't envisage living anywhere but Oxford. Was it possible to ease his way into her world, just as she was doggedly burrowing her way into the lives of those 19th century Englishmen? His confidence was not equal to his desire.

His nightmare was that he'd turn out like his father and give up if the going got tough. And in India, his road would surely be full of potholes every step of the way. As he sat on the silt-covered, litter-strewn ghats with a view of the mystical Ganges, he couldn't visualise himself living in India.

His mind turned to England and surprisingly sun-filled childhood memories of his father on holiday in Devon. Even with his good visual memory, Harry struggled to get a clear picture of him. He was fourteen when Roger left. He'd simply walked away without a goodbye. Harry had never heard a single word from him since and wondered how a father could do that to his son. When he was fifteen, his mother had tried explaining. He recalled that conversation with raw emotion.

'Harry,' she'd said, hesitating for a moment before talking to him as if he was an adult. 'Children tend to see their parents as omniscient but all human beings are imperfect. You and I love art and you know that even ugly scenes can be made beautiful. Do you remember me taking you to the V&A and showing you that sculpture of Samson slaying the Philistine? It's brutal but the work of art is beautiful.' He'd nodded, baffled but trying to understand. 'You remember how your father could be such fun? We hardly ever quarreled but when we did, we were rather like characters in a play; our emotions released with lots of

189

drama. You must have felt like you were back stage looking on. I trusted your father but...' She pursed her lips.

Harry could see his mother trying desperately to explain something to him. He just hadn't a clue what it was.

'In most marriages, couples do some job allocation. It's preferable to one partner doing everything; we shared our chores and I trusted your dad to look after our finances. When a cheque for the gas bill bounced, I couldn't believe it. I thought the bank must have made a mistake. They gave me the evidence and I confronted your father with it. Without a word, he walked out. You remember how we searched for him, starting with the hospitals, then all those missing person's posters we made? Well, someone finally recognised him and that man came to see me. His name was Graham and he opened the door into a part of your father's life that I didn't know existed.'

Harry put his head in hands. A memory was playing out, a suppressed encounter that lurked in the shadowy parts of his brain. Suddenly that back stage moment was playing at full volume and the sound from his childhood bedroom was of Sting and the Police. Harry could see his fifteen-year-old self eavesdropping from the top of the stairs as his mother talked to this stranger called Graham.

'There must be some mistake,' his mother had said. 'Roger enjoyed betting on the horses, but such an extreme amount of gambling? Are you sure it was him?'

'The Roger I knew was the man in those photographs.' The man pointed to the family pictures.

'But... I had no idea.'

'You'd be surprised at just how good we are at hiding it,' said Graham. 'Our excuses are plausible. My business went bankrupt before I faced the truth. My wife agreed to stand by me if I stuck with Gamblers Anonymous. I tried to persuade Roger to come along with me.'

'What did he say?'

'The usual. Everything was fine. He had a sure-fire bet coming up, and then he would stop. It was all a delusion. It always is.'

The next day his mother had sat him down and tried to explain. 'You might say he gambled and lost, and because of that, so did we. Actually, Harry, I take that back. We haven't lost. We still have each other, and we still have Aunt Julie, and we're almost back on our feet again, aren't we? I just wish I knew where he'd gone and what happened to him. Please God, he's alive. If he comes back, I can forgive him and I hope you can too.'

Sitting by the Ganges where pilgrims had sat for 4,000 years, Harry couldn't remember saying anything to comfort his mother. Faced with the reality of a compulsive gambler for a father, a man who had stolen his mother's hard-earned money and then couldn't face up to that truth so left the two people who loved him the most, Harry had silently vowed to walk a different path.

Terrified of becoming his father, he'd gone the other way. He hadn't risked sticking with his art but got a job as an art teacher. But the permanent positions with pensions and benefits kept slipping through his fingers and his rolling contracts left him vulnerable. With careful preparation, he'd opened Deco-rators which was now earning him an income and nicely diversifying into design consulting. But now, Ramma was asking him to take a leap on little more than a whim and a prayer. And he just didn't know if he could do that. Even if he could, he didn't know *how* to do that. Was he strong enough for Ramma? He didn't want her needing to forgive him, as his mother forgave his father. Not only that, money was becoming tight. After paying the shippers there wasn't as much of Selene's cheque left as he had anticipated. He didn't want to borrow off Ramma.

Agitated, Harry stood up and with his back to the river, set off into a narrow alley. He tried concentrating on the world around him. He found a simple café and drank masala tea. It was sweet for his taste but the spice in it gave him a healthy, optimistic boost. He opened a copy of *The Times of India*.

> *Rohit Bogilal, 29, Hindu from Gujurat. MBA*
> *A business consultant*

> *Namrata Pana from Kerala, Christian, 21, graduate in commerce*
> *Fair skinned. Good family*

Dismayed by the columns of advertisements for arranged marriages, he folded up the paper and firmly ran his thumb along the crease. Harry thought he'd overcome his prejudice. He knew these marriages could often be more successful than Western love marriages because they were about more than sexual attraction. That was the point of Gangabharti's challenge. Were they sure that their marriage could survive when things got tough and their lust less insistent?

Harry glanced again at the newspaper. How would he and Ramma appear in a marriage broker's book? Some of the adverts gave exact times and dates of birth. He knew Gangabharti was a sceptic and had joked about how Indian couples often cast their horoscope before setting a date.

Harry remembered the offices for astrologers and gurus. Leaving the café, he went further into the network of lanes. He saw a queue outside one office with a simple sign over the door, "Guru SaRam". Unlike others he had seen, there were no lists of his accomplishments, just two Sanskrit swastikas either side of his name. This looked intriguing and Harry was tempted. 'A bit of harmless fun,' he reasoned and joined the queue.

An attendant spotted him and beckoned him ahead of the waiting crowd. Harry felt embarrassed but the others smiled courteously and seemed to take no offence whatsoever. The guru sat on a bolster behind a long low desk. Behind him was a poster of Shiva and opposite, shelves full of files. The guru rose and gave Harry 'namaste'. In beautifully modulated English, he directed Harry to sit and looked straight into his eyes and he put his hands on Harry's hands. He beckoned his assistant who presented Harry with a sheet of paper on a clipboard and a pencil. Harry looked confused.

'What we shall do is as follows; you shall write down your two questions whatever their nature.'

Harry had not expected this and he was conscious of the crowd outside and of wasting this man's time, although he would of course be paying for it. He wasn't too happy with what he wrote but the questions were broad enough and specific enough to see if this man was a fake.

'What should be my biggest concern?'

'Where should I finally make my home?'

The attendant didn't hand the paper straight to the guru instead he put it in an envelope and sealed it before handing it to him. Guru SaRam placed his fingers on the unopened envelope and consulted a chart of Sanskrit symbols before turning towards Harry.

'When confronted with a difficult decision, you hope the problem will resolve itself and sometimes it does. But you know that this reluctance leads you to errors. If you recognise this tendency in yourself, you will make fewer mistakes. It will become less of a concern. As to your second question, all I can say is, you will not live where you were born. I cannot be more exact. You will have alternatives; that is all I can say. Also, you will not die at home.'

Harry hesitated. The guru nodded and the assistant gestured to the door. Harry stood up and gave a 'namaste'.

'Thank you, swami-ji. That was… interesting.'

After paying the assistant, Harry walked to a sculpture-covered temple, rather like a tapering iced wedding cake, and sat on the steps looking into the misty heat haze. November was in the cool season so it wasn't uncomfortable.

The guru hadn't even opened the envelope. That alone

was impressive. Harry considered his answers. It was true; his current problem was procrastination but that was because he hadn't got the answers. He must not put off the decision for long. The guru was right about that. He had not given him the answer as to whether to live in England or India but only posed the question. In the end, Harry had to determine his own destiny. His choice was to live in India married to Ramma or to return to Oxford alone.

*****

Back at the hotel, Ramma was waiting for him.
'Why don't we spend our last evening like our first in Varanasi by the river?' suggested Harry. 'I'm finding it less strange even if I have some strange tales to tell you. Let's walk there and talk about our day.'

'Accha' said Ramma, 'If we are going to walk, let me change into jeans and trainers.'

The night air was cool and fragrant. Ramma enjoyed Harry's stories.

'You had all these adventurous experiences while I was walled up in a library.'

'You are with me now and so we're bound to have a bit of excitement,' replied Harry.

Their hotel was about a mile from the river and turning a corner by a temple was the Ganges and above it, a lazy haze with the moonlight seeping through. Their eyes connected and Harry drew her to him and gave her a kiss filled with promise. To anyone watching it was plain from the depth of that look that here was a couple in love.

'Stop, Harry, this is India and we are near the holy Ganges,' protested Ramma.

'Sorry honey, I could hardly forget but how does everyone manage this self-restraint? Of course, they don't have you beside them.' They smiled into each other's eyes.

Rough hands grabbed him. Ramma screamed and a hand slapped her mouth shut. Harry was yanked back and to the side. Struggling to get to her, Harry tried to rip his arms free but his hands were already tied tightly behind his back. Then a fist knocked him back and out.

When he regained consciousness, he was in a grubby office, surrounded by four youths dressed in similar red T-shirts printed with a gold bow and arrow logo. Harry struggled but could not move. His arms and legs were tied to a chair.

'Where is Ramma, you fucking... what have you done with her?'

'We, the Army of Ram, ask the questions here and you will talk with respect or be sorry.'

In another room in the same building, Ramma was held by a large man with the appearance of a wrestler, while a small wiry man with black-rimmed glasses and a thin moustache above a concave sneer interrogated her.

'How can you behave like this? Have you no morals?'

'How dare you talk to me of morals? Since when has kidnapping been holy?'

'Shut your mouth, you shameless hussy. No self-respecting Hindu girl dresses like that,' and he pointed to her skin-tight jeans.

'I twist her arms a little, Arjun? Teach her some respect? After I finish with her she will learn the lesson.' The wrestler leered in broken Hindi.

Arjun spat at her and, pressing his face close to hers, wiped off her lipstick with a filthy handkerchief. He wrapped it around his index finger and used it to jab a bindi on the middle of her forehead.

Ramma choked on the fumes of cheap oil arising from his greasy hair and she felt soiled by the drip staining her face.

'Tou kaun hai – your name, jaldi!'

'Why should I tell you?'

'Because we are the moral police – theek hai? If you want that boyfriend of yours to leave here a man, you will answer me.'

He laughed as he made a sinister chopping motion. Ramma had heard of a shadowy group of Shiv Sena, in Mangalore, who had been harassing couples of mixed religion. Had their tentacles spread this far north?

'Ramma Sangupta. You people should like what I do. I am a researcher uncovering our pre-Mughal past and sharing it with India, and the rest of the world. Isn't that what you are about? Championing Hindu culture?'

Arjun left the room and walked down a narrow corridor with peeling paint and tangled electric wires suspended from the ceiling. Opening the door at the end, he joined the thugs holding Harry. On their travels, Harry's hair had begun to grow long and he had tied it back in a small ponytail. Arjun yanked Harry's head so far back, the pain of the position surged through his body. Harry tried not to call out. He took shallow breaths and tried to relax as many muscles as he could.

'Tell me the name of your whore,' sneered Arjun, relaxing his grip so Harry could answer.

One of the thugs slowly drew a knife out of his pocket. Ramma as a first name was not uncommon. The truth should be okay?

'Ramma.'

'And her family name?'

'Why do you want to know?

'Do you want to see your girlfriend again?' He pulled Harry's head back again and then forced it forward between Harry's knees. 'Answer me.'

Harry tried to keep his mind clear, even though his head felt like a drum being beaten. They must be after a ransom. He mustn't tell them her name. If they knew she was a famous singer's daughter, the demand would be huge.

'Okay. Ramma Sachdeva.

Arjun pulled him up and slapped him. 'That's not what she said.'

He must be decisive.

'The embassy is expecting me to call them tomorrow. I'm a visiting artist, part of a group of us from England exhibiting in Delhi. When I am reported missing, all hell will break loose.'

Arjun smirked but the others looked uneasy. Harry took advantage of the moment of hesitation.

'If you don't believe me give me a pencil and paper and I'll prove it to you.'

Now Arjun looked concerned so Harry said in a calm voice.

'What is it that you want with us? Money? We have some back at the hotel. Let Ramma go. One of you can accompany her and she can bring you what you want and we can forget all about tonight.'

'Who do you think we are?' Arjun looked offended and angry. 'A gang of common criminals? Our friends in high places don't approve of a beef-eating drinkers corrupting a Hindu girl who should know better.'

'Corrupting her? How? Her father has approved our engagement. We are going to be married.'

'I thought so – you be like those arrogant Americans coming here thinking they can buy people. You like them – a Christian – wanting to convert her.'

'Except I am not American and it's the other way. I'm agnostic and Ramma is teaching me Hinduism. Why else do you think she brought me here to Varanasi? I haven't eaten beef since I met her.'

Arjun's attitude visibly changed.

'Chalega. Learn to behave respectably.' He nodded at the others. 'Release him.'

'Not without Ramma. Where is she? I want to see her. You say you are moral so you'd better not touch her.'

'We shall see if her story tallies.'

*****

'Your boyfriend says you are to be married?'

'Yes, that is correct. What is it to you?'

'Stop giving me lip. I smell alcohol on your English-speaking breath.'

Ramma struggled to keep her composure. If only she had taken some lessons from her father's actress friends. She wanted to betray no emotion whatsoever. Arjun tried again to humiliate her.

'You traitor, how can you look yourself in the mirror knowing you want to betray your culture and marry a Christian? Maybe I can think of something to change your mind?'

*****

Half an hour later, they were pushed out of a battered car and left by the side of the road, not far from their hotel. Ramma and Harry stumbled back inside. The man on reception looked at them.

'Are you alright, sir?'

'No... Can you phone the –'

Ramma interrupted him. 'We need to talk, Harry.'

Back in their room, Harry checked her out, concerned but angry. 'Are you hurt? We mustn't let them get away with it.' As he let go of her, he stalked to the phone on the bedside table.

'What are you doing?' demanded Ramma.

'Calling the police, of course.'

Ramma took the phone from him, her hand shaking, and put it down.

'We can't let them get away with it. They'll do it to someone else,' fumed Harry.

'You don't understand. Do you want to bring shame on my family?'

'I bring shame on your family! How can you say that? What have I done to bring shame other than love you?'

'Harry, trust me. I feel dirty. No, not that,' she added wearily. 'He spat at me,' she pushed open the shower door. 'Can you order us a drink and then we can talk? Please, Harry.'

With his jaw clenched, he agreed. He splashed his face with cold water and changed his clothes. As he combed his hair, he winced in pain. In the mirror, he could see a large bump.

All of a sudden, he realized that he was ravenously hungry so rang room service and ordered a plate of samosas.

As she picked up her glass of water, Ramma looked as she had after Birmingham: the energy drained from her face.

'Harry, I understand why you want to go to the police but these people are attached to the Shiv Sena. They are fundamentalist Hindus. It is a contradiction really. We Hindus are free to believe what we like. Sorry, I gave you that lecture before.'

Ramma sank into a chair and whispered.

'A man from an extremist group like theirs shot Gandhi. They are fascists. They believe they are the upholders of Hindu culture, some purer version untainted by anything non-Hindu, as if such an India ever existed. It is not my Hindu culture nor is it the vast majority of everyone else's. Fundamentalism bounces back, just like the caste system. Ashoka got rid of it and reduced the power of the Brahmins but 1000 years later they were back in power and the caste system was stronger than ever.' She looked as if she was going to cry. If Harry hadn't been so enraged – he could still feel the blood pulsing in his temple – he would have taken her in his arms and comforted her. Instead, it took all his strength to just listen. 'It's mindless. And ultimately pointless because change is coming anyway. But they scare me. And to make matters worse, they can harm my reputation, maybe even destroy it.'

'How?'

'Look, Daddy-ji is unusual – we would not be here together

otherwise. It took a long time for me to realise how different his aspirations were for me and how liberal his attitudes. Most Indian fathers would be horrified by the idea of a daughter travelling alone with her fiancé, let alone sleeping with him. If it were put in the papers that Gangabharti Gupta's unmarried daughter was sharing a hotel room with an Englishman, it could ruin his career and my reputation. I would feel that I had betrayed his trust. Remember how he warned us to be careful.'

Harry put a hand on his aching head, groaned, and looked at Ramma through his fingers.

'No, I don't understand. How will going to the police lead to all that? I told you, I didn't give them your real surname. How could it end up in the papers?'

'If we report their crime, we shall have to give our correct names at the police station and if they are arrested, they will soon know our true identity and plaster it across the media. The police here are badly paid and easily bribed. Believe me! Daddy-ji will see unflattering reports of us splashed over the papers. The Birmingham pictures hurt him but this would be worse. I cannot let him go through that again. Why is it that people believe what they see written down even when it is slander?'

'But if we don't even try to expose them they will do the same thing to other people and the results could be even worse,' said Harry. He tried to read the expression on Ramma's face. He had hit a nerve.

In a quiet voice she said, 'Harry, *you don't understand*. This province is notorious throughout India. Many of its politicians have criminal records and the police protect them. Forget the rule of law. This is Uttar Pradesh.'

Harry gritted his teeth and muttered, 'You win. We won't go to the police but what shall we do?'

'Get out of Varanasi. Head for Nepal and rid ourselves of this nasty taste.'

That night, they slept facing in opposite directions.

CHAPTER 8: Quarrels on the Road to Lumbini

Simla, September 1886

I have acquired a translation of the writings of the Chinese pilgrim, Xuanzang. It is thanks to him that we know about the world's first international university at Nalanda. Its foundation in 300BC puts even Oxford in the category of recent! Xuanzang mentions Ashoka, but his quest was for the teaching of the Buddha, not for the man who founded Buddhism.

And I? I am curious of both men: the teacher & the warlord who created a new religion.

The answers to my questions would have been found in Nalanda if Muhammad Bakhtiyar, the so-called World Burning Sultan, had not set fire to the place, destroying not only the books but 10,000 monks so that their knowledge was also lost to the world. What makes men like Muhammad Bakhtiyar? Ashoka himself as a young ruler surely had more in common with Bakhtiyar than with the Buddha. How was he able to make that transition from warlord to pacifist? While my transition has not been as extreme or as sudden as his, I have found the journey from subject of the Raj to Ashokan devotee deeply confusing & fraught with guilt. I struggle to divest myself of Christianity & yet cannot fully embrace the implications of Mr Darwin's natural selection with its idea of creatio ex nihilo. I can no longer embrace the God of my youth, but equally cannot conceive of a world without Him. It has been akin to a grieving for what I have lost, as well as a rage for what actually lies the heart of Raj. I have found neither the solace nor strength that Ashoka did. Was the creation of Nalanda the cornerstone? He built an army, not of soldiers but of scholars & monks. From Xuanzang's account I have reason to believe the university was eight miles long. He describes an azure pool that wound around the monasteries, adorned with the full-blown cups of the blue lotus. "The dazzling red flowers of the lovely kanaka hang here & there, & outside groves of mango trees offer the inhabitants their dense & protective shade."

Xuanzang was impressed by Silabhadra, the monastery's superior, & studied with him before returning to China with 650 books in Sanskrit. What good fortune that something escaped the flames of Muhammad Bakhtiyar.

But the Chinese do not permit foreigners into the interior. Xian lies far into the heart of that mysterious land. I can conceive of no way I can travel there to study when I do not speak Mandarin, & for once I cannot conceive of a disguise that could hide my origins. With sun & the right dress, & speaking Hindi as I do, I can just about pass for a lighter-skinned Indian. But no matter how I try, I doubt I could pass for an Oriental. I regret this deeply as Xuanzang's pagoda in Xian is probably the one place in the world I am likely to discover an early account of Ashoka's transformation from warlord to founder of Buddhism.

Xuanzhang's account of Lumbini makes me wonder if it could be the birthplace of the Buddha.

Dora & I need a time apart. I shall recruit a small team to come with me. I have promised Dora that I will return in five months. Then we must decide what to do. The time to ponder without friction should help us both. Her book on the flora of the Punjab is progressing well. Kew appreciated the seeds that she has sent to them.

Lumbini was a 200-mile drive away. Harry was convinced he could drive there in a day but Ramma said their driver needed at least two days as the roads were poor and pot-holed.

The next morning, Harry went to greet Mahesh Dayal, an experienced driver recommended by the hire company. He looked doddery, past retirement age, and peered around as if he needed glasses. Beside him was parked a car that also looked long past retirement age. There was something familiar about it. Cowley in East Oxford was the home of the factory that gave birth to that model in the 50s, ten years before he was born. Harry remembered seeing these cars on Oxford roads as a child. He was doubtful it could see out the journey and said as much. The driver looked hurt.

'Sahib, my car is only two years old. India bought the Ambassador plant from Rover certainly some time ago. At this time, other makes of car are imported but when travelling in remote areas, timely availability of spare parts is a must, no? Otherwise you wait weeks for a delivery, haan-ji. The company uses the Ambassador for journeys like this. The parts are to be found everywhere.'

Mahesh shook his head from side to side in that confusing South Asian manner.

Harry found Ramma at reception checking out.

'Damn it, Ramma, I don't think I can be a passenger in that car with that man for four days. Let's hire a four-wheel drive and go by ourselves. After yesterday, I want to be on our own. How can we talk freely in front of a chauffeur? You say we have to keep quiet about what happened. That is going to be difficult.'

'Harry, I understand but where we are heading, if something goes wrong, we cannot call upon the RAC. This firm has agents everywhere.'

'Then why don't we rethink our itinerary and go somewhere I can bloody well drive? This passive role is a bit hard to take. I may not look it, Ramma, but inside, I'm a full-blooded independent bloke. In my business, I drive almost 20,000 miles a year. This isn't me, Ramma. You're starting to dictate everything. Is this how you want things between us?'

Ramma went outside and gave the driver some cash and told him to buy himself tea and chaat from the nearby booth. Standing among their luggage, Harry looked so miserable that Ramma was not sure what to do.

'Do you want to go back to Mumbai?'

Harry regretted what he had said.

'I have no idea what to do. I love you, Ramma, and you know how much, but do I have to love everything about this bloody country to be able to marry you? And after last night, I don't know what to think. I'm not sure I can be happy here anymore.'

Ramma had not seen Harry look this way before. This wasn't just anger at last night, although that was still there. It was... everything. And she understood. The freedom that Oxford offered them both would not be theirs in India. At the best, at the very, very best, it would be different. Tiny tears appeared in the corner of her eyes and she turned around to hide them, aware that people in the crowded foyer were beginning to stare at them.

A surge of tenderness arose in Harry and although he hated the prospect, he beckoned a porter. He gave him a generous tip and asked him to put their luggage in the Ambassador. Ramma turned to him with a look of gratitude.

*****

Sitting in the back of the car, Harry was silent and subdued. He recalled Gangabharti's warning about how he and Ramma should behave in public: 'Remember where you are. This is conservative India, not liberal England.' He, Harry, had forgotten it in of all places, a place of pilgrimage – Varanasi.

He had failed her father's challenge. Why had he forgotten? Why had he kissed Ramma in a public place when he had been warned many times? Everything had been going smoothly.

Facing disaster, he expected to be flying home alone.

Ramma was in a dark place. The vile experience of last night had shaken her to her core. Harry had not agreed with her reaction to it. Had she pushed him too far? Her father had taught her to be independent-minded. When she was born, Gangabharti wanted to name her Achla meaning "determined" but her mother chose Ramma. She wondered if she had injured Harry's pride. She had lectured him, led him and he had gone along with good humour. She doubted an Indian guy would be as relaxed at taking advice from a woman. If they were alone, she could tell him, show him how she appreciated him. But they were not alone. That was the whole point. Realistically, they would not spend time alone until the evening. No wonder Harry was quiet. Could he cope with Indian family life where there was little privacy? She needed to ask him.

What meaningful words could they say in front of their conservative driver? She wanted to tell him that she understood and to explain that those thugs were as rare as racist TV celebrities in England. Out of sight of the driver's mirror, she grasped his hand and used her fingers to express her longing and regret.

She had not confided in Harry what their captors had said to her; just as in Birmingham she hadn't told him about the encounter with Joe Buy. That was a mistake so why was she repeating it? If they were to be married she must be more open: that was what giving and sharing was about. When and how could she tell him?

After an hour of un-Indian quietness, Ramma broke the silence. 'Where would you say is about half way, Mahesh–ji?'

'We could overnight in Ayodhya, memsahib. It will put some few miles on the journey but the hotel there is a pukka place.'

She had seen an image of the god, Rama, on the dashboard and she thought that a night in Ayodhya, the birthplace of the god, should cheer up their driver, still gloomy after the morning's disagreement.

Ramma pointed to the image and turned to Harry.

'This may confuse you, but that is an image of a male god with a name similar to mine but pronounced differently. Rama's wife, Sita, was kidnapped by the evil demon Ravana and imprisoned on the island of Sri Lanka. The story of her dramatic rescue with the help of the monkey king, Hanuman, is one of India's favourites.'

'Ask Hanuman to come to our rescue in Ayodyha, will you?'

'Why not? We are going in peace.'

He had no idea what she meant and raised a quizzical eyebrow.

'Sorry, Harry, that was my attempt at a joke. In Sanskrit, Ayodhya means "not to be warred against".'

'Ha ha... whatever... it's fine by me.' Unusually for Harry, he was not in the mood for playful conversation but, wanting to change the atmosphere, he invited his history don to tell him a story. 'Tell me a bit about the town.'

Vivid storytelling was something Ramma enjoyed but her inner energy had been diminished by the encounter with Arjun.

Gangabharti's special talent had passed her by but she could usually mesmerise Harry with her soft melodious voice. Not on this day. The opportunity to change the mood faded as she told the romantic and dramatic tale of the Rammayana in a monotone manner.

Harry's next question didn't help. 'What will we see in Ayodhya?'

'There was a great temple in Ayodhya which was destroyed by the Mughal invaders with the materials then re-used to build a mosque in its place. Since that mosque, the Babri Mosque, had not been used as place of worship for thirty years some BJP politicians came up with the idea of pulling it down and rebuilding the temple. That provocation lead to the worst Hindu-Muslim riots in decades.'

'I thought the name had echoes.'

Desperately trying to lift the dark mood, Ramma said, 'There are interesting temples here and as a place of pilgrimage, Bartholomew Carew must have visited. Let's see what he thought of it and make up our own minds? We can take a look after dinner?'

'Ramma, Bartholomew Carew isn't going to give us the answer.' He sighed. 'But sure, let's take a look around.'

That evening, after being searched by security guards, they negotiated the maze of caged paths leading to the main temple.

'Do you know, Ramma, I'm getting fed up of being frisked by unsavoury looking men,' said Harry.

'You accept it everywhere else you go, even in England after the IRA threats. Do I really have to justify everything?' They had reached the path designed so that worshippers could only go in single file, so Harry didn't reply. That night, neither of them felt the desire to make love.

CHAPTER 9: A Mountain to Climb

Sravasti, December 1886

The Buddha is said to have lived here for twenty-four rainy seasons. The remains so far uncovered are all from the Gupta Period. Considering that the Guptas continued in the Ashokan manner of government, why & how had matters changed by the time the Chinese monks came here?

I may have found the answer just outside a dusty village called Kandhbhari. Here I found a Hindu shrine except it wasn't originally Hindu. Someone had placed a large Shiva Linghum inside the remains of a small Buddhist stupa. This is what must have shocked the Chinese pilgrims. There are no descriptions in their account of the Hinduisation of the sites. All invaders of India, not only the Mughals, have been prudish about Shiva's parts. The Catholic Portuguese cut off Shiva's creative organ when they found the Elephanta Cave temple.

The end of the Buddhist era was due I suspect, to the colonisation of the sites by the Brahmins & caste interests as they clawed back their power. A Brahmin ruler called Pushyamitra Sunga pursued a vicious campaign against Buddhists near Ashoka's capital.

Everything points to Lumbini being the birthplace of Buddha. I must learn from Nairn Singh's experience in Tibet & be more circumspect. European clothes will attract too much attention. I shall take Polonius's advice: Apparel oft proclaims the man. Best if I look Indian.

Ayodyha Dec 22: Received letter from Dora. She seems determined to return home soon. I did her no favours in marrying her. I must stop procrastinating. I must decide whether to accompany her. If I do, I am unlikely to return to India.

U p to that point, Harry's experience of India had been one of huge cloudless skies filled with dazzling light. But the following day, dark clouds shrouded the sun and a rising wind moaned. They lapsed into a grey silence, teased mercilessly by the sounds of threats coming from the heavens. The driver attempted a joke about the road giving them all a 'free massage'. In response Harry joked back that it reflected the roller coaster of the last four months. Makesh twisted and turned to avoid the deepest potholes. Ramma and Harry felt as if their beings had been shaken violently by the gods of the mountains. Were they looking down from Himalayan mountain peaks enjoying their confusion?

They stopped for lunch at Sravasti and afterwards they explored the site of the Jetavana monastery. Ramma referred to her notes but Harry's guide was subdued.

'So why are we here again?' he asked.

'The Buddha himself stayed here for twenty-four rainy seasons. See that raised platform? It is called a walking platform. The Buddha walked up and down it every day in contemplation.'

Harry tried a half-hearted smile. 'Then I'd better have a go.'

With that, he climbed up onto the brick dais and walked up and down. He had been half-joking. But once he stood where the Buddha had stood, Harry felt ashamed of himself. He was not religious and had never really understood 'sacred' but at that moment he experienced a connection to the past.

Ramma sensed the small change in the atmosphere.

'I have been reading Bartholomew's diary. This was a crisis point for him. His wife wanted to return to England and he had to make up his mind whether to return too. You remember that photograph you found of him in Indian clothes and wearing a turban. I think it was taken in front of those steps,' said Ramma pointing to a small doorway. 'They lead to the rooms where the Buddha lived while at the monastery.'

The driver was anxious to get on the road. It was only 115 miles to Lumbini but Makesh knew something about the road they didn't. It took six hours to reach the border with Nepal and they would be six gruelling hours with road conditions the like of which Harry had not seen even in India.

Lumbini felt like a disappointment after such an ordeal of a drive. Harry was actually pleased that he hadn't been driving himself, especially the last bit travelling in the dark trying to avoid holes in the road sometimes two feet deep. Harry suggested that they give Makesh a day off to rest and although this wasn't the end of their trip, he gave him a generous tip. The guesthouse was basic but welcoming. They both fell asleep as soon as they got into bed.

Ramma had been dreaming strange things since their ordeal in Varanasi. The words were Arjun's. Hussy... whore, all the demeaning insults he'd sworn at her rattled around inside her brain meshing with Harry's sketches of her, parts of her that she'd glimpsed in his book. She hated the association and could not understand how her mind kept putting the two together. She felt confused and hoped it was just tiredness. This journey was testing her resolve. She asked herself, 'Do I love Harry enough? We have to be absolutely certain of each other to be strong enough to face the future. That is what Daddy-ji understood. We can't know what challenges we shall face. Can we face them together or will they drive us apart?' Ramma was unsure of the answer.

After breakfast the next day they walked the short distance to the park entrance. There was a half-mile drive leading to the temple site. The path cut through the kind of forest described in the Buddhist myths. Long-tailed langurs swung from trees making piercing sounds, and families of them hunted for seeds by the side of the road. They passed the Telar River and stopped to watch the egrets. After so long spent cooped up in the car, it was good to stretch their legs.

The Ashokan pillar had been struck by lightning centuries earlier. Ramma examined it closely and took photos of the inscription. To Harry, there was something different about it. It was not shiny like the others he had seen. They had been made from mica and this one was sandstone. There were foundations of two early temples but having come so far, they had hoped for something exquisitely memorable. Harry surmised that their misery and lack of lovemaking infected their view of everything.

Then they saw the multi-coloured garlands of Tibetan flags tied to trees near a pool. They noticed people gathered around one of them and went over to join them. They were pilgrims from Japan and they shared greetings. Their tour guide spoke English. He explained that this was a bodhi tree and bodhi means 'wisdom' because in Bodhgaya the Buddha had received enlightenment beneath just such a tree. But there was a big difference. This was not just one tree. He pointed out how it was two trees with different root systems that looked like one tree. Not only that, the second tree was a banyan, not a bodhi. Harry looked hard and could see that the guide was telling the truth. These two fundamentally different trees had grown together as one, weaving their limbs, sharing nutrients, and casting the same shade.

It was his nirvana moment. He stared at it and then burst into joyous laughter. There must be a way for him and Ramma. Their backgrounds could not be more different but they too could feed each other and flourish while not abandoning their roots. He pointed it out to Ramma with a wry smile. He didn't need to say anything. Ramma understood. He whipped out his pencil and quickly sketched the braided trunks and branches, the graphite blending further the lines between the two. He signed it with a flourish and handed the pencil to Ramma who with a smile signed it as well.

*****

They took a picnic lunch to eat by the river and set out on a long walk. As they walked they began to talk. To begin with, they discussed Lumbini.

'Lumbini would have been abandoned and neglected when Bartholomew was here but he was convinced he had found the birthplace,' said Ramma. 'The inscription would not have been visible because the lower six feet were only excavated in 1896. The inscription was written in Brahmi and it says, "Here Buddha Shakyamuni was born." So he was right. It's a shame that he didn't live long enough to realise that.'

'I understand the reluctance to believe Lumbini was the birthplace. Buddha was born a prince but this place doesn't look at all palatial,' continued Harry.

'That's because Prince Siddartha's kingdom was based in Kapilvastu. That is where he grew up,' Ramma replied. 'It was destroyed even in the Buddha's lifetime.'

'To walk in the garden where the Buddha was born isn't something a working-class kid from Cowley could imagine doing.'

'There are ambitious plans to revitalise Lumbini: to excavate the sites of the monasteries and the Japanese want to restore the garden. You can see from the materials that it will all start soon,' said Ramma. 'Again, a shame that Bartholomew Carew never saw that either.'

'From his last letters to Dora, it's clear that they had quarrelled before he set off. She was threatening to leave him and return to England. Then off he goes to the high peaks and is never seen again. The accepted explanation is that he was killed by the harsh climate. But perhaps not. He was disappointed in his marriage and disillusioned with the Raj,' said Harry. 'Maybe he took his own life?'

'He doesn't strike me as the kind of man who would do that. He had been battling for acceptance of the Anglo-Indians in the Raj, and self-government for Indians. You've read his diaries, he was so passionate for change and never sounded depressed. Is that a man who then takes his life, even out of sheer frustration?'

'Good point.'

Walking in the footsteps of Ashoka and Bartholomew Carew at the birthplace of the Buddha, both Harry and Ramma hoped their spirits would return to harmony. Questions still swirled in Ramma's mind.

'After sights of barbarity, had Ashoka made a similar pilgrimage? The pillar he erected was intended to spread the message of tolerance.'

Memories of the sordid experience in Varanasi began to fade as they relished the natural beauty of the river. They paused to take in the view.

'Perhaps Bartholomew was on a spiritual journey. But Ramma, I'm not Bartholomew. I'm not sure that I even believe in God. I guess you'd call that Brahma: the breath of life – yes?'

Ramma nodded.

'Being here makes me wonder, but I have to be honest with myself and with you. I'm not into renunciation. I like the good things in life, and all its pleasures. I can't make myself believe in an afterlife or even in reincarnation. This life may be all we get.' Then he widened his eyes and raised his eyebrows. 'Crikey, Ramma, we're being so serious.'

Ramma stopped walking and turned to him looking at him straight in the eyes.

'If, as you say, we only get one life, we should surely overcome all difficulties to achieve as many of our ambitions as possible. I don't want to spend my life waiting for something to happen; I want to make it all happen. I love the way you make me laugh but we do have life-changing decisions to make. We cannot put them off forever.'

'Can we put them off for an hour?' asked Harry. The path had taken them into the Sal forest and there was not another human being in sight.

'Let's eat our picnic and chill out for a while?'

The atmosphere of peace exorcised the events in Varanasi from their minds.

'Lumbini is turning out better than my first impressions but I know I couldn't live anywhere this remote. If I'm honest with myself, I'm an urban person,' said Harry.

For a moment he was lost in thought. 'Where would I be without trips to the theatre, to concerts and exhibitions and meeting my friends at pubs?'

Ramma looked at him; he seemed to be laughing to himself.

'What are you thinking, Harry boy?'

'I was remembering something – a play at the Donmar. The lead actor tripped on his spear at a deadly serious climax and it tore his tunic in a rather awkward place. We just erupted.'

'What made that come into your mind?'

'Talking "urban"? The journey took us six hours to travel just 115 miles. I was comparing that to the Oxford Express to London, a bus every fifteen minutes to transport us to exhibitions and theatre land. Dr Johnson was quite right, you know. If you are tired of London, you are tired of life.'

'This could hardly be further from Oxford or London, could it? Everything about the Oxfordshire landscape is cultivated. The Cotswolds are like pimples compared to the Himalayas and the Thames like a trickle next to the Ganges. Chale chale, Harry. Come and get me.'

Ramma ran ahead to the nearest Sal tree and danced around it Bollywood style. Harry knew all the right movements and gestures but Ramma sensed he wasn't entirely with her in the moment and she was right. He swung her around and pulled her to the ground and combed his fingers in her hair.

'Can I adapt to a different way of life? Can I untangle my old life?'

Ramma was consumed by similar thoughts. She'd felt certain that Harry would marry her and stay in India, but since Varanasi she was conflicted with doubt after doubt, question after question. She truly didn't want to coerce someone to move just for her. She didn't want the responsibility of making Harry happy in India. With the guilt every time something went wrong – which it was bound to at times – the pressure would be emotionally exhausting and permanently distracting.

To think that two weeks ago when they left Mumbai, it had felt so simple.

*****

In the evening, there was nothing to do apart from read, talk or pray. Ramma showed him how to do Puja in a little Hindu temple. They lit joss sticks and placed them in the inlaid brass vases and draped wreathes of marigolds around the deity. They placed coins on the step beneath, which would go to the temple priest. Ramma taught Harry a mantra and as they sat cross-legged on the floor all thoughts of Oxford disappeared in the heavily scented candlelight. They felt love and intimacy. The distance between them melted and that night they comforted and enjoyed each other.

'North, south, east and west, I love you in all directions, Princess Ramma.'

'I told you not to call me that, King Harry. I need to punish you for that.'

After their quarrels, their lovemaking had delicious poignancy.

The following morning over a fresh, if spicy breakfast, cooked by the owner of the guest house, Harry asked Ramma, 'In which direction do we head now? It feels like we have arrived at the beginning rather than the end.'

'Somehow the journey is what it has all been about. We are heading in a strange circle – which seems very Buddhist,' laughed Ramma. 'We shall pass through Kushinagar where the Buddha died and then we must head for Nalanda before going back home to Mumbai.'

'Does that mean you have all the material needed for your thesis?' asked Harry.

'I have lots of ideas now but I am struggling with this book you brought from England, the one Charles Carew gave you. I know some Brahmi but have only read rock and stupa inscriptions and some of these passages have words I don't understand. There is one place that could help me. Nalanda was the site of a vast monastery complex and library, the one I told you about. When the Mughals invaded, they massacred all the residents and destroyed the books. So much knowledge was lost but it is having a renaissance. They have built a modern centre there, for postgraduate studies in Buddhism.'

'You think they can translate it?'

'This book is rare. You do not realise how rare. The library Hsien took back to China survived for centuries until...' Ramma sighed, 'until 1967 when the Red Guards burned them. They were acting on Chairman Mao's instruction to 'destroy the old'. Do you think Charles Carew would be upset if I gave his book to the library?'

'If it is properly looked after and put to good academic use, I'm sure he'd approve. That is why he sent it to you. He wanted you to use it.'

'That would be great. I need help with a few passages. The religious sections are not really for me with their endless rambling on about freeing ourselves from suffering. Once I have translated the stories of the missionary journeys going east, I won't need it anymore. Daddy-ji appreciated it but he is not sentimental. He would much rather it be put to good use.'

The end of their pilgrimage was in sight. Nalanda would be their final destination.

'Bodhgaya was where the Buddha found enlightenment. Without being disrespectful, I hope our next stop in Nalanda can do the same for me and that everything will suddenly become clear. Those two trees growing together like a single tree, can that be us, Ramma?'

*****

On the drive to Nalanda, they felt oddly connected to the enigmatic Victorian, as if he were an old friend. 'I do want Bartholomew to be at the heart of my thesis, reveal him as a great pioneer of the renaissance in Buddhist studies. What I like about him is how he was open to people who were not from his background. That was unusual in a man who probably died a hundred years ago. Do you realise that it was almost a century ago that he disappeared?' said Ramma. 'I wonder if the Nalanda academics have heard of him?'

Harry nodded but wanted to change the subject. 'I'm not sure about Bartholomew but a school report would mark our personal studies for your father "unsatisfactory".' His joshing didn't last as, once again, Harry felt inhibited by having a driver in the car. Personal studies? Was he turning into a stereotypical reticent Englishman? Just as on the first day of the journey to Lumbini, there were unusual periods of silence. From the first day they met, the way they were able to talk to each other had marked their relationship as special. Why the silence now?

Harry's thoughts turned to his old life in Oxford. How had the shop been earning without his inputs of fresh stock? What should he buy in India to sell in Deco-rators? He thought more frequently about Deco-rators than he wanted to admit to Ramma. His shop and all the friends that went through it were his life. It was more than just a shop, but almost a living, breathing entity that was part of him. The shop, he realised with some chagrin, was more than his financial security, it was his security blanket.

Luck was not with them. The car shuddered to a halt on the outskirts of a small town. Mahesh wasn't at all fazed. 'No problem, sahib. It will be repaired by morning; Mahesh does not lie.' It was mid-afternoon. After checking into a guesthouse, Ramma suggested they go to the only place of interest – the cinema.

'No subtitles but I can whisper the essentials to you. In any case, Indian films have lots of singing and dancing. The roles are choreographed, so you will follow most of it.'

'You do realise, don't you, that if I'm to live in India even part of the time, I'll have to learn Hindi. I wish I were a better linguist.'

'Don't worry. You'll have the very best teacher: me,' laughed Ramma.

There was a long queue; it was a popular film. A blockbuster by Bollywood standards.

'*Dilwale Dulhania Le Jayenge*. It means "The Brave-Hearted Get the Bride". You could pick up a few tips, Harry,' laughed Ramma. 'DDLJ, as it is known, is popular even though it was released in 1994. Four years later and it is still packing them in! That's Bollywood for you.'

Even Harry had heard of Shahrukh Khan, the heartthrob playing the leading role. He was amused from the start because the hero was called Raj Malhotra and he was a Lamborghini-driving Londoner! Sure. Didn't everyone who lived in London drive flash cars? He smiled as he remembered his accidental encounter with fame on a Bollywood film set and he whispered to her, 'Pass the cough sweets, Amita darling.' She could hardly stop herself laughing. The audience glanced their way and they quickly shut up. Harry followed the story easily enough. Raj falls for the heroine, Simran, a doe-eyed beauty.

Ramma whispered, 'Her father has committed her to an

arranged marriage in India.'

Raj forsakes his playboy ways and follows her to the Punjab. He is determined to marry her but refuses to elope – he wants her father's permission. It was all starting to ring bells; the hoops you have to jump through to please fathers in India! 'My life's a Bollywood movie, and a corny one at that. Except I'm not obscenely wealthy, I don't drive a Lamborghini, and I can't sing or dance.' The idea depressed him. But then, the love songs tugged at his heart despite his determination to resist them. Ramma was smiling happily beside him and he could feel her tapping her toes to the music. They left the cinema with a bounce in their step, knowing they wanted to be together somehow.

Mahesh was true to his word, the ambassador, valeted and repaired, was waiting outside the next morning ready for the last part of the journey to Nalanda. It was dark when they arrived and so they spent what was left of the evening in their hotel.

CHAPTER 10: Discoveries in the Library

Lumbini, March 1887

I have found what appears to be an Ashokan Pillar. The material is not Mica but sandstone, which raises questions. I hired a team from the village to excavate close by & may have found the birthplace. The brickwork we are uncovering is of the right period. Proving this is the birthplace of Buddha will not be easy.

The traditional story is that when the time for the birth grew near, Queen Maya wished to travel from Kapilavatthu, the King's capital, to her childhood home to give birth. On the way to Devadaha, the procession passed a grove, which was full of blossoming trees. The Queen asked her courtiers to stop, & she entered the grove. As she reached up to touch the blossoms, her son was born.

The terrain here fits the description & Lumbini would have been on that route. Why else would Ashoka have ordered a pillar to be erected here, albeit an inferior one?

Surprise does not adequately describe this encounter. A contingent of pilgrims from the remote kingdom of Bhutan arrived here & among the party is a young woman called Lady Yushika. She is of the family of the young prince, Ugyen Wangchuck, who has been consolidating his power in the kingdom of Bhutan & putting an end to the civil wars. His aim is to establish an elected Buddhist monarchy; surely this is something that Ashoka himself would have approved of: rule of law based on equality & respect for all. After signing a treaty with the Raj, the elites there are learning English. That includes the Lady Yushika — astonishing! We have spent many hours speaking & she is a rare conversationalist.

She has been promised in marriage but Ugyen Wangchuck has given her permission to travel with an entourage to explore & find inspiration from the Buddhist sites for a year. They have made their way here from Darjeeling. The Rinpoche is also of the opinion that Lumbini is the birthplace of the Buddha. I have been invited to visit them in Bhutan.

Once settled in a comfortable hotel, Harry asked, 'Why are we here, apart from seeing this library?'

'You want to eat my brain, my visitor from Oxford? Yours may be an ancient university but Nalanda was founded more than 1000 years earlier,' said Ramma. 'Remember the description I showed you by Hsien, the Tang dynasty Chinese pilgrim?'

'When was the Tang Dynasty again? What a lousy antiques dealer, having to ask that question.'

'I don't really know. What a lousy historian, not knowing the dates for that. But I do know that Hsien came here in the 7th century when Nalanda had already begun to decline from its zenith in the Gupta period.'

Ramma read from Hsien's poetic description. 'He described forests of pavilions, harmikas and temples which seemed to "soar above the mists in the sky" so that from their cells the monks "might witness the birth of the winds and clouds."'

'I'd love to paint that scene,' sighed Harry.

'According to Hsien, there were over 10,000 students and 2,000 teachers.'

'What did they learn here?'

'They covered every field of learning of that time and attracted pupils and scholars from Korea, Japan, China, Tibet, Indonesia, Persia and Turkey. That is why Nalanda is thought to be the world's first international university. The library was located in a nine-storey building where meticulous copies of texts were produced in the same way that medieval manuscripts were written in monasteries in England.'

*****

In the morning they set off to see the ruins of the world's first international university. 'It has only been partly excavated,' said Ramma. The kilometre that had been uncovered took their breath away. They passed a great stupa flanked by steps and terraces and even walked into Hsien's room. Walking along a narrow passage between high brick walls they arrived at where the great library once stood. Ramma held back the tears.

'The top half was wooden. In 1193, a fanatic called Bakhitya Khili burned down the library and that marked the end for Buddhism in India. All the books were destroyed apart from one. One monk was travelling and he had that with him. All the monks were killed and their knowledge died with them.'

'It all makes sense to me, Ramma. Ashoka was forgotten because India was no longer Buddhist and the records kept here had been destroyed. So the only evidence that remained was on the pillars, rocks, and stupas and no one could read them because they were in Pali and Brahmi.'

'You see why I want my country to know more about this civilization and Ashoka's ideas of good governance? And your countrymen, like Bartholomew, played a key role in recovering so much lost history. You do understand why this matters to me?'

There was a pleading look in her eyes. He wanted to kiss her in answer but nodded instead. He'd learned his lesson.

They spent nearly all day at the ruins trying to picture it in its heyday. Ramma wrote and Harry sketched. To passers-by, they looked like two people with not a care in the world. In the late afternoon they took a taxi back to their hotel in nearby Rajgir. On the way they passed a modern but not impressive building with a sign 'The University of Nalanda'.

'That is where I need to go in the morning,' said Ramma.

'There are plans to build a new campus near the old university site. The Japanese have promised help with the funding.'

The next morning, at the new university's library they asked to see the head librarian, who introduced himself as Dr Ramachandra. After ten minutes, they were taken to his office where they carefully unwrapped Charles Carew's book and handed it to him.

He puzzled over it. Then for the first time in centuries the title of the book was revealed. 'It's called *The Pillars of Ashoka*. Brahmi is not my strongest language but even I can translate that much. Where did you find this?' the incredulous librarian asked. They told their story and Ramma said, 'We are considering giving this book to the library. But first, I hope you can help me translate some of the more difficult passages. I want to quote it in my doctoral thesis.'

Delighted and smiling broadly, he picked up the phone and asked for the visiting Professor of Ashokan studies. Unfortunately, she was away at a conference. Ramma and Harry could hear the voice at the other end coming through the receiver. 'The professor's PhD student comes from a family who are expert in Brahmi and Pali. I suggest I send for him. He should be here tomorrow morning.'

Dr Ramachandra turned to them. 'Did you hear that? Can you come back in the morning?'

'No problem. We're here for a couple of days,' said Harry.

Ramma wanted to stay at the library to work but was concerned that Harry would be bored. Harry fancied a break from history and travelling. He had in mind Selene's request for him to look out for talented Indian artists. He was directed to a series of small workshops in the town. They were situated around a courtyard and in the middle of the courtyard was a gnarled but beautiful Banyan tree. Each workshop was open at the front and visitors could wander in and out as they pleased. Harry appreciated the skill of what he saw laid out but felt that most was best described as craft. The miniature paintings were exquisite but they were reproductions of the art and style of an India long past. Harry valued what he felt was best from the past although that wasn't fashionable. A thought nagged at him as he looked at a reproduction. Maybe his style was fresh but was he, as an artist, still in the past? He wanted his art to be relevant to the approaching millennium. He didn't want to abandon brush and paint. Somehow he had to use them in a way that would have immediacy and not be a pastiche of past styles. He had not yet found a way to do it that was true to himself and was convinced it had to come from within.

Harry passed workshops making gleaming copper bowls and blue pottery but knew that his customers were unlikely to buy them. 'They won't fancy cleaning the copper,' thought Harry. 'In India, the middle class has servants. That changes what people buy.'

At the far end, there was a yard containing massive blocks of stone and marble. Harry heard the click-click of a chisel and followed the sound. Emerging from a block of marble was the head of an elephant. The piece was huge, life-sized, and the sculptor was making it entirely by hand. In England, the sculptors Harry knew who worked with stone, did the initial work with power tools and only finished the fine detail in the manner of this Indian artist. Harry introduced himself and asked if he spoke English.

Holding out a dusty hand to Harry, the sculptor replied in modulated tones, 'Namaste. Pleased to meet you.'

Harry looked closely at the emerging elephant. 'I love your work. I'm an artist, too, but couldn't do what you are doing. How long has this taken so far?'

'Three months and with timely intervention, eighteen months to complete, no?'

Harry glanced around looking for sketches of the work in progress but could see none.

'How do you do it without outline drawings?'

'I cut away everything that isn't elephant.'

There was silence. Harry and the sculptor looked at each other without saying a word. The seconds ticked past. There was such a tumult in Harry's head that he couldn't break his eye lock with the sculptor. The dust motes spun and caught the light and then, as the silence held, settled. Finally, Harry spoke.

'How do you know what isn't elephant?'

The sculptor ran a hand along the marble, as if stroking away the not-elephant bits. 'I do not know until I do it.' A tiny puff rose beneath his hand, fuzzing the air. 'You have to understand what's captured inside, and trust it to come out.' He gave a small smile as he picked up his chisel. 'I release it.'

That evening he told Ramma, 'I spent the afternoon just thinking about him freeing up what's inside. This man takes two years to complete his sculpture. There is something wonderful about his dedication and his philosophy. Do we make everything far too complicated? Perhaps we should be thinking about taking away the bits that aren't elephant?'

Ramma hadn't a clue what he was on about. Harry tried to explain. 'It's about getting to the essence of things.' Ramma sounded doubtful but it was because she didn't really understand what he was talking about. She was an academic at heart, and the sweeping metaphors of Harry's interior world confused her. But she was willing to try anything and the contentment they had recovered in Lumbini had not left them.

The next day they arrived at the library by mid-morning. Dr Ramachandra invited them to take tea with him in his office while they waited. Ramma explained the nature of her research and the librarian suggested that the student, Bhamaya, could discuss it with her. A knock came at the door. He turned to Ramma and Harry to introduce them.

'This is Bhamaya Cari. Bhamaya, these people have come from England bearing a precious gift that I want you to see.'

The young man put on a pair of white gloves, picked up the book and turned the pages with great respect. He examined it carefully. Then he looked at them in amazement. 'Thank you for bringing this. What a discovery. Where did you get it?'

Given the student's name, they were surprised by his East Coast American accent. As briefly as he could, Harry told the story of the well-travelled chest of drawers and the consequences of him buying it.

Ramma enquired about Bhamaya's name given his Western appearance and accent.

'I'm partly of Bhutanese ancestry. I understand that you're interested in donating this book to the university.'

'Before I do, would you be kind enough to translate these pages. They will be useful for my thesis on the rediscovery of Ashoka. I can read a little Brahmi but not well enough to read this book,' said Ramma.

'Translating this will be such a pleasure. My PhD thesis is on the edicts of Ashoka so our work is complementary. I specialise in the Ashokan period and I understand that you are working on how the story of Ashoka was rediscovered in the 19th and early 20th centuries?'

Ramma and Bhamaya discussed their work with such enthusiasm that both their faces glowed with energy and inspiration. Ramma obviously liked him, he was of the same age, and what's more they shared a passion. Harry assumed that for Bhamaya, the linguist, India would present no challenges. He was aware of the other man's good looks and they somehow seemed familiar. Harry did not want to acknowledge the feelings welling up and forced himself to smile as happily as possible.

Ramma turned to Harry. 'I would like to stay here and go through the passages I need help with. Bhamaya and I can join you for lunch. Is that alright with you, Bhamaya?'

'Do you mind, Harry?'

Harry did mind; he felt superfluous. Biting his lips, he left them together and went for a walk. He was jealous – yes that was it – the green-eyed monster.

After an hour Harry felt he had walked off his temporary insanity. Ramma wouldn't change her feelings for him so quickly, would she? He was being stupid. She was passionate about her career and he should no more be jealous of that than she should be of Deco-rators.

By the time they met for lunch, Harry had forgotten his surprise at his first sight of Bhamaya. But now, as he walked into the restaurant and saw Bhamaya's profile, he was forcibly reminded of an uncanny likeness. It was the jaw, the set of the neck, the angle of the head. It spoke to him.

Harry rummaged in his briefcase and drew out a photograph of the handsome young adventurer, Bartholomew Carew. And he then lost his nerve and slipped it under his hat and sunglasses resting on the table.

'So where do you live in the States?' Ramma asked.

'Boston, Massachusetts.'

Harry was disappointed but a touch relieved at the same time. The probability that Bhamaya was related to Bartholomew was in the realms of unreality. No one from the Carew family had migrated stateside. Harry was glad that he hadn't shown the young man the picture.

Bhamaya continued. 'But originally, my father is from Bhutan and went to study in the States. He met my mother while he was at Harvard. She's American.'

Harry's eyed widened. 'So...' He paused, uncertain about what questions to ask to get to the bottom of the mystery. Ramma filled in the silence with her own questions.

'How did their parents respond when they discovered that they were getting married?'

'My Bhutanese grandparents were not pleased. Don't get me wrong, they liked her but it was hard having a son and grandchildren so far away. My American grandparents weren't thrilled either but that's for a different reason,' and here he gave that easy laugh that Americans have, 'and it's a different story.'

Astonishment spread like a shadow across Harry's face.

'And your great-grandparents...' he prompted.

Ramma and Bhamaya looked perplexed at his question but Bhamaya answered readily enough. 'I heard many stories about one of my great-grandfathers. I didn't know for certain if they were true or were old wives' tales. I was told that he was English-born but became a Buddhist back when that was rare. I know for certain that he was a scholar and worked for King Ugyen Wangchuck. I was named after him: Bhamaya Cari.'

'Do you mind if I ask how old you are?' interrupted Harry.

'Twenty-five,' answered Bhamaya. Harry continued to stare at him and then handed him the photograph of the clean-cut explorer.

'Bartholomew Carew was thirty-three when that photograph was taken. Sixteen years later, in 1888, he was last seen a few hundred miles northeast of here. He was presumed dead. Looking at you, I can't help believing that he survived. This book was given to us by Bartholomew's grandson, his English grandson.'

The graduate student examined the photo in the same manner that he examined the book: thoughtfully and with considerable focus. Harry couldn't help wondering if this is how Bartholomew went through India: overly intense, fully engaged and with a roiling intelligence. Bhamaya finally lifted his head with his eyes wide in amazement and continued his story.

'I was told that he first met my great-grandmother in Lumbini. Her journey was unusual. In the 19th century, foreign travel was almost unheard of unless you were a merchant. She was the first woman in the family to step outside Bhutan.'

'Do you happen to know what year that was?' Ramma asked. Harry knew that she was double-checking the dates in the diary.

'I do, actually, because I wrote my Master's thesis on it. 1887.'

'Published?' Ramma enquired, one scholar to another.

He nodded with quiet pride and she inclined her head in recognition of his achievement.

'She was a devout Buddhist and persuaded her father to let her visit Lumbini. Her Rinpoche suggested that was where the Buddha was born. She had agreed to marry the man of her father's choice but begged him to let her pursue her pilgrimage first. She must have been kick-ass, don't you think?'

'So she married the Bhutanese man?' asked Ramma.

'They say there was an arranged marriage planned to a much older man. Some of the stories hint that she was not keen on him. But how much of this is true, I've no idea.'

Harry's mind was racing ahead. 'Could it be that Bhamaya's great-grandmother and Bartholomew set out for Lumbini with similar motives? She was putting off an undesirable marriage and he was escaping from a loveless one and both were seeking a Buddhist mind set, which they hoped could lead to contentment.'

'The Englishman was alone but my great-grandmother had members of the household staff and an uncle with her. Romance must have been tricky. I really don't know how much of this is true – stories become myths with time, don't they?'

Ramma and Harry were listening in disbelief. If Bhamaya Cari was who they believed he was, they were discovering the reason behind Bartholomew Carew's mysterious disappearance.

The waiter came with their food and for a few minutes they had to pause their conversation but they were tense with expectation. Bhamaya began to eat. An impatient Harry asked, 'Did Bartholomew follow her?'

'Not immediately. He turned up nine months later. Few ordinary people had even seen a white man, so he caused quite a stir. He was a lot taller than most Bhutanese and he had a beard. He didn't look like that picture you showed me. He certainly wasn't dressed like that or at least, not in the few pictures that were taken of him in Bhutan. In those, he always wore

Bhutanese clothes.

'What I know for a fact, because they are in the palace records, was that he was able to perform a service to the nation. People in and near the palace were dying of typhoid. It's on the record that Bhamaya Cari found the cause, a polluted water supply, and ended the epidemic. The King was so pleased with Bhamaya that he appointed him chief engineer and scientific advisor. That I know is true. After he accepted the position he married my great-grandmother. Her intended husband had died – a victim of the typhoid outbreak. As for the rest of the story, it happened such a long time ago and I heard many different versions before my parents took me to Bhutan.

'Punakha was the old capital of Bhutan but the family moved to Thimphu when it became the capital and I've only been to Punakha once. The story I've told you contains threads that run through all the accounts I have heard. My parents can probably tell you more.'

'Do you know when this happened?' asked Ramma.

'They married around 1892. I think he was twenty years older than her but they didn't keep birth certificates in Bhutan in those days. I am told that they lived happily until he died in 1919. My great-grandmother lived for another twenty years. My father's marriage to an American is unusual and he identified with Bhamaya. That's why he named me after him.'

'Well,' said Harry handing over the photograph of the young Bartholomew Carew, 'you should keep this. I feel certain that this is a picture of your great-grandfather, Bhamaya Cari, whose name in England was Bartholomew Carew. We admire him very much and we know someone in Oxford who would love to meet you: the man whose book has brought us together.'

The conversation carried on all afternoon as Ramma and Harry told Bhamaya all they knew. When he left them, to telephone his parents, he asked if they would mind writing down some of the things they had told him.

*****

'Ramma, honey, I'm not a religious man,' said Harry as they walked back to the lodge, 'but you know we say "a bolt out of the blue" as if the gods are taking aim? I feel that I've been well and truly speared.'

'Do you mean by the surprise?'

'I was remembering how adamant I was that I didn't want to buy the chest of drawers. Despite knowing that Kathy would hate it, I bought it. Now, we've resolved a 100-year-old mystery. Somehow, it feels like we were meant to be here today.'

'Harry, you are becoming a Hindu, attributing events to fate! I may be Indian but I want a say in my destiny.'

'You have more than a say in your destiny: you determine my life too. I'm not superstitious but after all that has happened, don't you believe we are meant to be together? Bartholomew's story has inspired me. I feel more positive than at any time since we left Mumbai.'

CHAPTER 11: Head to Head

Simla, February 1888

I was present to wave goodbye to Dora & Douglas from Bombay docks. That does not mitigate my failure at not being there when they arrived in India. I have filled half of the chest of drawers with my research notes, papers & correspondence & I shall make use of the remaining six drawers for my photographic equipment & my photographs. The shipping company will collect it next month & deliver it to Dora in London.

I have decisions to make but find excuses to avoid making them. As always, I feel pulled between passion and duty. Any compromise I thought possible has proved elusive.

The sun was setting as they sat with a drink after their evening meal in the garden of the Hotel Gautama: Harry had come to love this time of day in India. The heat had dissipated leaving a warm and lazy glow. He understood the chameleons stretched out on the wall. They would suddenly emerge from their stupor and dart away and disappear. Harry wanted to adapt like a chameleon.

Back in their room Ramma gave Harry a deep, slow massage as she thought about his comment on fate. 'After we have relaxed we must talk about that karma you described.'

They sat on the balcony and tried to make sense of everything that had happened to them and what was happening.

'The way Daddy-ji phrased his test of our commitment implied we should live here because that is what he would like. He would not try to stop us living in Oxford but it would make him sad, even though he wants to be happy for us. It reminds me of what Bhamaya said of the Bhutanese family's reactions to his parents' marriage. My father needs you to understand the sacrifice you are asking of him. I love you Harry, I want to spend my life with you but I adore my father too. You know that we are closer than most fathers and daughters, probably because of losing Mummy-ji. But he is not possessive, yes? If he were, we would never have met. And it is true also that a career in India has greater prospects for me.'

'Let's go inside, I want us to hold each other as we talk this through.'

As they lay on the bed with their arms around each other, the moment to focus on the important questions was lost. After making love they were reluctant to move. Ramma asked Harry, 'What do you think happened to Bartholomew in Lumbini?'

'I'm not sure but I have a feeling that the spirit of Bartholomew will subconsciously come out in my paintings. How about you? Can you get inside his head?'

'What a challenge! A twenty-four-year-old Indian woman gets inside the head of a macho but brilliant Victorian! You are as bad as my father, are you not? Daddy-ji sent me into research and now you want to send me into my imagination. I like challenges so you never know. You start me off. Try. What do you think happened?'

'I don't think Bartholomew was all that macho. If he had been, he would have had more of a problem with Dora. She was up for adventure. Think of her determination travelling to India alone and with a small child!' Harry looked sideways at Ramma before adding, 'I bet that Dora was cold sexually – not wholly her fault. The Victorians wanted their women to be domestic, to be upright mothers, to run efficient households but not to have sexual feelings. Middle and upper class women were often denied the opportunity of strong emotional bonds, even with their children.'

'Or...' Ramma paused and struggled to put her thoughts into words. 'She was unable to let go. She had such passion for botany and despite not having any support, not even from her husband, managed to submit new flora from India to England – and it is not as if other botanists were not attempting the same feat. When, for one reason or another, Bartholomew did not follow through on his promises, she must have been resentful. Could she have been confused about why being a wife and mother was not enough for her when it was for seemingly every other woman? The constant struggle with herself and her world could have hardened her, robbed her of sensuality or playful tenderness. I sympathise with her.'

Harry gave her a strange look. 'I sympathise with both of them. They could have been best friends, built each other up and been a power couple of 1880s India like Richard Burton was with his wife, Isabel. But the Carews just couldn't figure out how to be partners. Maybe because Bartholomew was highly receptive to Indian ideas, including Khajoraho and uncovering the stupas, and Dora wasn't. You can see from his writings that his eyes were opened by India.'

'You mean to the racism of the Raj?' asked Ramma.

'That and more. India awakens senses and possibly made him aware of his loveless marriage. He was genuinely passionate about Ashokan ideas of government and tolerance. That's transparent in his letters but his work also provided an excuse to escape. When he headed for Lumbini, could he have recognised who he was – or what was elephant? Had he begun to use his research as a means of avoiding making decisions about his personal life? We can relate to that! We've been doing the same thing; we're avoiding the elephant in the room by discussing Bartholomew.'

'I do wonder if the answer to our own problems would become transparent if we focused on Bartholomew's decision to go to Bhutan.'

Harry decided that Ramma might be on to something. 'If I work out why Bartholomew was prepared to live in exile and start again in a completely new life it might help me,' he thought but said aloud, 'Divorce was scandalous in Victorian England. He cared about Dora or he wouldn't have exited in the way that he did. He had a plan that set them both free. He knew Dora could cope without him and expected her to thrive if he were declared dead. He discovered a personal connection with a Bhutanese woman, a woman from a completely different culture: a bit like you and me. They connected just as we did. By pretending to die, he liberated himself and Dora.'

Ramma nodded in agreement but said, 'It must have been tough on poor little Douglas.'

'Boys from his background were all sent off to boarding school and sometimes didn't see their parents for years. I expect his life was not so different from his fellow pupils. Our idea of fatherhood is an intimate emotional bond, but the Victorians weren't into that. They suppressed emotions out of a sense of duty.'

Ramma ran a finger across Harry's upper lip. 'A lot of Indians have a stereotypical view of English men and women as cold. Perhaps that is why.'

Responding to her humour, Harry momentarily stiffened his face but as he relaxed, he looked sad. 'Douglas told Charles about his father playing cricket with him and that sounded full of regrets. Maybe Bartholomew had become disillusioned with Victorian ideas of relationships. I know what it does to you, when a father deserts you. I haven't forgiven my father for walking out on us, just like Bartholomew did.'

'Oh, Harry, come here. I promise that I will never leave you.'

*****

That night, Harry woke up disturbed by dreams of when his father had walked out. Most bizarre was a persistent sound, a chink-chink like a chisel reverberating in his head, his father's face emerging from an elephant's body, ghastly, terrifying. Harry jerked awake, opening his eyes to the darkness, unable to unsee his father's elephant-face. Creeping out of bed, trying not to disturb Ramma, he splashed his face and the nape of his neck with cold water but the fear didn't evaporate with the moisture.

He sat for a while on the balcony. He sensed that Bartholomew had appeared in his dream too. When he'd said "Goodbye" to Douglas, was the explorer no different from Harry's father? No, that wasn't fair. Bartholomew was a Victorian and his disappearance wouldn't have made Douglas's life much different to his schoolmates'. Bartholomew was adventurous but not a gambler. He'd left Dora and Douglas financially secure and with hope for the future.

When Ramma awoke, she was surprised to see Harry sitting on the balcony.

'You're awake early. Is everything okay?

'I had an odd dream and it's made me think about the difference between risk-taking and gambling. Let's take a risk on an Indian omelette, shall we?'

CHAPTER 12: What Next?

Simla, 1888

Cursum perficio. I have deposited my will with Bolby & Sons, & they will make sure it is sent to their London office. I said my goodbyes to some old colleagues from the Survey. They were oblivious to the finality of my farewell but commented on the firmness of my handshake. I am proud to have worked alongside courageous & dedicated men, both Indian & British. I would like to think that when Douglas becomes a man he will be judged by his actions, not by his station in life or race or nationality. I hope also that he will one day discover his father's diary & know that he was loved and forgive me.

The next morning, they met up with Bhamaya. While he worked with Ramma translating the passages she needed, Harry asked if he could sketch them. From his subconscious, something flowed. Francis Bacon, the artist, said the first brushstroke was all-important; nothing else had that kind of immediacy. Harry remembered Ramma's confused reaction to his description of Bacon using ripped photographs for his models, not beings in the flesh. She hadn't understood his volumes of sketches of different parts of the body.

'Maybe Ramma has a point,' thought Harry as he looked up. 'I need to make a whole of the parts.'

He felt an energy travel through the nerves of his arm. He was inspired by what was in front of him, not simply being an illustrator. Harry knew that to Bartholomew, Bhamaya's great-grandmother must have been what Ramma was to him. That communion invaded his sketch.

Looking at it afterwards, Bhamaya looked bewildered.

'But it doesn't look like me. I'm not sure it even feels like me but it has a strong emotion.'

Harry smiled.

*****

During their siesta, Ramma commented thoughtfully, 'That picture was different from your other work, wasn't it? What does it mean?'

'Do you remember my encounter with that sculptor, the one who carves elephants by cutting out all that isn't elephant? I can't get it out of my head. What is it that I want to achieve? What is important to me?'

'But what in your life isn't elephant?

'The more important question is figuring out what is.'

He pulled Ramma close to him. 'You are my elephant. I don't want to live without you. Without you, I won't be a whole man.'

Ramma seemed to melt into him. Then he whispered, 'For a moment, I forgot how the desire to live drained out of me when you left. I felt an outsider here and I was afraid that I could unravel if I gave up my roots in Oxford. I was fazed by the challenge of living here and panicked that I might do to you what my father did to me. I have this terror that I'm like him, you see.'

'What are you trying to tell me, Harry? You can't live without me but you can't live in India. I have to choose between you and Daddy-ji?' Ramma's voice was small.

'No honey, but I need a meaningful life, not one following you around. I watched you and Bhamaya working together and saw your commitment. I don't want to get in the way of that. If India is to be our home then I need the same kind of commitment. I'll relish the Indian family life but that is not enough, not by a long shot could I live in your and your father's shadows. That's what your father in his wisdom knew and I've discovered on this journey. We mustn't find ourselves in a situation where I resent the pressure to stay here. He was right to doubt me.'

'You have come to a decision?' asked Ramma, her eyes wide.

'Bartholomew Carew has helped me to do that. Giving up travelling must have been incredibly difficult for such an adventurous man. When he risked everything he knew himself and what he most wanted in life. That self-knowledge was what I lacked when we set out from Mumbai. I suspect that Bartholomew was driven to follow Yushika to Bhutan for the same reason that I followed you to India. They wouldn't even have enjoyed what you and I have, but they connected. It was a chance encounter, or destiny, or karma, or the gods rolling their dices, whatever you call it, it changed his life, just like me stumbling over you and you changing my life.'

Ramma was mesmerised by what she was hearing.

'If I were a statistician, I'd try and work out what were the tiny odds of Bartholomew and Yushika meeting – or you and I for that matter. But what made Bartholomew act on his feelings? He must have known there was little chance they could be together. Somehow, he untethered himself from his old life to experience whatever chance threw his way. I must find some of his courage and do the same.

'Do you remember this morning, when I told you that I was struggling with the difference between taking risks and gambling? I see it clearly now. My father was a gambler, and when he lost so did my mother and I. I've been frozen by my fear that I could become like him. I see the difference in Bartholomew. He was prepared to take huge risks but he wasn't irresponsible. That painting this morning? I felt free to risk doing things differently. Am I finally free from the fear that I'm like Dad? It's a strange contradiction but I have to become a risk-taker to secure our life together.

'People describe me as entrepreneurial but in truth, Ramma,

I've been careful – you've risked far more. I haven't taken unnecessary risks. What looks accidental was in fact well-planned. I only left teaching when I had the means to afford the lease on Deco-rators. I knew where I stood and I was rooted in Oxford, a city I love. I was the opposite of Bartholomew and you with your love of adventures in archaeology.'

'From reading his diary, I think that Bartholomew changed too, and became even more high-risk. Your journey sounds like his,' Ramma mused as she imagined Harry in the guise of the Victorian adventurer.

Harry smiled, pleased with the comparison. 'I doubt Bartholomew regretted his decision, although he must have had difficult periods of nostalgia for places and people he'd loved. But he built a fulfilling life and a family. He was a compassionate man. Maybe Buddhism helped him to find peace, to figure out what did and didn't matter.'

'That is so lovely, Harry.' Ever the historian, Ramma added, 'We cannot be certain but it has a ring of truth, does it not? But go on. You have told me that you struggled knowing what to do but you seem decisive today. Am I right?'

'You're right. If I want to live with you and I want to make you happy, I have to be prepared to cut out what is superfluous about my old life. Think of Ashoka. How did he change his thinking and turn his life from a warlord to a peacemaker, how did he find out what was truly important and what was harmful and useless? I have to believe that I can make changes to my life. I've got to take that risk. I may have to confront an uncertain future in India but I had some good news, which could help me.

'I went to an internet café when you were working with Bhayama. There was a message from Selene. The container has arrived. She loves it all but was intrigued by a painting I sent her. A friend of hers at Christie's took a look at it and it's rather valuable. That gives me confidence that I can make a living here. But I don't want you to have to choose between your father and me; that would be unfair. You have already lost your mum and I know how that feels. I'll build a new life here in India with you.'

'Oh, Harry, thank you! Thank you!' Ramma clasped his hands and looked lovingly at him. 'In India, it is usually the girl who has to abandon her life and adapt to her husband's family. I can't believe this is happening.'

In the evening, they picked up their conversation where they had left off but it felt more positive – this time the mood was expansive as the Indian sky.

'Harry, something happened to give you a sense of possibility here even before the news from Selene. What was it?'

Harry turned his warm gaze on her.

'Like I said, it was the elephant in Nalanda. And did you know that "Nalanda", means "self-knowledge"? Seeing that sculptor, knowing that he felt it worthwhile spending two years of his life on that one piece, made me feel cheap. I enjoy painting and you've seen my efforts at sculpture but I haven't given art that kind of commitment. The need to earn a living got in the way. My paintings give a lot of pleasure. My customers tell me what fun they are but I need to be braver. I must throw myself into an art that I can be serious about. But I have to earn a living and nowadays it's hard to be a serious artist and make money without being sensationalist.'

Ramma nodded her agreement. 'Tell me, what kind of art do you want to do?'

'I want my art to have immediacy but to be true to how I feel, it must also have humanity. I believe that the serious artist in me can develop here, possibly better than in Oxford. Everything in India is exposed in technicolour. When I sketched you and Bhayama, I was driven to add brilliant colour. There is something vibrant about colour in India. But in the end, wherever I am, it has to come from within me. Of course I was already aware of that as a fact but because of everything that has happened in the last two months I now have more self-knowledge. It's as if I've released that piece of me that was being held inside.'

Ramma not only understood but also felt in awe of the change she saw in him. Harry continued, 'I can trust now and, like Bartholomew, open myself to chance – I didn't trust before. And it was me I didn't trust. I couldn't.

'None of this changes the facts; it won't make it any easier in India earning a living as a serious artist. As long as I have some time to try and develop that side of me, I believe I can thrive here. But I have to save Deco-rators. It wouldn't be fair on Kathy to let it go now. I owe her so much. I could sell the business to Kathy bit by bit. At the moment, I don't think that she could do it by herself because her kids are too little. So I'll need to spend two months a year in Oxford and earn enough to employ someone to replace me. But I've got to give her time. For now, if I can buy and sell art I can keep the business solvent.'

'I can come with you, Harry. I can write up my research and attend conferences. But I need to understand your art just as you have understood my love of history.'

When Ramma had first seen Harry's sketchbooks, she had wondered if he could be some kind of a pervert. How could she have been so wrong? How could she show him that she really understood that art was at the heart of his being? Now she saw the depth in the art she had thought could be perverted.

'Harry, I have not always been easy. There have been some things I have not really understood about you but I believe I do now.'

She felt herself dissolving in his arms as he kissed her ear. She made a resolution that she couldn't have made even a week earlier.

'If you want to sketch and paint me, I am ready. I am yours. But please, to begin with, just for your eyes only. I am not quite ready to be revealed to the world.'

A desire to open herself up to him, give herself, confide in him was swelling in her body. She had the feeling that she would make self-discoveries in the process. That night when, for the first time, he drew her naked, all of her, was special. It was liberating. The figure on the paper was dancing amid a blur of yellow and orange. Was it even her? Swirling black hair half curtained the face. Yet the pose was hers and there was something about the spirit of it that touched her.

'I glow.' Ramma was exceptionally pleased with the painting. As she examined it, she realised that the figure looked comfortable in her own skin, radiantly so.

She liked this confident version of herself that combined mind and body. Was this her 'elephant'? She had thought she was free because unlike most Indian parents, Gangabharti had not tried to control her. Ramma realised that she had, in response, desperately wanted him to be proud of her. In effect, she had controlled herself, single-minded, unwavering, tunnel-visioned to the point of rigidity. She knew she wanted to be the free spirit in the painting. She felt confident that she could be that person and that it would inspire her work. Her DPhil could be exceptional thanks to the discovery of Bartholomew Carew and that would never have happened without adventuring into life beyond academia. Exposing herself to Harry, allowing herself to be vulnerable, it had not made her weak but confident and free.

Harry was looking hard, not at her but at the painting.

'I'll need to work on this,' said Harry. 'Do it on a bigger scale. The movement is not just you, Ramma, but the dancing figures of Khajoraho. I'll never forget the agony of that time, not knowing what had happened to you; I thought I'd lost you for a second time. Varanasi and the drive to Lumbini knocked my confidence but there's no way I want to lose you again.'

When he said "confidence" a thought floated to the surface of his mind – a realisation that he had always enjoyed painting but rarely respected his own work. That needed to change.

'I love you. Thank you. This is special. I don't know where the inspiration came from if not from you but this work is fundamentally different from anything I've done before. It's like you've untied a knot for me; I have let go of the part that is not elephant. I don't really know how to describe how I feel. Unburdened? A free spirit?'

Ramma caressed him and she looked different too: relaxed. 'That was special for me too. You, Harry, have shared my passion and now you have given me something more. You have given me permission to let go and be more than an intellectual. We are going to be good for each other. We bring out parts of ourselves we didn't know existed.'

AUTHORIAL COMMENTS

I was moved by the reaction to my first novel, *Brushstrokes in Time*, from young people from what some label "mixed parentage". I was able to write about Little Winter and her daughter Sara with sensitivity because when my wonderful sons, Justin, Adrian and Paul, were growing up they were often defined by their father.

When Justin was six months old there was a knock on the door of our Handsworth (Birmingham) home. A reporter from *The Daily Mail* wanted to question me about my marriage. I am usually a hospitable person but I didn't ask her in. She asked me how my parents had reacted to me marrying "an Indian". The implication in her voice was that they should have disowned me. I replied that I didn't marry an Indian, I married Atam. She didn't like that response and left. Her feature was published and among her victims were a so-called "mixed-race couple" we knew well. When I read the way she sensationalised their marriage, I realised that I may have been young but I had been wise.

When Barack Obama was elected he was proclaimed the USA's first "black" president. His father was definitely of African ancestry but his mother? Does she have to be whitewashed out of his life? In my eyes Barack Obama is Barack Obama who, like everyone else, is a unique individual. Atam's PhD was in quantitative genetics so I know that my assertion is based on science and not on my subjective opinion. Despite everyone's uniqueness, cultural differences impact in subtle and unexpected ways. I felt the desire to write another novel that could appeal to young people who don't want to identify with just one part of their background.

I wanted the story of Cowley-born Harry and Mumbai-born Ramma to be caused by a chance encounter much like my own story. People don't set out to marry someone from a different nationality, colour or religion. Half of this novel is set in India where pursuing your desire – your kama – is acceptable in Hindu philosophy.

The contemporary story is set in 1997-98 before social media and I needed a link to the parallel historical story – that comes in the form of the well-travelled chest of drawers bought by Harry. When I was working in the art and antiques trade I bought just such a chest of drawers that had been to India and back. Its contents become essential to Ramma's research into early Indian history. Why the historical story? My generation of school children was taught history that was informed by the underlying racist narrative of "White Supremacy." Civilisation apparently began in Ancient Greece with a nod to agriculture in Mesopotamia and to exotic Egypt, which is seldom recognized as 'black history'.

Now that China is the world's second largest economy and will soon become what it once was – the world's largest – people elsewhere in the world will become more familiar with its history. I would like more people to be aware of a lost civilisation that spread Buddhism across Asia, including into China. That civilisation was Indian and knowledge of it was lost. Jesus did not create Christianity, St Paul did, and similarly the Buddha did not create Buddhism. Ashoka was responsible for that.

ACKNOWLEDGMENTS

Thanks to **Sushma Gaba** and **Achla Chadda** for accompanying me on a Buddhist tour of North India and Nepal and to Anil Sachdeva for helping us organise it.

Thanks to **Mukta Vasudeva**, my fellow student on the Diploma in Creative Writing (Oxford), **Heather Rosser** and **Linora Lawrence** of the Oxford Writers Group and **Caroline Henney** of Antiques on High for their support during the writing of *Sculpting the Elephant* in all its reincarnations.

Thanks to **Brandon Lindberg (Christie's)** for giving permission for me to feature the real Ingrid Lindberg in this work of fiction.

Thanks to **Dr Jim Bennett** of the Museum of the History of Science for pointing me in the direction of the Great Trigonometrical Survey of India.

This book would not have been possible without **Katie Isbester** of Claret Press superbly aided by **Joshua Hunter**, **Isobelle Lans** and **Oliver Lane**.

Thanks to the generous people who have given precious time to read and endorse *Sculpting the Elephant*.

Thanks to my family especially to **Elizabeth Vetta**, the artist who drew the cover illustration: **www.elizabethvetta.co.uk**

GLOSSARY

Some Hindi words and references used in *Sculpting the Elephant*

Namaste: Greetings, Hello

Theek Hai: Okay, fine

Accha: Good, well, nice

Beti: Daughter

Jaldi: Quickly

Prana: Food

Urdu: One of 22 official languages recognized in the Indian constitution. It is a Persianised version of a standard Hindustani and the national language of Pakistan.

Laxmi: The goddess of wealth and good fortune

Brahma: The Hindu creator God

Kama: Wish, desire or longing

Dhamma: Usually refers to right ways of living, duties, rights, laws, conduct and virtues. To Buddhists it refers particularly to the teachings of the Buddha.

Raga: A melodic framework for improvisation in Indian music.

Mirza Ghalib: (1797 –1869) A prominent Urdu- and Persian-language poet during the final years of the Mughal Empire

ANTIQUE REFERENCES

Art Deco: A style of visual arts architecture and design popular in the 1920s and 1930s.

The Pottery Ladies: Charlotte Rhead (1885-1947), Susie Cooper (1902-1995) and Clarice Cliff (1899–1972).

Keith Murray: (1892–1981) A New Zealand born architect, aviator and ceramic designer.

Etling: A firm founded by Edmond Laurent Etling. It had a retail shop at 29, rue de Paradis, Paris in the 1920s and 1930s. It commissioned art deco works in glass, ceramics and bronze.

The Martin Brothers: Britain's first professional studio potters, Martinware Pottery (1873–1923).

William Morris: (1834–96) Artist, designer, philosopher and socialist. Morris was the driving force behind the British Arts and Crafts Movement.

William Benson: (1854 - 1924) Encouraged by Morris, Benson established a successful foundry. Many of his designs were patented. He designed the first British table lamps to use electric light bulbs.

Gabbeh rugs: Persian hand-made rugs for domestic use not commercial sale.

SOME NOTABLE VICTORIANS MENTIONED IN *SCULPTING THE ELEPHANT*

Charles Darwin: (1809–1882) An English naturalist, geologist and biologist. The discoveries and insights he made on the voyage of the Beagle led him to write *On the Origin of Species* (1859), considered to be the foundation of evolutionary biology.

Richard F. Burton: (1821–1890) Explorer, inventor, soldier, poet, archaeologist, diplomat and adventurer, Richard Francis Burton was one of the most remarkable men of his age. He made a dangerous pilgrimage to Mecca in disguise and explored the Nile with Speke. In relation to India he is best known for translating the Kama Sutra.

Isabel Burton: (1831-1896) An adventurous woman who accompanied her husband, Richard Burton, on many dangerous journeys. Her writings include *Richard, The Life of Captain Sir Richard Francis Burton*. The reputation of this intelligent and capable woman was marred when, after his death, she burnt much of his work on sexual practices.

George Everest: (1790–1866) Surveyor General of the Great Trigonometrical Survey of India from 1830 to 1843. When the Royal Geographical Society decided to rename Peak XV 1865, his successor as Surveyor General put him forward to be honoured.

Ernest Binfield Harvell: (1861–1934) An influential English arts administrator. Under the pen name E.B. Havell, he wrote numerous books on Indian art and architecture, and was heavily involved in the reform of art education alongside Abanindranath

Tagore. His work led to the foundation of the Bengal School of Art, which built on his use of Indian rather than Western educational models.

Sir Henry Edward Landor Thuillier: (1813-1906) Surveyor General of India from 1861 to 1878. Under his direction, 796,928 square miles of India were surveyed, including difficult mountainous, forest, and desert regions, often for the first time.

Nain Singh Rawat: (1830-1882) A surveyor trained by the Great Trigonometrical Survey of India. Indian explorers, often known as Pandits, were employed particularly in the Himalayas. His most notable achievements were in Tibet.

Radhanath Sikdar: (1813–1870) The Indian mathematician who is best known for calculating the height of Mount Everest.

James Prinsep: (1799–1840) A brilliant English scholar and the founding editor of the Journal of the Asiatic Society of Bengal. He is best remembered for deciphering the Kharosthi and Brahmi scripts.

Alexander Cunningham: (1814–1893) An engineer with the British Army who would later become appointed Archaeological Surveyor to the government of India. Whilst working in the military, he became passionate about uncovering the history of India and its archaeological legacy, and after his appointment he organised what would later become the Archaeological Survey of India.

Monier Monier-Williams: (1819-1899) The second Boden Professor of Sanskrit at Oxford University, best known for his Sanskrit/English dictionary.

Max Müller: (1823–1900) A German born philologist who helped found the disciplines of Indian Studies and Comparative religion in Western Academia. His works on Indology ranged from the scholarly to the popular, including *The Sacred Books of the East*, a 50-volume set of English translations prepared under his direction.

Florence Nightingale: (1820-1910) A nurse famous for her work in Crimea and for being the founder of modern nursing. However, she was also a statistician and social reformer and as such had opinions on the causes of famines in India.

Samuel Bourne: (1834–1912) A British photographer known for his prolific seven years' work in India, from 1863 to 1870. Together with Charles Shepherd, he set up Bourne & Shepherd, first in Shimla in 1863 and later in Kolkata.

George Frederick Samuel Robinson: (1827–1909) 1st Marquess of Ripon. When, in 1880, he was appointed Viceroy by the Gladstone administration, Ripon sought to reverse the Afghan policy of his predecessor Lord Lytton. He devoted himself to the task of liberalising the Indian administration. He had a pragmatic and humane approach to solving problems but left India disillusioned when he failed to remove the racist and discriminatory applications of the law in India.

Sir Ramakrishna Gopal Bhandarkar: (1837–1925) A scholar who in 1866 was part of a group that publicly denounced the caste system. He also campaigned for female education and for the abolition of child marriage.

BUDDHIST REFERENCES

Ashoka: (d.232 BC) The Mauryan emperor who spread the teachings of the Buddha across Asia thus creating the religion called Buddhism. The story of the rediscovery of Ashoka is told in *Ashoka: The Search for India's Lost Emperor* by Charles Allen, *Pushyamitra Sunga and the Buddhists* by Ram Kumar Mishra and *A History of India* by John Keay.

Silabhadra: (529-624 CE) A Buddhist monk and philosopher. He is best known as an abbot of Nalanda monastery (in India) and for being the personal tutor of the Chinese Buddhist monk Xuanzang.

Xuanzang: (602-664 CE) A Chinese Buddhist monk, scholar, traveler, and translator who travelled to India in the seventh century. Modern knowledge of this period of Indian history is to a great extent thanks to him. Before the destruction of the great library at Nalanda by Muhammad Bakhtiyar, Xuanzang made careful translations of Indian Buddhist texts to Chinese as well as recording his travels in Great Tang Records on the Western Regions. The Buddhist texts he bought back with him to China were housed in the Great Wild Goose Pagoda.

ABOUT THE AUTHOR

Sylvia's first novel Brushstrokes in Time, published by Claret Press, was inspired by in-depth interviews with the Stars artist Qu Leilei. He is one of the inspirational people Sylvia sent to her mythical island of Oxtopia. The castaway series was published by The Oxford Times between 2007- 2016. The 120 life stories were reproduced in three books.

Details of all her books are on **www.sylviavetta.co.uk**